BLOOD RED SARI

Ashok Banker's books have sold over 1.4 million copies in twelve languages and fifty-seven countries. He is currently best known for his multi-volume retellings of epics. But long before he became India's favourite epic storyteller, he was the author of the first Indian crime novels in English, one of which featured Sheila Ray, India's first female private eye. Sheila Ray returns after a twenty-year hiatus, as do other series characters such as Anita B. and Nachiketa Shroff who previously appeared in short stories published on mystery fiction websites and in magazines.

With *Blood Red Sari*, Ashok reinvents the action thriller in a new global all-female avatar. In the Kali Rising Series, the sequels *Burnt Saffron Sky*, *Rust Black Heart* and *Silver Acid Rain* are already complete and awaiting publication. Ashok can be contacted via his website ashokbanker.com. One of the most accessible and reader-friendly authors, over 41,000 readers have corresponded with him till date. He looks forward to hearing from you!

BLOOD RED SARI

Kali Rising

Book 1

Ashok Banker

HarperCollins *Publishers* India

First published in India by
HarperCollins *Publishers* in India

4th Floor, Tower A, Building No. 10, Phase II,
DLF Cyber City, Gurugram, Haryana -122002
www.harpercollins.co.in

2 4 6 8 10 9 7 5 3

P-ISBN: 978-93-5029-321-8
E-ISBN: 978-93-5029-926-5

Typeset in 10.5/13.5 Charter BT
InoSoft Systems Noida

Printed and bound at
Manipal Technologies Limited, Manipal

I think I should select from my poems as my favorite 'The Emperor of Ice Cream'. This wears a deliberately commonplace costume, and yet seems to me to contain something of the essential gaudiness of poetry; that is the reason why I like it.

– William Carlos Williams
(Letter dated 6 January 1933)

For

May Smith, grandmother
Sheila D'Souza, mother
Bithika Jain, wife
Yashka Banker, daughter

You made me the boy I was,
The man I grew up to be,
The husband and father I have become,
And the person I aspire to be someday.

And for Willow,
Who taught me that even 'human'
Is too narrow-minded a classification.

We are all one in our separate skins.

One of the undersides of globalization, human trafficking exists in at least 127 countries ... the second most lucrative illicit enterprise in the world after drug trafficking, it is also the fastest growing, with global profits estimated at $44.3 billion USD per year.

– International Labor Organization and United Nations

The number of people held in slavery worldwide is estimated to be between 12 and 27 million, more than at any time in world history. A large proportion of the victims are women and children.

– U.S. Department of Health and Human Services

India's home secretary Madhukar Gupta remarked that at least 100 million people were involved in human trafficking in India. 'The number of trafficked persons is difficult to determine due to the secrecy and clandestine nature of the crime.'

– cnn.com

India may be the epicenter for human trafficking.

– freedomcenter.org

iam redit et Virgo
Translation: Now returns Justice

– Virgil

Prologue: India

Kali Pujo

An Appeasement

ON A SEARING AFTERNOON in May, I caught a tram to the oldest neighbourhood in the city. This is the place for which Kolkata, or Calcutta as the British pronounced it, was named. Kali-ghat, the sacred burning ghat of goddess Kali, which is now just another debilitated inner city neighbourhood, still houses the ancient Kali temple which once formed the centre of the city. It was a Sunday and the streets were quiet and deserted as I got off the tram and walked the last few kilometres through winding cobbled streets. Heat shimmered on the street, making the departing tram seem to levitate before it passed into obscurity. A stray bitch, teats bulging with unconsumed and probably hardened milk, muzzled a pile of rotting watermelon rinds beneath a fruit seller's handcart. I glimpsed a trickle of blood oozing from her swollen genitalia as I passed by. If the swollen lactose glands didn't kill her, the haemorrhaging certainly would.

The fruit seller, dozing on the footpath beside the cart, glanced up at me with bulging Bengali eyes, clutching his watermelon knife. The blade had been re-sharpened so many times that it was little more than a crescent sliver. 'Melon khaabey?' he asked hopefully. I ignored him and walked on. My destination was the temple, where I meant to offer pujo and express my gratitude to the goddess as promised. I had fasted all day to keep myself pure for the offering.

Kali, in ancient Indian mythology, is one of the infinite forms of Devi, the eternal goddess, repository of all feminine power. The Puranas, literally 'ancient tales', tell of a time when the devas, the myriad gods of the Vedic pantheon, were troubled by new enemies. The asuras, their eternal rivals, had four great champions with great powers of destruction. Try as they might, the devas could not defeat the new threat. The demons rampaged and ravaged the realms of the gods and mortals for an eternity until finally, exhausted and at their wits' end, the devas took refuge in Almighty Brahma, the Creator. The other partners who made up the great Trimurti of the Vedic pantheon – Vishnu the Preserver and Shiva the Destroyer – combined their fury with that of Brahma and the other gods, and a terrible brilliance emanated from each of their faces. Combining with the evanescence of a thousand suns and the spiritual strength of the great sage Katyayana, the devas produced a mighty new champion in the aspect of the goddess Kali. From the deva Mahendra was formed her face. From Agni, Lord of Fire, came her eyes. From Yama, Lord of Death and Dharma, her hair. From Vishnu, the champion of mortalkind and upholder of life, her eighteen hands. From Indra, the general of the army of the devas, her viscera. From Varuna, Lord of the Ocean, her hips and thighs. From Brahma the Creator, her feet. From Surya, the sun god, her toes. From Prajapati, the seed-giver of all life, the teeth. From the eight Vasus, her fingers. From Yaksa, her nose. From Vayu the Lord of the Wind, her ears. And from the ascetic tapasya of Maharishi Katyayana at whose ashram their energies converged, she received her seductive eyebrows.

She was given gifts too – weapons and objects of beauty and great power – by the various devas. When her creation was complete and her armaments assembled, she mounted a lion and went to the highest peak of the Vindhya Range, from whence she launched her campaign of vengeance against the supposedly indomitable asuras – an epic rampage of bloodlust that has few equals even in the blood-spattered annals of Hindu mythology. She was given many names, the foremost among them being Durga, Katyayani, Chamundi, and of course, Kali.

It was to her shrine that I now came, to perform pujo, the prayer ritual to appease and please her. I paused at the entrance to the narrow alley that led to the temple precinct. The last time I had come here, it had been with rage in my heart and a curse on my lips. I had furiously demanded that Kali deliver to me the goal I desired, *or else*. So frustrated had I been at that time, I had threatened the goddess herself. It was the nadir of the worst phase of a not wonderful life.

Now I returned bearing gifts and a light heart. I had in the folds of my sari a gold chain that I intended to give to Kali. I had bought it at a jeweller's in Park Street for more money than the fruit seller I had walked by would probably earn in his lifetime. The comb, kohl, lip colour and other cosmetics that one customarily gifted to the goddess during the ritual, I would purchase from the pundits at the temple. I also intended to put five thousand rupees into the daanpeti, the donation box of the temple. I would pay to feed all the residents of a girls' orphanage in Dakshineshwar once a week for a year as well. And of course, how could I forget the sari it was customary to gift the goddess: a sari in a colour that matched her blood-soaked rampage.

There were other offerings too, for I had money to spend and to spare. And limitless gratitude. It had been a good year. A very good year. The more so since it came on the heels of a hard and dangerous life. Not everything that had happened in that year had been good. Some awful, terrible things had taken place. I had made two of the dearest friends I had found in my entire life and lost one of them under circumstances so tragic that it still made me cry in impotent rage when I remembered. There had been a series of events epic enough to rival the tortuously winding story-cycles of ancient Indian Puranas; and when trapped within the deepest, darkest days of that period, I hadn't expected to come out of it alive. Yet somehow, I had not just survived, I had prospered. Hugely. And now I wanted to show my gratitude, to share the overwhelming sense of relief and joy I now felt, with the goddess I had cursed and abused before leaving Kolkata.

The line was short. The annual Durga Puja festival had just ended – nine days and nights of celebration devoted to nine aspects of the Eternal Goddess – and my fellow Bengalis were mostly home recovering. The woman in front of me in the line was young, barely more than a teenager. She had a Blackberry clutched in her hands and was pressing buttons non-stop, tweeting about her first trip to Kolkata, her first visit to the Kali temple, the fashionable club she was going to party at with her posse that night, how she couldn't understand why people clung to these ancient pagan customs in this modern age, yada yada yada. The last glimpse I had of her screen, she was updating her Facebook status to continue the grumbling there as well. I resisted the urge to grab her and shake her by the shoulders. In many ways, I was her; I was less than a decade older, perhaps, but in other ways, I was centuries older. And had always been. I was relieved when her turn came and she moved on, head still lowered, punching away.

The temple bells began to toll as I stood there, steel thali in hand, the heavy Bengali silk sari feeling awkward on my jeans-and-shirt-accustomed body in the sweltering sunshine. Before, they had always sounded to my angry ears like a lost goddess raging to an unjust world. Now, they sounded sad rather than angry, like a dirge, a toll, a commemoration of lost friends, and an ending.

I climbed the steps of the temple, the ancient stone cool beneath my bare soles, its surface worn smooth by the footfalls of countless devotees over the centuries, seeking solace, appeasement, virility, wealth and the thousand other things people prayed for. I had sought only one thing when I came here last, and somehow, impossibly, I had received it. I had looked into the hot eyes of Kali and demanded, cried out for justice.

Or was it vengeance?

Sometimes, it is hard to tell the difference.

Karkidakam

Day of the Dead

One

1.1

EVER SINCE SHE WAS a little girl yay high, she had loved Karkidakam.

Ever since she was a little girl yay high, she had hated Karkidakam.

She hated it for being the death knell of summer vacations, the months when they could be as lazy as fat flies. When mangoes were in season and they could have their fill, just wander into the kitchen reading a dog-eared copy of a favourite book, pick up a mango from the crate – the top layer had the ripe ones – bite into it, skin and all, and feel the sticky juices spill down their chins. When they could tumble out of bed and race the dogs down to the beach, toothbrushes and Colgate clutched in their fists, and brush their teeth in the surf while jumping sideways like crazy crabs every time the tide roared in. Afternoons they might spend collecting coral or reading and dozing and talking or all three together in the shade of the palms on the cliff, while the dogs lay upside down for their tummies to be scratched. Sometimes, they caught a ride out on Achchan's boat to fish. Once, Lalima brought a karachemmeen one-and-a-half times as long as herself; and then they ate karachemmeen for breakfast, lunch and dinner the next three days. Evenings they ate sukhiyan at Mathews's and watched the sunset. It was an unspoken rule; they never missed a sunset and never ate sukhiyan anywhere except at Mathews's, don't ask why.

But then came Karkidakam and amavasi, and Varkala was overrun by hordes of the Undead. That was what Lalima called those who had not made it to the other realm one summer and the name just stuck. Ezhu had returned from one of his trips from Do-Buy with one of those shiny new bissyaars – a National Panasonic with *remote!* (he always said it that way, italicised and with the exclamation at the end) – and one of the tapes he brought back was *Night of the Living Dead*. They watched it one breathless night without Atta or Acchi knowing, and for weeks afterwards, 'They're coming to get you, Barbara!' became a permanent fixture in their vocabulary. So when the hordes of pilgrims began falling off the buses and rolling through their backyard on amavasi, their lives came to a standstill. The beach, *their* beach, was gone, taken over by an army of the Undead, lurking around, praying, offering vavu bali, indulging in papanasam, eating *their* sukhiyan at Mathews's, stealing *their* sunset. The horror, the horror. And afterwards, even though the invasion lasted for barely a day or two, the beach and its environs were always so filthy with the refuse and leftovers that it just wasn't the same. There were neat mundu-sets left everywhere, ostensibly for departed relatives, and while they understood the reason why people did it, it was irritating to keep tripping over little piles of cloth everywhere in their backyard, not to mention the fact that none of these mundu neriyathu could actually be used by any living person because that would be inauspicious.

So Anita also hated Karkidakam, though hated is probably too strong a word. It was just that it marked the end of the summer fun. The fact that it was on an amavasi day in Karkidakam that Lalima's parents left for the UAE, with her in tow, only served to permanently etch the day in her memory as a really sucky one.

So of course, it had to be on vavu bali day that she got the news that Lalima had passed away. Philip called. He didn't have her cell phone number so he called the old landline. She stood by the telephone in the living room, still holding the instrument in her hand as the dial tone droned sonorously into her ear. Finally Mrs Matondkar stopped rocking, turned to look at her, and barked, 'What, you're having silent conversation?'

She put down the phone which rattled on the cradle before settling in. Mrs Matondkar saw the news written on Anita's face like a creepy crawly on a business news channel. 'Who died?'

How to describe Lalima? How to sum up a relationship, a person, a lifetime of memories – even if most of that lifetime had been spent apart? How to put it all into one concise word, neatly embossed on a plaque or a tombstone? Best friend? First love? The sister she had never had? All of the above? How could she convey what Lalima had meant to this old flatulent landlady who regarded same-sex relationships as an abomination in the eyes of God?

'My best friend.'

Anita sat down on the little cane stool she kept by the telephone stand. For some reason, it was a foot high while the telephone itself was placed on a jutting wooden stand four feet high. It left her sitting with the telephone above her head, like a hovering bird. The stool and the telephone were in the main passageway of the flat, just inside the front door, and as she sat there, a package slid through the mail slot and fell with a heavy thud to the floor. It was a yellow manila document envelope with her name written on it with a black marker. She ignored it and buried her face in her hands and stayed that way for a while. She didn't hear Mrs Matondkar wrestling herself out of her rocking chair, but at some point the old lady appeared beside her and placed a heavy hand that smelt of roasted channa on Anita's head.

She said nothing; just kept her hand there.

After a moment or two, she turned and shuffled back to the rocking chair. She farted as she lowered her not inconsiderable bulk into its welcoming embrace. The squeaking began again. That was Mrs Matondkar's way of consoling her. It was more affection or sympathy than she had shown Anita since she had come to stay at her place as a paying guest seven years ago.

Finally, Anita rose from the stool, somehow avoided hitting her head against the telephone stand, picked up the envelope from the doormat, and turned towards her room. She would call the airlines to book a flight to Thiruvananthapuram, or maybe just pack a small bag and head straight to the airport. It being late evening on a weekday, Mumbai traffic would be horrendous as always, and the sooner she got going, the sooner she could be on a plane heading home. It would be the first time in thirteen years that she was going home. It felt like a lifetime.

The Undead would have left by the time she reached, although the piles of cloth would still be choking the beaches.

Somewhere in there, perhaps, was a pile for Lalima.

1.2

THE SECURITY GUARD OF the building was waiting when she pulled into her parking spot. He salaamed her as she shifted herself from the driving seat of the car to her wheelchair. He knew better than to offer to help and stood by watching with sympathy till she had completed the transfer, locked the car door, and started rolling towards the entrance of the building. It was early yet, and though some idiot was accelerating too fast and honking too much as he roared past, Sector A Pocket C was one of the quietest, most peaceful parts of Vasant Kunj. Most of the residents of the old Lutyen's era building were high court lawyers who operated out of their chambers at the court premises. She was the only one who 'worked from home' even though she lived on the Gurgaon–Mehrauli highway. She used this apartment as an office. It was against regulations to operate a business practice and she had experienced some grief over it from a few of her less tolerant neighbours at first, but her physical condition and history helped ameliorate their attitude; the fact that she only saw clients at the chambers and used this place more for research and as a kind of back office pacified them. Now, she got a few glares from time to time, but those were mostly for the dogs.

She recognized the security guard as the one who usually worked the night shift, a tall Jat who was more polite than most of his brethren.

'Madam, kisi ne aap ke darwaazey pe pishaab kiya hai.'

She frowned, pausing to look up at him. Was he serious? Even with his heavy Haryanvi accent, she had had no difficulty understanding him at all – despite her Gujarati primary schooling, English-medium secondary schooling and college education, she had picked up Hindi and most of the north-Indian dialects quite well in the past few years. With the kind of clients and cases she got, it was a necessity. But why on earth would someone piss on her front door?

He saw her expression and mistook her lack of response as stemming from the language barrier. This was the first time he had actually spoken to her, since he was mostly off duty by the time she came to work. 'Man come to madam office in night time, trying make piss on office door.'

She resisted the urge to cover her mouth. However polite he may be for a Jat, she didn't think he would appreciate being laughed at openly. She managed to turn the action into a touch of her forehead.

'Where is the man now?' she asked.

He flapped his hand, imitating a bird flying away rather than a man running away. 'Not here. Gone. I wait for you to come. You want make police complaint?'

'Nahi, ji,' she said. 'There is no need. Thank you, Shri ...?'

'Rajendra Powar. Most welcome, madam. It is my job.'

She nodded and started rolling towards the entrance. He followed her a few steps, still speaking.

He grinned widely, displaying paan fragments stuck in his front upper teeth. 'I am matric pass, madam. Wanted graduate. But having to do job. Came Dilli.' He spread his arms, indicating the world, the city, his uniform, the universal condition of humanity.

She felt uncomfortable at his following her and spilling uncalled-for personal information, but didn't want to seem impolite. She mustered a polite smile. 'Thank you, Rajendraji,' she said, and rolled into the foyer.

The power was out, of course; after all, this was Delhi. The lift cage and stairway was in darkness, only a glimmer coming down through the stairwell, but she knew the place like the back of her hand. She turned the wheelchair right, then left again around the generously curving passageway. The old-worldly spaciousness and accessibility were a blessing. No new office building in the heart of Delhi could ever provide her with this much space on a ground floor, apart from the quiet and peace. She turned again into near-pitch darkness and slowed the chair. There was only this last stretch of the corridor and all the three doorways lined up in a row belonged to her 'office' apartment.

The strays had smelt her and came forward eagerly out of the darkness to greet her, ragged tails wagging, the tapetum in their eyes glowing in the darkness. Her eyes were still adjusting to the gloom and she didn't want to run over any of the pups, so she paused to pat and cuddle them. They were all gets from the same middle-aged bitch she called Justice. As in, *Justice is a bitch*, her patent line, delivered so many times over the years that it had become her trademark, her calling card, and at times even an insult yelled at her across crowded smoky bars. *Justicebitch!*

Justice permitted her sons and daughters their licking and yelping and tail-thumping for a moment or three, then barked, the sound echoing up the stairwell of the empty building. When they didn't comply, she began nosing and snarling them out of the way. Nachiketa thanked her and rolled towards the office door. As she unlocked the heavy padlock and yanked back the rusting bolt, she the pungent odour of male urine hit her. She grimaced as she tried to imagine a man standing here in the dark, unzipping himself, pointing his penis at the door and urinating on it. The dogs must have been out foraging at the time, otherwise Justice alone would have made a hasty snack of the man. That was why even the security guards discreetly allowed the dogs and even helped feed them at times – there is no better helper for a nightwatchman than an adopted stray.

She rolled into the office, only Justice following behind. The younger dogs knew well enough to remain outside the sacred sanctum, where they sat patiently, tails thumping happily on the wooden passage floor, awaiting their usual breakfast of biscuits. Justice escorted her imperiously through the musty outer room filled with glass-fronted wooden cabinets and sagging desks, all packed and piled high with bulging files full of legal documents. On Shonali's desk, an ancient Pentium III computer acted as a repository for the practice's entire store of electronic files. In the innermost room, a master bedroom converted to her private office – her *chambers,* as Shonali grandiloquently referred to it – where her ageing but wonderfully comfortable old chair awaited before her desk piled equally high with files and more files, she opened the drawer in which she kept the doggie stuff and tore open a fresh packet of biscuits.

'These are wheat,' she said to Justice, who watched patiently. 'Healthier for you than the usual glucose biscuits. These have fibre.'

She placed the opened packet on her lap and manoeuvred the wheelchair back through the office, expertly avoiding the desk corners and dangerously piled stacks of files that threatened to topple over at a sneeze. Putting down the economy-sized packet of Britannia Vita Marie biscuits, she sat back and observed Justice watching with maternal pleasure as her brood consumed its breakfast gratefully. Only when all the pups had all finished did the proud bitch eat her share. 'That's Justice for you,' Nachiketa whispered, nuzzling the dog one last time before turning around. Time to get to work on that brief.

She felt the right hand wheel of her chair encounter something bulky and stopped, wheeled around, and then backed up to try and spot it. It was difficult to see clearly, but it appeared to be a yellow manila envelope on the ground just inside the doorway. It had probably been pushed in through the mail slot, though it looked almost too big to fit. Couriers would do that sometimes rather than come back the next morning to deliver, and they would scrawl an indecipherable signature on the proof of delivery slip themselves. Nachiketa had bawled out more than a few courier delivery boys for doing that before, and her forehead puckered with the folds of irritation that always formed when she was bothered.

She peered and strained, trying to see if it was something important. She considered trying to pick it up. But it had slipped partly under the edge of a table. Picking it up would be awkward and best not attempted; she would have to wait for Shonali or the peon. Somehow, in the dim gloamy light drifting in through the cracks in the shuttered wooden windows, she could see just the label on the front of the envelope. Her name was on it, neatly printed with black marker but no address. That was odd; it meant that the package had been hand-delivered rather than sent via courier or registered AD, the usual choice for legal documents.

Justice trundled over, sated with wheat fibre biscuits, and sniffed curiously at the package. When she snorted and snuffled loudly, Nachiketa realized that the package had caught some of the spill of man-urine from the door. The bastard must have stuck his penis into the mail slot to do his nastiness. She grimaced and backed away. That decided it. She wouldn't be touching the package until someone had opened it and gotten rid of that pee-soaked envelope. And if the contents were pee-soaked too? Well, she would deal with that later – or Shonali would. She sighed, patted Justice, and rolled off to switch on the generator and start her day.

1.3

THERE WAS AN UNUSUALLY large number of cars and bikes in the side lane adjoining the gym when Sheila drove up that morning. Since the gym occupied the entire three-storey building and the other shops in the lane were grocery and general provision stores, she assumed that the increased parking occupancy meant increased attendance at the gym. That was usual for post-holiday Monday mornings. After the long weekend spent partying, indulging and overeating, people invariably felt guilty and hit the gym hard. That was also the reason why new memberships spiralled during the first week of January, after the party and holiday season ended, apart from, of course, the ambitious new year's resolutions. By mid-week, regular attendance would even out, and the mad January rush would always ease off by

March when the financial year-ending required many to put in longer hours and overtime and the newbies began to feel frustrated by the lack of noticeable change even after three months. Most people lapsed in March, not realizing that physical fitness and weight loss are ongoing lifestyle commitments, not short-term goals to be achieved and then forgotten.

Salt Lake City, Kolkata, was probably the most modern part of this ancient city and its residents were all immigrant professionals who had come here to work on short- or long-term assignments. That meant that they were more focused on furthering their careers than keeping fit. Though it was named for the salt water marshes that had been reclaimed to accommodate the commercial interests that dominated the conscience of modern Calcutta, its more intransigent residents still preferred to call the area by its old name, Biddhanagar, partly because the old guard found it offensive to share a name with an 'Amrikan' city.

She took a moment to walk around the building, checking that the glass-fronted windows had been cleaned well, the sign was working, and the facade spic and span. Glancing up, she could see lycra-suited members on the long line of treadmills and cross-trainers, sweating away in air-conditioned comfort behind the tinted glass. The glass front was a better advertisement than any hoarding or press ad as the building faced a key side road that connected a major residential neighbourhood to a main arterial road. Most of her clientele came from that residential neighbourhood and their being able to actually look into the gym and see the people working out there as they drove by was a powerful incentive to come in and sign up. Sheila thanked her stars that she had been able to get this property on rent at a time when Kolkata's real estate had not yet begun to try and play catch-up with the rest of the country's skyrocketing realty prices. Her lease was secure for another year-and-a-half at the present rate, and though she knew that the owner would expect a substantial increment, she was more than willing to pay. She had broken even this year, and if all went well, the gym would be profitable enough for her to pay more rent as well as open another branch or two. She had been looking for suitable properties for the branches and she was determined to find places that had glass-frontage similar to this Salt Lake City one. If possible, she would make that the signature of her *She's Here* chain of gyms.

She took the stairs and was greeted by her employees at the reception and foyer. She was that rare variety of boss: tough but fair. She treated her staff well and paid them decently and led by example. It had been hard at first, finding women trainers in Kolkata. Harder still re-training them to meet the standards she wanted to work by. But the difficult days were past now, and she had a very good team here. The well-groomed and well-toned young women in the gym's stylish red, grey and black tracksuit uniforms who stood out among the members working out on the first floor were constantly approached by rival gym chains now, offering higher-paying jobs at Gold's, Sykz, Zaf, or whichever new franchise was aggressively setting up shop in the small but growing eastern market. It was a matter of pride to Sheila that her attrition rate was less than 10 per cent annually.

She took a moment or two to walk around the floor, greeting members warmly regardless of whether she knew them. At this time, they were mostly younger corporate executives working out before going to work. In a couple of hours, they would all be gone and the more matronly Bengali housewife crowd would arrive to put in a futile effort at combating the growing middle-age bulge. Sheila found it hard to work with those women, but this crowd she enjoyed. In turn, they loved having her work out with them because her superior fitness level brought out the competitive spirit in them. She caught one or two of them glancing at her and flashed quick smiles of greeting, guessing that there were some who probably desired to do more with her body than match its fitness level. The fact that *She's Here* was LGBT friendly was a major part of the reason for its success – although in the early days it had seemed a negative point. Two of its three floors were women-only and the third was mixed. In fact, Sheila suspected that even the negative buzz about her establishment being a 'lesbian pickup joint', as some wags called it, had only helped make it famous. Not to mention the hordes of misguided middle-aged Bengali men who joined up with obscure fantasies and absurd assumptions that lesbian women were nymphomaniacs who slept with women only because they couldn't find suitable men to satiate their lust! She knew that most people, like the two young women over by the shoulder press machine checking her ass out as she walked across the floor, assumed she was of a same-sex persuasion herself. She did nothing to discourage the notion and, in fact, it made no difference to her at all if people thought of her as a lesbian. Sure, she was completely and unequivocally heterosexual, but so what?

She finished the round and went into the back office area, breezing past the administrative staff with quick hellos. In her office, she opened the blinds and blinked as the east-facing windows let in the bright early sunshine, buttery warm even through the tinted glass. She watched the traffic on the road for a moment, idly going through her chores for the day. She had an appointment with the KMC ward officer to get formal permission for the renovations and slight expansion she wanted to carry out. Some bank work. Miscellaneous things around the gym. A new batch of trainees to induct before she handed them over to her chief trainer's capable hands. A meeting with the chartered accountant to go over tax-saving measures before the financial year ended. Some calls to make to the equipment suppliers about irregular servicing and other matters. But before all that, the best part of the day: her workout! She was already dressed in her track and sweatshirt with the gym's logo, so she was good to go.

She put her handbag down on the desk and saw the yellow manila envelope addressed to her. It looked thick and important. Documents? She couldn't recall anything that was supposed to come her way except perhaps ... yes, it was probably something related to accounts. She hoped it wasn't income tax forms from the chartered accountant; she hated those fucking things. Whatever it was, she would look at it later. Right now, workout!

She was pretty sure that before she finished, the two attractive young executive types who had been checking her out earlier would try to proposition her. She was used to it. She might even flirt with them awhile before turning them down ever so gently and coquettishly.

Two

2.1

ATTINGAL HAD CHANGED SO much in thirteen years, she almost began to correct the cab driver before she realized he was going the right way. Not just Attingal, NH-47 had changed. Hell, Kerala had changed. She liked the wider roads, the vaulting flyovers and swooping bridges. She didn't like the hoardings leering like mendacious highwaymen at every bend in the road. For every man or woman in a set-mundu she saw one in tee shirt and jeans. The cars, the same models that had turned Mumbai roads into roaring rivers of steel and chrome, were here. Expensive tourist taxis ferrying foreigners from the airport to five-star resorts. Volvo buses carrying white faces under blonde hair peering out through tinted windows. The bristling profusion of advertisements that formed a welcoming committee at Trivandrum Airport had already informed her of the fact that most of the world's leading hotel and resort chains now worshipped at the altar of God's Own Country. The new terminal itself, fully air-conditioned and as modern as Mumbai's own Chhatrapati Shivaji Airport, had intimidated her almost as much as the body search. The other changes she viewed en route evoked mixed feelings. On the one hand, she was proud to see Kerala finally making an entry into the 21st century. Yet at the same time, she couldn't help but wonder if it had been brought or bought.

The turn off to Varkala looked much the same except for the oversized hoarding advertising a housing colony with the dreadful name 'Papanasam Paradise'. 'All apartments sea view!' boasted the signboard. She wondered where those sleek glass-and-steel multi-storey towers were scheduled to rise. Surely not here? Still, the crunching of sand beneath the Esteem's tires, the glimpses of the blue ocean behind the swaying palms, the smells of drying fish, and that peculiar odour that was home eased her heart and made her resolve to act calm and dignified. She owed that to Lalima's memory. Whatever else had happened here, it took away nothing from what Lalima and she had shared for that one glorious summer. She bumped her nose on the half-wound window trying to see the cliffs as the car took the last curve; and suddenly, as the old mossy gateposts appeared, she felt a terrible longing to see Lalima's fifteen-year-old face again, laughing with her tongue out in that peculiar canine way, just for a minute or two, just one glimpse. Oh damn. Oh fuck. She couldn't do this alone. She had to, she must, she would. *Damn you, Lalima. You ditched me and left. Again. And this time you went so far, even a passport and visa won't get me there.*

The old house looked the same, barring one or two minor changes. There was a dish antenna perched on one corner of the roof and most of the roof tiles were broken or displaced, no doubt during one of the several winter monsoon storms that hit this part of the coast hard three years ago. She had read about the storm and felt vaguely guilty for not being there, as well as relieved that she wasn't. Looked like Philip, Graham and Isaac hadn't gotten around to fixing it yet, or perhaps, judging by the overall rundown condition of the garden and grounds, the rusting iron gate off its hinges and overgrown well-mouth in the courtyard, they simply couldn't be bothered. She admonished herself with a pang of remorse: *There could be another reason and you know it. They might not be able to afford repairs.* But a part of her, the mean bit, snorted and said, *Yeah, sure, but I bet they found money to drink every day. Besides, how much would a few tiles, some general maintenance cost?*

She walked around the house, putting off the inevitable as long as possible. The ancient Chevy Nova – its tires gone, resting on rims that had warped over time, streaks of rust like veins of copper in a mine visible beneath a thick patina of encrusted dust, leaves and bird droppings – was in the back garden, which now resembled a wilderness. It made her sad to see the vehicle in that condition. They had had quite a few happy times in that car, before Achchan fell ill and died and things went from sad to fucking miserable in the Matthew household. She remembered one particular long trip that they took to Mariam Appachchi's house in Mundakottukurussi where the Big Fight happened. It was undertaken before the night of the Big Fight, and that trip was pure gold, or as close to it as was possible in the Matthew household. She could still remember how happy she had been, thinking that maybe now things would be all right, they would be a real family at last, the way Lalima's family was, or Varkey's. For the first several hours of the trip, things had actually been wonderful, with all of them singing old songs and everybody still sober, and the sheer pleasure of going somewhere, anywhere, had suffused her with a warm, fuzzy hope. But after they stopped for lunch, 'just one quick beer' had led to another and then to several more, and then they were back on the road. And as the kilometres sped by, the exhilaration of being together rushing headlong along a country road had begun to wane, and the bickering and drunkenness began, and then the arguments and fights and slapping and punching and abusing and shrieking and threats of murder and maiming. It was then that she had come to realize with growing horror that it was actually worse than before; she was trapped in this metal coffin with her mad, violent family; and now, looking back, she knew that it had been then that she had finally accepted that she must leave this madhouse and seek a new life elsewhere. It had taken her another three years to get out, but that day had been the beginning of the end, even before they actually reached Mundakottukurussi and the Big Fight happened. As for that delightful event in the Matthew family history ...

She shuddered and was about to turn away from the rusting hulk when something caught her eye. She leaned over, frowning, and peered through the murky filth coating the rear left passenger window. What was that? It looked like a chain of some sort, attached to a leather collar. Yes, a dog collar and chain. What was it doing inside the car? Had they been keeping a dog in there? But why *inside* the car? And those brown splotches and dried patches on the faded dirty upholstery, surely they couldn't be ... *blood*?

A gust of sea breeze, redolent of salt and fish, swept

through the grove of kallu palms behind her family's property, and the resulting shirring sound was a soothing reminder of childhood afternoons spent daydreaming or reading with Lalima. It made her grieve again for those lost years and for the years that could have been, should have been. Perhaps that was why she didn't hear someone approaching behind her.

Something cold and hard pressed down on her right temple, causing her to freeze instinctively. Her eyes cut right briefly and she had a sense of a pair of long dark cylinders looming in her peripheral vision.

'Well, well,' said a raspy voice that she instantly recognized as Isaac's. 'The prodigal daughter returns. Didn't you read the sign, sister dearest?'

She kept her voice deliberately casual and sarcastic, knowing that displaying fear would only worsen her situation. 'I forgot my glasses in my ass. Could you fetch them, please?'

He cocked the shotgun in response; she could feel the reverberations of the bolt in her skull, the barrels were pressing that hard against her head.

'I referred to the sign that read "Trespassers will be Prostituted".'

She kept her hands still, but moved her fingers just enough to snap them smartly. 'Of course. And you would be the friendly neighbourhood Pimp-in-Charge, right?'

He made a harsh throaty sound, then the pressure of the shotgun left her head just long enough for him to swing the length of the gun around to whack her with the wooden grip; a hard whack, hard enough to dislocate a shoulder or concuss her.

She was ready for it, though. And moved cobra quick to meet it.

2.2

IT WAS ONE OF those days. Due to the renovation work going on in the courtroom that was usually used for regular hearing matters of the category, court was being held in the extension building where accessibility was never as good as in the main complex. Then, someone had unloaded several boxes of court documents from a vehicle on the access ramp and Nachiketa had to wait several frustrating minutes for the boxes to be moved so that she could roll into the building. Finally, some good Samaritan did the needful, and she gritted her teeth and thanked him, hating how it made her feel, hating that someone had to take pity on her. She promised herself that she would file a complaint, but even as she rolled into the courtroom, she forgot all about it. *They* were there today. In force. The whole lot of them.

The Shah family: her mother-in-law glowering at her with those beady thyroidical eyes; her two sisters-in-law, both with their mother's bulging optics and almost comically identical glare; assorted uncles and aunts and cousins and god knew who else; and of course, at the end of the line, looking a little bit fatter and angrier as he seemed to look each time she saw him, her great pati parmeshwar – husband who was like a god. Never mind that he was a mean, nasty, misogynistic, money-grubby son of a bitch, he was her husband, and that itself made him a god according to the 'values' of their community. She dearly wished she wasn't confined to this wheelchair only so she could prostrate herself before him, touch his feet one last time and then grab hold of his ankles and send him crashing to the floor, hopefully breaking the bastard's neck. She let none of this show outwardly, of course, greeting the court clerk politely and slipping him the case brief and waiting patiently till he informed her that her case number was indeed on the top of the docket for the day. That was satisfaction enough for her, because today was judgment day, hopefully, and it would be so, so sweet to see the expressions on their fat faces as Justice D.K. Pathak laid down the law.

But when the judge swept into court, she realized with a shock that it wasn't D.K. Pathak. It was Honourable Mr Justice R.K. Jain instead. How had that happened? She tried to catch the clerk's eye, but he was engrossed in the usual business of sorting and sifting through briefs to pass on to the chair in the correct order. She thought of sending Shonali an SMS asking her what was going on, but it would have been pointless. Besides, the DHC had probably started using the much-threatened jamming device due to the ongoing Judges' Assets case that was going on *in camera*. In any case, court was already in session now and the clerk was already reading out the list of case numbers and noting the extension dates for each one.

Then she noticed the expressions on *their* faces. The Shah dynasty of Shahibaug. They seemed curiously content. That was when she felt the first whiff of suspicion. She tried to rack her brains to remember if R.K. Jain was one of those rumoured to be a 'pliable' judge, which was the preferred euphemism among her esteemed colleagues. She had no idea, but surely their mass presence here, combined with the unexpected change of the presiding judge, that too on judgment day, signalled that something black and squirmy had likely fallen into the lentils, na? By then her number had been called and the judge was already making disapproving noises at her and the defending party's lawyers, who were all suited-booted hotshots from a firm large enough that her entire practice would probably fit into a single overnight case used as carry-on baggage by one of their junior-most assistants. She suddenly lost all the good mojo she had brought with her and knew that fate had just tossed the horseshoe at her skull. Clang.

'Begging your pardon, but Honorable Mr D.K. Pathak is well appraised of this matter and was about to pass summary judgment, so please Your Honour.'

The Honourable Mr Justice R.K. Jain stared down at her bleakly from his bench, and in a long-suffering tone mumbled something about D.K. Pathak proceeding on indefinite leave for personal reasons and that he would be taking over D.K. Pathak's caseload, if, of course, Madam Attorney-at-Bar Mrs Nachiketa Shah had no objections to the same. That drew a few titters from the front row, and she hardly needed to turn her head to know the source.

She tried again, asking for an extension, a continuation, time to review, etc., but she was summarily turned down each time with a bored, disdainful yet curiously methodical precision that told her all she needed to know about the good justice R.K. Jain. Bought, sold, sealed, delivered. Gift-wrapped with a red ribbon.

She was on the verge of giving up – if only for the day, that is, she had come much too far to ever truly give up – when she caught sight of a familiar set of faces. That perky young news reporter from NDTV News – or was it CNN IBN? One of the English news channels, at any rate. And several others. A whole shebang of TV and print news reporters all lined up and ready to byte. Of course. They were here for the Judges' Assets matter. It was big news, headline and breaking-news stuff. Not her piddly little nobody-nothing case. But they were here nevertheless. And so was she. And if she was going to be railroaded and outmanoeuvred yet again by the great Shah dynasty, she was damn well going to kick in a few teeth, even if only metaphorically.

She turned back to the bench. 'Honourable sir, I request you to consider the primary facts in the case one final time before passing summary judgment.'

R.K Jain frowned, and even the court clerk blinked rapidly and raised his head to peer owlishly at her from above his stacks of files and papers and chits. But before anyone could object, she was launched and rolling like an Olympic ski racer down a too-fast slope.

'That man, my husband Shri Jignesh Ramchandra Shah, married me for one reason and one reason only: to use me to siphon off my family's money. The truth was revealed immediately after the ceremony itself. Our honeymoon was cancelled because he cashed in the tickets and hotel reservations and kept the money, just as his mother and sisters took away every single one of the wedding presents. Over the next few weeks, every single thing of value I had brought with me, including my personal jewellery, they took – by cajoling and pleading at first, then by demanding arrogantly, and finally by use of force. Then the demands began. He needed cash to shore up his new venture, a new car, a new flat. My parents were not badly off, but they didn't possess unlimited means either. When my father tried to put his foot down, the abuse began. At first, I was only harangued and yelled at and slapped around a few times each day. Then I was beaten and locked into a storeroom and left for days without food or water or toilet facilities. Then the real horror began. My husband left on a business trip and my mother- and sisters-in-law came into the storeroom where I was sleeping in the dead of night and began to beat me mercilessly with cricket bats and stumps. All the time, they kept yelling at me that if I wouldn't pay in cash, I would pay in kind. "Tara hadkanu maas kadi leisu" was a favourite phrase they shouted over and over again – which translates into "We will take even the marrow from your bones".

'When they had finished with me, I had seventeen major fractures, including two on the skull, a shattered hip, a smashed spine, a ruptured spleen and pancreas, a damaged kidney, a collapsed lung, three broken ribs, and I had miscarried and lost the foetus I had been carrying, of which even I was not aware at that point. I required fifty-eight stitches, fourteen hours on the operation table, three months in the ICU, over eight months in hospital, and another two years in physiotherapy before I was even fit enough to use a wheelchair independently. I am disabled for life and can never bear children or enjoy a normal life.

As a result of the considerable amounts already given to my husband's family, and the medical expenses that followed, my family was thoroughly bankrupted. My father suffered a stroke and was subsequently paralysed. He died within the year after the Shahs attacked me. My mother developed a heart condition and succumbed to it three years later, and there is no doubt that the shock itself had reduced her life. I consider what the Shahs did to be nothing less than murder. Had they shot my parents dead, they could not have killed them more effectively. As for me, I have spent the subsequent eight years, not including the three years of hospitalization and therapy, attempting to bring the Shahs to justice for their acts. Today, finally, I came to this venerated court room to hear the summary judgment on my case. I await your Honourable decision with all grace and humility. Thank you, Your Honour.'

And she rolled back a metre from the bench, keeping her head down and eyes averted, praying that she hadn't gone too far, that her little 'performance' had served to draw the media's attention to her otherwise nondescript case and the judge's attention to the presence of the media, in the hope that whatever backdoor deal the Shahs had worked with this R.K. Jain, it wouldn't be immune to the glaring eye of the fourth estate.

2.3

SHEILA WAS DOING ABS when the men entered the gym.

She did cardio and abs three days a week, legs twice, weight training six times weekly, one major body part and one minor. Today was chest and triceps day. She had started with a ten-minute warm up on the treadmill, just to get her heart rate up and a little sweat going. Then she had started with flat bench presses: three sets of 60, 80 and 100 kgs, fifteen reps each set, thirty seconds between sets, then a two-minute break and a couple of tiny sips of an electrolyte drink to keep her salts balanced. She tended to sweat a lot once her heart rate crossed 135–140 and hence dehydrated easily. After that, incline bench presses, same weight, same reps and time. And finally, decline bench presses.

That earned her and her spotter a five-minute break each, during which she exchanged hellos with regulars and kept an eye on the trainers, both the private ones who got paid extra for every forty-five-minute workout session as well as the floor trainers who only got a salary. She preferred to promote floor trainers to private trainers because that motivated the salary earners who were eager to work hard and prove that they deserved their own set of clients and a cut of the extra fee paid for private training. She also paid a better percentage to the private trainers – 60 per cent as against the 30 or 40 per cent most gyms reluctantly shared. She was routinely called by private trainers from other nearby gyms, eager to bring their roster of clients with them to earn the extra commish she paid. But she rarely agreed because in her view the extra commish was to reward her own deserving trainers who had worked hard to build their own list of clients, rather than an incentive to poach trainers and clients from other gyms. It kept other gym owners from getting too resentful of her quick success and at least one had visited a couple of times and expressed grudging admiration for how she ran the place.

Five-minute break over, she did flat bench dumbbell flys, three sets of 25 kgs (two dumbbells made 50 kgs), 30 kgs and 35 kgs, twelve to fifteen reps each. The same thirty-second break between sets, two-minute break to sip on Enerzal. Repeat with incline, then decline. Then another five-minute respite, during which she greeted a group of young women who had just entered for their workout: the Dakshineshwar athletes in training. These were India's best women boxers, wrestlers and weight lifters, many of them world class, all national-level or at least state-level champions, and Sheila had offered them a month of free workouts if they won a gold medal at the Commonwealth Games. They had won not one but two golds, one silver and a bronze, and she had generously upped the offer to three months of free workouts. The girls came by bus all the way from Dakshineshwar just to workout here, and livened up the place. It was great publicity and inspirational for the regular members to see these international-class athletes pushing the same weights and sweating it out on the same mats every day. New memberships had quadrupled by the second week before stabilizing at about twice the normal sign-up rate. Cheers and high-fives went up all around as they greeted her one by one and made the usual jibes about the 'old woman' who still liked to keep in shape. She was well liked by them all, not just for the free workouts, but because of something she had done for two of the girls a year ago, just before she started the gym, back in her 'earlier life', as she liked to say, though she never talked about that earlier life.

By the time the Dakshineshwar athletes settled into their own routines, good-naturedly joking in Bengali as they peeled off their tee shirts and stripped down to their shorts to reveal dark brown and near-black bodies compacted and tightened to perfection through hard training and punishing discipline, Sheila was on her third session: cable crossovers. Giving in to the temptation to show off a bit, she went way over her usual top pulling of 120 kgs, and tried for 160 kgs – 80 kgs on each end. The athletes whistled and cheered her on as even the members on the bank of cardio machines at the far end stopped looking at their plasma screens and Blackberrys long enough to watch, some with sneers of naked jealousy but mostly with bemused amazement.

She ended the session drained, and slumped down on

the floor, sweat staining her pullover from under both arms, right down to her waist. Her breath steamed inside her hood as she sipped the orange-flavoured drink from a Bisleri bottle and got her wind back. Fuck. Who said she was too old? At thirty-seven, she could give most women half her age a run for their money. Mits, her spotter, crouched beside her, patting her on the back proudly, happy to be sharing the limelight with her boss, and rambled on about some new scandal in Bollywood. Sheila could never understand how Hindi films had encroached even into parochial Bengal which had once had a flourishing film industry of its own and whose bhadralok had refused to speak any language except their own beloved Bangla. Yet there it was: Mits spoke reverentially of Bollywood stars and films the way her fellow bhadralok had once revered Satyajit Ray and Mrinal Sen. Sheila sighed. The world had changed. The dampness started to feel cold in the air-conditioned gym and she began to take off the pullover, then stopped herself: the scars. Exposing them would invite too many questions. Let the past stay past.

She gave herself a break on the triceps. Over-extending her limit on the cable cross had already given them a pretty good workout. She settled for doing bench dips which worked out both her abs as well as strengthened her triceps further. She was in the middle of the fifth set of fifty with one more set to go after that when the men walked in.

She knew right away that they were trouble. For one thing, men weren't allowed on this floor or the one above – strictly. Their entry meant that they had roughed up the receptionists to get in, because that was the only way Shailly and Meenakshi would have let them past. Then there was the way they looked. Two of them moustached, one bearded, two clean-shaven but with badly groomed oily hair. They were dressed in pant–shirts – except for the guy leading them who was in the staple white kurta–pyjama that most politicians favoured – all chewing paan at eight in the morning, and had that certain macho swagger that she knew well. It was the strut of political party workers or uniformed policemen, of off-duty military men or gangsters, men whose job entitled them to the use of force and violence, and who thought that hurting other people made them more powerful, superior in some way.

She watched as they strolled through the gym floor, looking at the women working out, ogling openly, exchanging lewd glances, wiggling eyebrows, staring openly at breasts in sports bras and bums in cycling shorts. Several of the members stopped working out to gape disapprovingly at them, and at least one snooty Park Street princess unleashed a barrage of Bengali, complaining about the invasion of her privacy. One of the men made a comment in street-crude Bengali about how he would like to *really* invade her privacy and the other men laughed.

What the fuck?

Sheila lowered her feet to the floor and rested her butt on the bench, watching them make their way towards this side of the floor. Mits glanced at her nervously and asked if she wanted her to go upstairs and fetch Ashutosh and the others. She meant the male trainers on the mixed floor, the only other men in the building apart from Jiteshkaku, the security guard who wasn't really old but not quite in his prime either.

Sheila shrugged and said okay, then reached out and gripped Mits's forearm. 'But quietly jaabo, no panicking, huh.' Mits slipped out discreetly, glancing back anxiously over her shoulder as she went.

The men were amongst the Dakshineshwar boxers now, who were neither intimidated nor upset by their presence. These were girls who had risen from the toughest backgrounds, many of them brutally abused by close family members, male relatives, or total strangers, brought up in the filthiest, poorest slums and backwaters: to them fitness and sports were survival, not a means of looking good or some macho power game. They fought to survive, to live. They had seen the likes of these assholes all their lives; they had dealt with them. They knew how to take care of them. The men seemed to realize this and their stances altered subtly. Instead of the open catcalling and eyebrow twitching, they resorted to verbal insults, questioning the feminity of the boxers, wondering aloud if there weren't penises – the Bangla word was 'boga' – in the girls' pants, challenging their womanhood. The girls drew closer, fists tightened, ranks closed, and just when violence threatened to explode, Sheila stood up and identified herself.

'Aami Sheila Ray aachey, owner of this establishment,' she said. 'Are you looking for me?'

The man who seemed to be in charge, a hefty fellow with mutton moustaches and a mouthful of paan, glared one final time at the boxers, then looked at Sheila with calculating, droopy eyes. Sheila thought he might be high on something other than just the tobacco in the paan.

'We are come to tell you shut up,' he said in horribly accented English. It was obvious he was trying to demonstrate that he was no less familiar with the language of Bengal's past oppressors than anyone else present.

It took Sheila a moment to absorb this. 'Shut up?' she asked, resisting the impulse to laugh because that would have been a disaster.

He waved his kurta-clad arms around. 'Gym! Shut up. Bandh koro! Closing time. Finish.'

That was clear enough. 'On whose authority?'

He reached into his pocket and pulled out a chai-stained sheet of pulp paper, folded into a small irregular square. A loose cigarette fell out when he pulled out the paper and opened it. 'Kolkata Municipal Corporation. KMC. Myself Assistant Ward Commissioner Raghuvendra Choudhry. Myself authority.' He sneered as his companions agreed loudly.

Sheila was at a loss for words. What was that short form everyone used in text messages and on Twitter and Facebook these days? *WTF*. This was a WTF moment, if ever. She started over to the man, reaching out for the paper, even though she knew already that she had been fucked over but good ... but by whom, and why?

Three

3.1

ANITA BENT HER HEAD to duck beneath the trajectory of the approaching gunstock, moving diagonally off to Isaac's right in the same motion. This put her out of the approach of the heavy wooden grip aimed at her skull, along with taking her just out of easy reach. As she passed him by on his right, she reached up with both hands, gripped his arm which by then was stretched out and starting to turn to adjust to her movement, and yanked upwards, hard. She pushed her hip into his groin, overstepping his right foot with her own, and anchored his lower body to the ground, even as she shoved his upper body up and back as hard as she could. Isaac's snarling expression changed to a look of shocked surprise as he found himself flung back and bent over. A sharp twist to his wrist and he lost the grip on the shotgun, issuing a small yelp. Then she stepped back, removing her foot and releasing his lower body while turning sideways and kicking his foot with her left boot. Bent over backwards at a thirty-degree angle, one foot kicked out front, he tottered for a moment like a slapstick character on freeze, then fell with a crunching of dried leaves to the ground. He stared up uncomprehendingly for a moment at Anita, who was now holding the shotgun that he had released. She pointed it at his chest and cocked both barrels before putting her finger on the trigger.

Isaac's hands shot up in front of his chest. 'Hey, kutta! I was just ... fooling with you, men!' He used the Malayalam term of endearment for a sibling – when used for a girl, it implied a mocking tone.

She looked down at him down the length of the barrel. 'Of course, kutta dearest,' she said, giving it back with interest. 'Same old Isaac. Always a bully, no? I think maybe you forgot that last time you tried to bully me, I taught you the lesson of your life. Remember?'

Anger flared in his eyes even as the colour deepened in his fleshy jowls. He had put on weight, a lot of it, and was running to fat now, she saw. Isaac, who had once been so vain about his appearance, so proud of his muscle tone and physique; who had strutted in his bikini briefs on the beach during tourist season, showing off his Charles Atlas bod to the blonde aunties and more than once rented out the use of his masculinity in exchange for a few days of five-star comfort, room service and a crumpled $100 bill at the end. Isaac, who had tried more than once to fumble with her breasts or caress her ass – and Lalima's too – when he'd had a few too many, bought with the remnants of those aunties' 'tips'. Her big brother, asshole of Varkala.

She racked the shotgun, enjoying the way the sudden movement and sound made him – hands held up before his face – cringe and whimper. The shells popped out and she caught them easily in her right hand. She racked it again, but there were only the two shells. She tossed them high into the grove and saw them disappear into dense shrubbery, then swung the shotgun back to rest on her shoulder. He had opened his eyes briefly to peer up between his fingers once he realized she wasn't going to shoot him, but when she swung the gun, he cringed again, until he realized she was laying the gun on her shoulder, not swinging it down like a club as he'd thought. He relaxed then and his face changed again to a snarl as his fingers turned to claws.

'Bitch-cunt,' he said. 'Back from whoring yourself in the big city and acting like you are Queen of Sheba! Purakottu poku! Why don't you just go back to your whore-city!'

She grinned at his sudden revelation of his true feelings. 'Kshamikkanam, kutta. I am so sorry! Did I injure your big strong shoulder?' She clicked her tongue sympathetically. 'Jnaan maappu chothikkunnu. Please, please forgive me kindly.'

His eyes flicked past her and she turned at once, just in time to see her mother emerge from the back door of the house, the one that led through the storeroom and kitchen. Iris Matthews – face wrinkled like a prune, dressed in a sloppy nightgown with rubber flip-flops on her feet – looked like she'd aged thirty years rather than just thirteen, her hair wild, tangled and completely white. A half-burnt cigarette smouldered between her fingers which resembled a chicken's claws and were stained almost as yellow from nicotine. She stared at Isaac, then raised her eyes to Anita's face, and in that short action, Anita saw her countenance change so dramatically, it was as if a switch had been turned on.

'Ente kutti! What have you done to my son, you bitch?' The voice was cracked from smoking and nowhere near as husky or Shirley Bassey-ish as Anita remembered it.

'He was the one who tried to bash my skull in with this thing,' Anita retorted. 'What the hell are you 'll doing with a shotgun, anyway? Who keeps guns in Varkala for Christ's sake?'

Iris Matthews crossed herself as she clutched the crucifix dangling from her neck. 'Don't take the Lord's name in vain, you ... you vaishya!'

Anita sighed. 'The whore references are quaint but really quite inaccurate. Just so you know.'

Her mother approached her from a wide circling angle, like a fisherman looking to toss a net across a school of fish without frightening them away. She looked drunk or drugged or both. Anita stepped back, putting a distance of a metre or two between herself and Isaac so Iris could approach her. The back door opened again and a man who closely resembled her father in his younger days came out, and for a moment Anita actually believed it was him; but of course, it was only Graham, her older brother who was younger than Isaac, looking more like Achchan than ever, right down to the pale skin with mottled red cheeks and prodigious beer belly. He was snapping on his belt, and had a crumpled magazine under his arm, as if he had just come out from the WC; he stopped short at the sight of Anita with the shotgun on her shoulder.

'Hi Graham, killed any kittens lately?'

He flushed, his acne-scarred cheeks turning bright red under his European-fair complexion. Graham had taken after their Anglo father unlike the rest of them who were as

Indian-dark as their Malayali mother, and it made Anita sad to see him look so much more like Achchan as he grew older.

'Philip said you were coming,' he said, snapping the belt buckle. He had missed a loop, but Anita didn't bother to inform him of the fact. 'What is it you are wanting from us now?'

'She has come to disgrace her Achchan's name, shameless vaishya that she is,' cried their mother, squatting beside Isaac who was now sitting up, holding his arm and wincing. 'She will not rest until she prints her whoring stamp on this good family's reputation. I always told her father he should have taken her and thrown her into the tide the night she was born. She is the devil's get, on account of your father covering me during Lent. Good for nothing but whoring and blasphemy. Look at how she attacked her own kutta! Witch!'

'He attacked me, actually,' Anita said calmly, though her heart was pounding at sprinting speed and bile churned in her belly. Why had she ever thought that things might have changed here? Everything was the same as it had been when she ran out thirteen years ago. Home sweet home.

'Bitch broke my arm,' Isaac said, getting to his feet by pressing down on his mother's shoulder. Iris promptly lost her balance and thumped down on her ass, legs splaying out and nightie riding up to reveal heavy cellulite-jellied thighs marked with thick green varicose veins. Isaac ignored his mother as he stood up to glare at Anita murderously, squeezing his shoulder with his left hand.

'Illa, it's not broken,' Anita said, 'you probably just pulled a muscle.'

'What do you want here?' Graham shouted, going over to help his mother up. Iris cursed him with a very un-Christian-like epithet and struggled to her feet on her own, hawking and spitting a gob of phlegm in Anita's direction. 'Why didn't you just stay away? There's no share for you in this, you know! You might as well just leave now. Purakottu poku!'

'Shut up, Gram,' Isaac said, glaring at his brother. 'Just shut your trap.'

Graham frowned near-sightedly at his brother. Anita realized that there was another reason why he resembled Achchan so much at first glance – he wasn't wearing his spectacles. *Must have left them back on the washbasin in the WC.* 'Is it not obvious? From someone or the other, she heard about the offer and now like a vaishya she comes to claim her pound of flesh! I am simply saying—'

'*Bitch*!' Both Isaac and Iris shouted at once.

Graham stood breathing heavily, then turned back to peer at Anita again.

All three looked at her with varying expressions of hatred and loathing. Anita sighed inwardly. Coming here had been a mistake after all. She should have known better.

She began to walk away without saying anything – there was really no point in bandying words with them – when the sound of a motorbike grew louder and Philip came in sight, riding Achchan's old Norton that looked as if it had been well cared for and sounded well maintained. Even with the bike goggles on, she could see him reacting to the sight of the family reunion.

He got off the bike, put it on its stand and stood looking at the four of them.

She looked at him, shook her head wearily and tossed the shotgun to the ground at his feet before walking away. She headed in the direction of the dirt road that led back to the main road which in turn led back to the highway, and didn't stop even when she heard their angry voices shouting, arguing, bickering behind her.

After a while, she was out of earshot and there was only the sound of the wind in the palms and the distant calling of gulls on the beach.

She walked on without looking back.

3.2

IT TOOK NACHIKETA SEVERAL minutes to fully comprehend what the judge had just said. He seemed to realize that she hadn't responded to his last query, paused to glance down at her from the bench over the rims of his half-spectacles, and asked if she was all right. His tone was kindly and that, more than anything he said, cut through the blurring noise that had begun to fill her head as he had read the summary judgment. She found that she had been holding her breath and let it wheeze out in a whistling rush, then gasped and breathed several more times, finding it hard to resume a normal breathing pattern. She had never been able to breathe quite as naturally since the attack and, from time to time when under duress, she tended to wheeze, sounding to herself like a battered tea kettle with a faulty whistle. But this was the first time she had let it happen in court and it was a measure of the shock she had received that she found herself not really caring about what the courtroom thought.

Her brain, which had frozen stiff somewhere in the first few minutes of the judge's reading of his own judgment, suddenly restarted with a diesel chugging, and she felt her motors coming back to life.

Did he say he's found for the complainant? He couldn't have said that, could he? No, no, no, no, it's not possible.

But it was indeed possible. And he had said exactly that.

After eight years of legal wrangling, of judgments and appeals and counter-appeals, stay orders and legal manoeuvring and blocking and tackling, after all these court dates and filings and procedures and struggle and toil, after all the seemingly futile and endless scrabbling at the pitiless stone feet of the blind bitch, could it be that she had finally, ultimately, eventually, inevitably ... *won*?

Could it possibly be?

Apparently it had.

She had.

He had.

The verdict was in at last. The 'phinal-phinal' verdict as Shonali always said, deliberately mimicking the Hindi 'ph' mispronunciation for the English 'f' sound. Oh, there was still the Supreme Court after this, and quite likely, the Shahs would go on to batter at the stone feet of that blind bitch as well. But for now, quite conclusively, decisively, she had, it seemed, won.

'... in full, with interest, legal fees ... *and reparations*!'

The magic words, glowing in foot-high 3D alphabets as they floated above her eyes in mid-air now, like superimposed titles in an American TV series, dancing across the courtroom from right to left looked good enough to pluck and eat.

Reparations!

Not just the amount she'd demanded for the medical expenses, plus the money and other gifts her parents had been compelled to give the Shahs under duress during her marriage – now regarded by the court as 'dowry' and therefore illegal – plus legal fees, plus a fair allotment as per alimony awards for a daughter-in-law of such a family as the Shahs, but also reparations in lieu of the mental, emotional, anguish she'd suffered! All of which amounted to ... *how much?* Well, equivalent to all the declared and known assets of the entire Shah family – which, being a Hindu Undivided Family, perforce possessed joint assets and cash holdings under income tax laws – which of course represented probably a third of their total value, two-thirds of the bulk almost certainly being socked away in black money and grey investments. The judgment even hinted at this without actually stating it up front in so many words, but implied that even after awarding their entire 'official' holdings and assets to their aggrieved ex-daughter-in-law, the Shah family would no doubt still be able to manage quite comfortably with their 'savings'.

There were the expected noises of outrage from the smartly turned out young lawyers of the big MNC law firm, and much hand-wringing by the Shahs themselves, and even a few tears and wails of grief, but Nachiketa saw from the stunned glassy eyed expressions on the faces of her ex-husband and ex-mother-in-law and ex-sisters-in-laws that whatever they might have expected, this was not it.

In a rush of blood to her own befuddled brain, it all made sense to her.

This judge, R.K. Jain. *He* was the honest one.

It was the previous one, whom he had replaced at this late juncture, who had been the one the Shahs must have bribed, and about which they had hinted heavily to Shonali in the last settlement conference – which Nachiketa had routinely refused to attend on principle and which she had permitted even Shonali to attend only because the judge had demanded it over the years. The judge had recently fallen prey to the Judges' Assets scam that came to light thanks to a public interest litigation filed under the new Right to Information Act. The Shahs had expected this to be their day in court; instead, it had turned out to be Nachiketa's all the way.

'Yes, yes, yes,' she said now to the judge who had started to look somewhat concerned – her face was probably contorted by now – not quite sure what she was agreeing to and not giving a damn.

She had won!

Everything!

They would have to pay their entire official 'white' fortune to her now, even if they still had unofficial 'black' assets tucked away. The resulting public shame and community embarrassment would be even more expensive, because in their Ahmedabadi sub-caste, if dowry murder by itself was not considered a blot on a family's reputation, financial loss certainly was. For them to have been defeated in open court by her, the 'pagli', the mad daughter-in-law, a woman who had dared to go up against the might of the community, was the ultimate humiliation. It would blacken the Shah name forever. They would be the laughing (sniggering) stock of the community and of Ahmedabad at large.

She had won!

Nachiketa spun her wheelchair around in a dizzying circle, startling the lawyers – waiting for their matter to be called next – standing behind her, and pumped her fist in the air, throwing her head back, tossing her hair off her face, and yelling to the packed courtroom: 'Yes!'

3.3

IT WAS PAST NINE that night when Sheila returned to the gym. The building was in darkness and neither Jiteshkaku nor the night watchmen were anywhere in sight. She assumed they had simply walked away rather than get involved in a possibly sticky political situation. Politics is a life-or-death matter in West Bengal, even in this second decade of the 21st century. And if there was one word that terrified people more than even the dreaded T-word – which denoted terror and its associated activites – it was the mighty M-word: Maoism and its various manifestations. Maoism is to India what the Irish 'troubles' had been to Britain in the last century. If she had had any doubts this morning, she had no doubt at all now: she was up against the dreaded might of the Maoists, albeit their most genial public face, the CPI

(M), Communist Party of India (Maoist). But the genial party face was just the front for the hydra-heads of the biggest grassroots-level violent armed rebellion India has faced in its history. And if she didn't lie back and take it now, the main body would rear up and crush her like a mite. That much had been made clear to her this day itself.

She stood for a moment on the gym floor, letting the events of the past several hours sink in. She had spent the whole day running from one bureaucratic office to the other before finally ending up back in front of the same asshole, Raghuvendra Choudhry, who had laughed uproariously when she entered his cabin, and had then proceeded to lay out the facts of the entire affair. She had still not absorbed everything he had said, and that was why she had returned here – to try and make sense of the whole mess. If things went badly for her – and by today's reckoning, they had already hung a sharp turn past Fucked and were well on their way to Totally Fucked via that picturesque old detour Royally Fucked – then she would probably lose the gym altogether. She had had to come back if only to try and figure out how things had gone pear-shaped so suddenly.

The glass windows let in enough ambient light to illuminate the outlines of the equipment. Without people working out, without the constant ambient chatter of voices talking and weights clinking, without the bright lights, pounding music and plasma screens flashing music videos and Bengali soaps, the gym was nothing more than a graveyard of hard-core branded tombstones. *She's Here* had been proud of the fact that it was the first gym in the neighbourhood to stay open eighteen hours a day, and was shut only between midnight and 6 a.m. Situated on the edge of Sector V, Salt Lake City's IT hub, it drew a number of members who worked odd shifts and liked to workout immediately before or after.

Sheila herself had grown accustomed to staying around till closing time, and even kept a cot, TV set and bookshelf in her office where she had begun routinely spending the night several times a week of late. Her flat in Sector I wasn't that far, especially with the roads being good and the traffic in Salt Lake City being minimal at night, but she found the still, empty flat in a dull residential-only neighbourhood boring after the vibrant hubbub of the gym. Besides, she couldn't cook to save her life, apart from the fact that eating alone only underlined the loneliness of her private life. She enjoyed eating in the locker room at night with whichever trainers and staff were on their dinner break, catching up on their personal updates, local gossip, or just chit-chatting and kidding around. At times they would discuss sexual matters and all the women's voices would grow hushed until a new arrival entered and enquired quizzically if there was a séance in progress, which comment would be greeted by embarrassed peals of laughter. It was during these sessions too that Sheila learnt what was in fashion and what was not, which were the best places to shop for cheap accessories, or knock-off winter wear from Tibetan immigrants, cheap Chinese electronics on the grey markets, and even the latest Sabyasachi formalwear worn on the ramp by the season's reigning supermodel. On one occasion her staff, egged on by a member who owned a beauty salon, had even attempted a makeover for Sheila. She had run laughing from the room when she realized they intended to turn her into a replica of the current Bengali actress who had recently scored a major hit in Bollywood; she had locked herself in the toilet and they had banged on the door of the stall and attempted to coax and cajole her out unsuccessfully for the next half hour.

She smiled now, remembering that horseplay. After her workout, that was her next favourite part of the day. After the last members had left, she would oversee the closing up, wave goodbye to the departing staff, and let the night watchmen fill their water bottles from the water cooler before locking the glass reception doors from the inside and retiring to her office. She would watch TV for a while if there was something on she was following – she had started to enjoy a couple of Bangla soaps of late – or read a book till she fell asleep. There were days she considered giving up her apartment and simply staying at the office. But she retained the lease on the outside chance that she would have a relationship again; one that lasted more than the three-week average of her past relationships. Until then, she felt more at home sleeping at the gym, and if that was pathetic, so be it.

Now, she sat on the cushioned seat of a lat-pulldown unit, surrounded by the ghostly shapes and silhouettes of the machines that were her livelihood, and realized just how good the past couple of years had been. Perhaps the best ones of her life, barring maybe those few years of middle childhood back in Daman when her mother was still around and before her father had been transferred to Mumbai and begun doing undercover work and everything had fallen to pieces. Now her life was beginning to crumble again, and though she was a grown woman now, there seemed to be almost nothing she could do to tackle the situation.

There's always something you can do. Always.

Yeah, sure.

The roots of her present predicament lay not in the

superficial municipal licensing laws and regulations she had allegedly violated, as today's notification listed out, but with a case she'd worked on several years ago, back in Dakshineshwar. At least, it had ended in Dakshineshwar. The case had begun in Assam where she had been hired by a very eminent north-eastern politician, ex-chief minister of Assam, now a wealthy industrialist and head of the party's north-east office, to find and retrieve his runaway seventeen-year-old daughter. Sheila had tracked the girl through the region for a month, finally locating her at Dakshineshwar in east Kolkata where she found her living in a contented same-sex relationship with a woman boxer of Bangladeshi origin. She had got to know both young women better and soon realized that running away from home had been the smartest thing the young girl had done in her short life. The father was knee-deep in dirty political dealings and underworld activities, and was that certain noxious type of Indian male whose one-sided sense of morality had frozen fast around the time that Rabindranath Tagore won the Nobel Prize for Literature, and to whom same-sex relationships were a gross aberration, incomprehensible and unacceptable under any circumstance. What made the situation even worse was the fact that the young woman boxer his daughter had chosen to leave him for happened to be a Bangladeshi Muslim. Sheila knew that once she reported back to him that his precious only child was spending her nights in bed with a lesbian Muslim Bangladeshi, if the bastard survived the shock, he would almost certainly want the other woman killed on the spot. He would then force the daughter into marriage with a suitable boy of his choosing, no doubt managing to find an alliance that furthered his own political and business interests at the same time, and that would be that. Sheila had done her share of bad things and had seen worse done, including some done to her. She had no intention of being part of the summary justice that the father would undoubtedly mete out to his daughter and her lesbian lover once he came to know of the truth.

Sheila made her choice. The daughter was five weeks shy of turning eighteen and becoming a legal major under Indian law. Sheila called Shillong and told the father's secretary that the daughter had gone to Pondicherry with a boy. Shortly after, she had gone down the east coast herself in hot pursuit, sending back periodical updates and increasingly optimistic reports as she apparently narrowed the chase. Once the daughter was legally eighteen, Sheila abruptly reported back to the father's sprawling Shillong tea estate mansion that the girl was not in Pondicherry and had probably changed her name to marry a man from another community, perhaps even departing the country for foreign shores under the new name.

The father had ranted and raved and refused to pay her the last part of her fee, which Sheila hadn't given a damn about; beyond that, there wasn't much more he could do. But Sheila knew that the father suspected, and the secretary was near certain that she had played them. In truth, the daughter *had* changed her name and religion – but she had converted to Islam, which they weren't capable of even dreaming of, so they never did track her down despite their subsequent efforts with other investigators. But over time, they had learnt enough through their independent enquiries to know that Sheila had led them up the garden path and, quite naturally, they had borne her a blood-grudge the size of a shopping mall.

Now, it was payback time. She had learnt today that the

paan-chewing feudal-age bureaucrat who had strolled into her gym and shut her down today was the nephew of the politbureau chief of the eastern division of the CPI (M). And that gent was married to the sister of none other than the same ex-chief minister-turned-aggrieved-father and Sheila Ray's former client. What was more, the secretary of that aggrieved father was now in Kolkata heading the group's new thrust into realty development and IT. He had moved here from Shillong quite recently, less than a month ago. As it appeared, he had wasted no time in settling the score with Sheila and he had all the power and weight of his employer's considerable political and allied network to do to her as he pleased.

There was still one way she could appease them and be spared complete ruin. The nephew, aka Raghuvendra Choudhry, assistant ward commissioner, KMC, had spelt it out to her in no uncertain terms: if she could lead them to the long-lost daughter even now, she would be spared. All she had to do was write down the address on a chit of paper. Email it. Fax it. Text it. Write it on a pair of pink panties and drop it from a passing Kolkata metro train. Just tell them where to find the absconding bitch and they would do the rest. She would play no part in it; in fact, he had told her quite reasonably as he chewed his paan noisily, she would only be completing the assignment that she had begun four years ago. What could possibly be the harm in that?

She sighed and pushed herself to her feet, heading in the direction of her office.

The bright fluorescents made her blink owlishly after the past hour spent in near darkness. She felt like switching them off, but needed the light to get around. Her room always had a few boxes of unpacked equipment parts lying around and she didn't need to break a toe or twist an ankle moseying around in the dark. She waited till her eyes adjusted, then spent the next half hour pottering around pointlessly, trying to think what she should do next. She knew that the one thing she could *not* do, absolutely *would not* do, was give up Gauri and Tasneem. Or Marhabha and Tasneem as they were now named. She would rather have her own teeth and nails pulled out with pliers one by one than give them up to these bastards. Which left ... what? Go to war? Against whom? The entire CPI (M) cadre in West Bengal? The entire nationwide network? She almost laughed aloud at the idea.

She realized that she hadn't eaten or drunk a thing all day and that she was dehydrated. She reached for the bottle of packaged water on her desk and when she picked it up, the bottle hit something and knocked it off the edge of the desk. She bent to pick it up and saw that it was a hefty yellow manila envelope.

Four

4.1

ANITA SPENT THE NIGHT at a hotel near Papanasam Cliff.

On the long walk back to the highway, she had half a mind to take a taxi to Thiruvananthapuram and catch the first flight back to Mumbai. But Lalima stopped her. She had come here for Lalima, and the least she could do was pay her respects before going back. *Tomorrow,* she promised herself, *tomorrow after I light a candle for her, I will go back to Mumbai.*

And after that, never again would she come back to the place of her birth and childhood, never again face those Munsters, the Addams Family, as Lalima and she had called them.

They had come up with the name one summer after Ezhu had brought back two videotapes filled with cartoons taped from TV. She still remembered how goggle-eyed they had been at the thought of a channel dedicated to cartoons and which ran all day and night – 24/7 as one would say now – and how they had sat together on the leaking couch in Lalima's house and watched Wily Coyote and Road Runner, Yogi Bear, *Spongebob Squarepants*, Bugs Bunny, Foghorn Leghorn, *Speed Racer*, Daffy Duck, *Tweety and Sylvester*, *The Addams Family*, Elmer Fudd, *The Munsters*, Porky Pig, *The Perils of Pauline*, all day long for two whole days, rewinding the tape over and over again until Lalima's amma had grown weary and thrown them out of the house, telling them to go spend some time in the sun. Watching *The Munsters*, Anita and Lalima had looked at each another and waggled their eyebrows as they did when they found something mutually amusing. Neither of them had actually said it out loud, but from that day onwards, they routinely referred to Anita's family as The Munsters. As in 'The Munsters are at it again' or 'I can't come over today, The Munsters are forcing me to go to church with them'.

That was also the night Anita became fully aware of her sexual proclivities.

While watching one of those tapes later that night, they had paused the VCR between cartoons because Anita had to go use the loo and in the meantime Lalima had discovered an image left over from the programme that had previously been recorded on the tape. Apparently, Ezhu had taped the cartoons over a blue film. The errant bit of undeleted film didn't show very much, just a bare-chested girl with part of what appeared to be a male appendage poking into the frame. The image was blurry enough that the said appendage might just be the man's finger, or it might be what they both assumed it was. Excited and whispering to avoid waking Lalima's mother, they kept pressing the cue button to fast forward frame by frame, but there were only two or three frames, blurred and grainy from the over-taping, and it was hard to be sure. The hardest part was suppressing their irrepressible giggling to avoid waking Amma. Ezhu denied it hotly when confronted the next day, but Lalima said she had seen a magazine once in his suitcase, peeking out between piles of shirts, and the portion of the cover she had glimpsed had said 'PLAYB' in big bold type.

That errant image left over from the alleged blue film – which Ezhu insisted was a National Geographic documentary on African tribal mating rituals – had marked the first year that they had openly begun talking about the 'S-word' and all things related. Later that night, about to fall asleep facing each other on Lalima's cot, Anita had been overcome by a wave of new emotion, a great desire to reach out and caress her friend, accompanied by a sweet aching in her groin. Unable to resist, she had reached out and put her hand on Lalima's shoulder and neck, then leaned into her warm intimate space to kiss her on the lips. Lalima, who became a zombie once she was very sleepy, mistook it for friendly affection, and thumped Anita on the side of the head roughly. The blow made Anita's ear ring and she realized what she had been about to do – or guessed at it, since she had no real idea what these feelings meant or might lead to – and she blew a soundless whistle up Lalima's nose, making her sneeze. Then she turned over and went to sleep. From that day onwards, Anita began to grow aware of the fact that she might not be a typical Malayali girl in certain respects. An understatement, to be sure, but even the most historic changes often begin with a nondescript event. Looking back later, she would always pinpoint that moment when she had tried to kiss the half-asleep Lalima as the moment of realization that she was gay.

Now, unpacking her bags on the bed, she was suddenly overcome by a wave of emotion. There was a whole bunch of things mixed up in it: her family, the past, the present, Lalima ... She slumped to the cold tiled floor, spine hitting the skeleton of the bed, and dunked her face between her knees. She thought she was going to cry, but no tears came. She focused on breathing slowly, taking deep, calming breaths. It helped a little. It had been a long day and an even longer month. She had just come off a case in Mumbai, investigating a murder in a tony private club on behalf of a media group that later turned out to want the crime covered up rather than exposed because the killer was a major advertiser in their group's publications and TV channels. The fact that the murderer was also a serial rapist who used his Page 3 celebrity status to gain his victims' trust didn't bother them in the least. Anita had turned the evidence in that case over to a person who she knew wouldn't hesitate to wreak vigilante justice on the bastard. The media group had suspected her of doing it and had refused to pay the balance portion of her fee, which had crimped her finances. She was short of cash and had no other job in hand – none that would pay decently, at least. There were plenty of messages on her voice mail from spouses wanting their wives or husbands or significant others followed, but sleazy infidelity cases rarely paid enough to cover the aggravation of dealing with jilted wives and cuckolded husbands. More often than not, the aggrieved parties blamed *her*, the messenger, for the message, as if by clicking pictures of the illicit trysts of their partners, she had made them happen. She had had it with those cases. But if she didn't get something soon, she would have to pick the least sleazy of them and try to make a rupee or two. Mrs Matondkar was patient about her missing the rent mostly, but she could also get cranky occasionally. That usually had something to do with Anita being overdue more than three months. Right now, she was at two-and-a-half months, which meant she needed to give the old bag some cash or endure nagging lectures day and night.

She had no idea when she fell asleep.

She opened her eyes to find herself lying asleep on her side, crouched in a foetal position with the bed against her spine and the room in pitch darkness. Even so, she instantly knew where she was: *I'm in a room in a hotel in Papanasam; I'm here for Lalima's funeral.* Her cell phone was buzzing somewhere close by and there was a knock at the door. She had sleep grit in her eyes and her breath smelt awful to herself, but the impromptu slumber had refreshed her. She grabbed her phone as she stood up, noting by the flashing screen that she had slept the afternoon and evening away, almost seven hours, and that Philip was calling. She happened across the light switch while patting the wall to find her way to the door and switched it on: cold fluorescent lighting bathed the room.

She fumbled the door open.

It was Philip.

'Chechi,' he said, shifting from one foot to the other. 'May I come in?'

Someone dropped a spoon in another room – their door was open, the sound of a television playing also audible. The clattering made him glance over his shoulder in a way that suggested pursuit. She let him in.

They sat sipping filter coffee. Ordering some filter coffee first, Anita had taken a moment to pee and then splash some water on her face. She had forgotten her toothbrush and had settled for rubbing her finger over her teeth. The filter coffee was hot and smelt wonderful. She had missed filter coffee in Mumbai. Mrs Matondkar had some kink about filter coffee and refused to let Anita make it in her kitchen – one of her many small eccentricities. And the only places that still served good filter coffee in the city were the handful of Udupi joints that hadn't caved in and morphed into restobars, and there were fewer of those each year.

Philip looked thirty years older since she'd last seen him, which was about thirteen years ago. He had put on some weight, all in the wrong places, and his watery grey eyes looked even more dog-sad than they had before. His hairline had receded considerably and he hadn't shaved in days. He sat rubbing the skin of his palms with his thumbs, an old nervous tic he had had as a kid. He looked haggard. He would pick up the cup of coffee, sip it noisily, then put it down quickly and go back to rubbing his palms. Anita didn't need to be a psychiatrist to know there was something seriously fucked up about him. Then again, her whole family was fucked up. *It's The Munsters again, Lalima, they just won't quit.*

Finally, she reached out and touched his knee gently, barely a fingertip. He winced as if struck by a belt.

'Want to tell me what's up?' she said.

He looked around, then sat up, leaning forward awkwardly in the low cane chair. She could see a bald patch beginning at the back of his head. It was shiny. He looked at her and she was shocked to see his pupils looking huge, like a schoolgirl's eyes in an anime cartoon. *He's hopped up,* she thought. She knew the signs. *But on what?*

'The package,' he said. 'Lalima must have sent you a package. Where is it? I have to give it to them. Otherwise, they'll fucking kill me, chechi.'

4.2

NACHIKETA WAS STRANDED AT the Delhi–Gurgaon border toll plaza when she got the call. Traffic was bad as usual on NH-8 but what irked her was the proliferation of Qualises filled with foreigners blocking every single toll lane. The huge hoardings told her what all the firangs were here for: the Annual BPO World Convention. Bad enough that they descended in tens of thousands upon an already choked traffic and infrastructure system, but did they have to block all the toll lanes too? Really? Couldn't they simply queue up and occupy eight or ten of them? She wasn't the only irked driver: people were honking angrily all around her.

A Sikh driver in the adjoining lane got out of his Honda CRV and walked over to the nearest Qualis to knock at the driver's window. The driver looked like a Jat; he ignored the Sikh. The turbanned sardar said something through the closed window. The driver ignored him, then lurched the car forward into the space left by the car in front as the line crawled forward. The Sikh mouthed what was clearly an abuse, gave the Qualis driver the raised finger, which gesture, since the car was moving forward, was extended to the blonde and brunette foreigners packed into the back seats as well. They glared at him in evident shock and one of them said something to the driver. Nachiketa saw the driver lean back and reply, saying something that made them smile.

Probably telling them in Haryanvi-accented English that all sardarjis are crazy. And at some point, they'll meet a Sikh who'll tell them that all Jats are crazy. Welcome to India. We all hate each other equally. Please to be paying in USD, sirji.

The Qualis in front of her lurched forward and she inched the car ahead. Her phone rang just then and she was tempted to ignore it. She was too euphoric from the judgment today to want to deal with another client. This was her day, whatever was left of it, and all she wanted was to go home, crack open a bottle of Sula and listen to some Rahat Fateh Ali Khan. During the weekend, she was going to meet up with the girls and part-ay! But she happened to glance at the screen of the Blackberry and it was flashing 'Office – Direct Line', which meant the landline on her desk. That had to be Shonali.

She slipped the Bluetooth earphone over her ear and pressed the button. 'Yeah, Shonali?'

Silence.

The Qualis in front of her had stopped moving, but hadn't put its brakes on; the vehicle rolled slowly back towards Nachiketa's Civic. She hit her horn with the heel of her hand

and the red brake lights came on at once, though she could see the driver's eyes glaring at her through his rear-view mirror. This one looked like it was filled with Swedes. Every passenger was tall, thin and blonde. They reminded her of the cast of the movie based on a Stieg Larsson novel, the original Swedish one starring Noomi Rapace, which she had loved – and *whom* she had loved. She was dreading what Hollywood would do to the US adaptations.

'Hello, Shonali? What up, girl?' She wondered if she was crying. Shonali could get emotional at times, usually over a man. Though she was cut up about her mother, the fact was that after ten years of fighting cancer through successive courses of chemo, radiation and ultrasonic treatments, she had pretty much exhausted her reserves of emotion on that front. The news that the cancer had metastasized yet again, this time to the brain and lungs, wasn't exactly earth-shattering. *Don't be bitchy, Nachos,* she told herself admonishingly. People might say 'it's better she went soon, she was suffering so much' all they liked, but the fact was dying was dying and gone was gone forever.

Still no response.

An argument appeared to have broken out four or five lanes to her right. She couldn't see much because all the Qualises fencing her in were higher than her eye-level. But she thought it must have something to do with the Qualis convoy blocking up all lanes. She could hear the angry raised voices even through her closed window, air-conditioning and the soft rock playing on 107.1 FM on her car radio.

Dogs barking.

Not here, not at the Delhi–Gurgaon toll.

On the phone.

Dogs were barking in the background. Close by.

It sounded like Justice and her pups. One grown dog's high-pitched hoarse ruff and a chorus of smaller ruff-ruffs pitching in for support.

'Hello? Who is this, please?' she asked sharply. With one hand, she switched off the radio and used the other hand to cover her open ear to block the rising noise of the argument outside. People were getting out of their cars to peer in the direction of the fight. All the firangs stayed inside their Qualises, no doubt terrified of being massacred by sardarjis. She would have probably been out there if the effort of shifting to the wheelchair, then lowering herself out, then coming back and doing it all over again wasn't so Olympian.

'Hello, will you please answer me? I know you're calling from my office. I can see the number on my caller ID. Who are you?'

The dogs stopped barking briefly. In that moment of respite, she distinctly heard the sound of someone breathing. A man. It sounded like a man breathing with the phone receiver held to his ear.

'I can hear you breathing, you bastard. Mard hai to kuch bol, gaandu! If you're a man, then speak up, assfucker!'

The Hindi abuses and challenge to his manhood did the trick. He spoke up at last, speaking in a coarse Punjabi accent.

'Where is package? We want now. Tell us.'

Who was this guy? What package was he talking about? A dozen recent and some not-so-recent cases passed through her mind, but none of them had anything to do with any packages. All were about women: those were the only cases she took. Women's rights, battered women, sexual abuse, sexual harassment, rape, spousal abuse, a few high-society divorces to help pay the rent ... but no packages she could recall.

'I don't know what you're talking about,' she replied.

The man said something in Punjabi, but not to her, to someone else with him in the room – *in my office, the fuckers!* – then came back on the line.

'Soni kudi hai. Bada mazaa aaya. Ab bol tu phataphat. Package kahaan hai. Gudiya ki jaan pyaari hai to bataa varnaa bye-bye bol abhi.'

She was struck dumb for a moment, then recovered. 'Who is this? Kaun ho tum? Main abhi issi waqt police ko phone kar rahi hoon. You won't get away with this, you bastards!'

He sounded unimpressed by her threats.

'Package! Madam, package is where? Please tell fast-fast. Time is short.'

'I don't know what package you're talking about,' she said. 'But if you hurt even a hair on that girl's head—'

The man on the phone said something to someone else in her office.

Then he disconnected the line.

The Qualis in front of her moved forward. The fight appeared to have escalated because she could see heads bobbing over the tops of Qualises, people clearly fighting, even some arms rising and falling, then the distinct sound of glass breaking and something heavy striking the metal body of a car. The car behind her honked long and hard for her to move forward. She glanced to the right: she was boxed in on that side. But on the left, there was a gap similar to the one in front of her, caused by the driver being distracted by the fight and forgetting to move forward in the queue. Horns were blaring everywhere now, adding to the chaos and confusion. The driver in the car beside hers had opened his door and was standing on the seat to get a better view. He was grinning and passing a running commentary to the other occupants of his car.

Nachiketa put the paddle shift into gear and eased out of her line, cutting across the car to her left and swinging around. She cut around it and U-turned, then drove back the way she had come, earning several horn blasts as drivers reacted angrily to her lack of civic sense. But most were distracted by the fight and the confusion, and in the chaos, she was able to slip back and turn into the lane heading back towards Delhi. In another moment she was back in the flow, heading towards Delhi Gate. She thought she could be in her office in half an hour at this hour, maybe even less. Tears began spilling from her eyes as she accelerated, overtaking car after car in rapid succession. She wondered what people made of the 'handicapped' sign on her rear windshield when she overtook them: they probably thought it was a joke. Crippled drivers didn't go racing on one of the world's deadliest highways. Her knuckles were white on the steering wheel. She had never done anything like this before and her heart was pounding.

Then again, nobody had ever broken into her office, taken her assistant hostage and then called her to say in guttural Punjabi: *'Lovely girl, this one. We had a great time. Now you speak quickly. Tell us where the package is. If you want to see this girl alive again, speak fast or say your goodbyes.'*

She made it in twenty-two minutes.

4.3

IT WAS LATE BY the time Sheila dropped the last photocopy on the dishevelled pile beside her. Her habit of neatness made her gather up the pages and slip them back into the envelope. Then she stared at the thick envelope, stupefied. Her stomach had stopped complaining about half an hour ago though she had forced herself to stop reading and order some takeout from the Chinese restaurant around the corner. She had the tendency to get acidity if she missed a meal. That, and the fact that she had barely eaten all day, had worked out harder than usual, and she had burnt as many calories from stressing as from physical activity. But right now, food and calories were the last things on her mind. She was just too stunned by the contents of the yellow manila envelope.

She sat back, leaning her head against the wall. It was difficult to rest her head because the inside of the wall was coated in those faux half-stones used for weatherproofing that resembled stone walls of some ancient castle or fort. This side of the building leaked during the monsoon and she had had the waterproofing done just three months ago. Now, how the hell would she recover that cost? Forget that. How would she continue her business with these goons breathing down her neck? Assuming she didn't give up the girls – which was a given – how the hell was she going to survive? Everything she had was invested in this place. She would lose it all.

Yet she wasn't able to think about that either.

All she could think about was the contents of the manila envelope.

And what they meant.

She sat like that for several minutes, barely aware of the passing of time. The sound of someone calling out roused her. It was coming from the front of the building. She frowned and got to her feet and walked out of her office to the adjoining yoga room which was empty except for a pile of rubber mats neatly stacked in a corner. She had booked an up-and-coming power yoga instructor from the city to come down on alternate days for two sessions of fifty minutes each day. The classes were over-subscribed already and not, she assumed, because the instructor happened to be male and charismatic. Now she would have to call him to cancel and let him swallow the one month's advance she had had to pay to book him.

The yoga room had floor-to-ceiling glass and brushed-aluminium French windows running along its length. She slid them open and stepped out, leaning out to look down at the front of the building.

A man was standing, peering up at the lit windows of her office, the only part of the building still illuminated.

'Hello?' she called out, waving to attract his attention.

He turned and saw her, and held up a plastic bag in one hand. 'Parcel?'

Of course. The place was locked up. She had come in through the rear service entrance, but he must have been foxed by the locked front door and dark entranceway. She pointed to the rear of the building and said in Bengali: 'Go around to the back. There's a door there. I'm coming down.'

He nodded and began walking in the direction she had pointed.

She shut the French windows behind her and went through the gym room back to her office. Her handbag was on her desk. She unzipped it and pulled out her wallet and left the office.

He was waiting outside the rear door when she came out. Little more than a kid, thin and gangly. 'Sorry to confuse you,' she said in Bengali, 'I forgot that the front door was locked up.'

He smiled at her awkwardly and she noticed his distinctly south-Indian features.

'Bengali?' she asked.

He smiled again and shook his head. 'Chennai,' he said by way of answer.

She nodded and paid him. This was the new Kolkata where nobody watched Bengali films anymore and Hindi movies ran to full houses, and your home delivery was more likely to be dropped off by a young man from Chennai than a native Bengali. After all, she was in Salt Lake City, the most modern township in the region, built entirely by Yugoslavians on contract. Anything was possible.

The bill came to Rs 267 and she had given him three hundred-rupee notes. He was counting off the change when she saw the red light flashing, reflected in the glass window behind the delivery boy. It seemed to hover in mid-air, disconnected from any other object, floating steadily in an arc as it approached. It went down the bylane and then was hidden from her view by the building.

She didn't need to go to the front of the building to know that it was a police wireless van with the red light blinking on top, or that it had stopped outside her gym, or that it meant the police had come for her. She should have expected things to escalate quickly once she didn't cooperate immediately with the municipal thugs. It was obvious that the big guns meant business this time. Their harassment, she might have endured stoically. But by sending in the cops, they had upped the ante, forcing her to fess up or get fucked. They knew her history; they knew she wouldn't bear scrutiny by the authorities. They knew that Kolkata Police would love to take her in for questioning and hold her for as long as the big guns wanted her held.

The delivery boy handed her the change.

'Keep it,' she said, starting to walk away quickly. She didn't look back or turn around or hesitate, just began walking towards the rear wall of the compound.

'Thank you, madam,' she heard the Chennaiite say before she went out of earshot.

The rear wall was barely five feet high. She vaulted over it easily, and was in the compound of the adjoining property, another office building which was closed for the night. She walked through the empty compound all the way to the far wall, then crossed over that as well. That led her to a back lane which wound its way circuitously through various bylanes before connecting with the main road. She continued walking, meeting almost nobody except a security guard or two and a few stray dogs who sniffed excitedly at the bag of food in her hand. They reminded her that she was carrying her dinner and after a moment's thought, she dropped the bag and continued walking. The sound of the strays tearing open the packets of food followed her for several yards.

She thought quickly as she walked: if they had stretched out the long arm of the law to reach for her at the gym, they would already be at her house. There was no point going there either. Luckily, she was carrying her wallet. She had no idea if they could or would go to the extent of freezing her bank accounts, but she wouldn't put it past them. All it would take was an income tax order. If they had planned this as thoroughly as it appeared, the order would have been issued weeks earlier, ostensibly dispatched to her office or home address via registered post but cleverly diverted either to an incorrect address or intercepted and torn up en route. She remembered using an ATM somewhere in this locality a couple of months ago. She found it nestled outside a bank branch that was shut for the night. The security guard barely glanced at her and she was relieved to find that cash was still there in her account. She withdrew the maximum limit allowed by the card, fifty thousand rupees, dividing the red thousand-rupee notes into two bundles, folding each in half and stuffing it down the front pockets of her jeans. She used the respite to look through the wallet which was too thick to fit in her pocket. It was mostly stuffed with various papers and stuff related to the gym. She tore them all into strips and discarded them in the waste paper basket overflowing with ATM receipts, pulled out the couple of thousand rupees cash, all her credit and ID cards, and stuffed those into her rear pockets before dumping the wallet too.

She felt as if she were bulging at the buttocks as she exited the air-conditioned ATM cubicle and stepped out into the balmy night air, but a quick glance at her reflection in the glass door showed only a slightly fuller look. Nothing that would attract unwanted attention – well, at least not *unusual* unwanted attention.

Her car was back at the gym. She would have to forget about that as well. She was on the run now and would have to assume everything she owned or possessed was gone for good. She had always realized this day might come someday, but the last year or so had lulled her into thinking that maybe, just maybe, it wouldn't. That was why she had stopped taking her usual precautions – stashing money away in off-site safe places, moving house every six months, etc. This has been the longest she had stayed in one place since the Munshi kidnapping. Since Bhasker had died. She would have to assume she no longer had a home, workplace, car, possessions ... nada. Just the clothes on her back and the cash in her jeans. Period.

She was crossing the highway when she remembered that she had left the contents of the yellow manila envelope behind as well.

Five

5.1

'WHAT PACKAGE?' ANITA ASKED.

Philip looked at her with a vicious shine in his eyes, as if she had just asked him who he was and what he was doing here. 'The one she sent you, crazy whore.'

She was taken aback by the sudden nasty streak. 'Hey, take it easy. I'm asking because I haven't a clue.'

He sniggered and wiped his nose on his sleeve, curling his elbow and wrist in a peculiar way which reminded her of a spin bowler. That was old. 'Yeah. You just came here for the fucking funeral.'

She stared at him silently until he realized she wasn't speaking and looked up at her.

'What?' he asked sullenly.

'I *did* come here for the fucking funeral,' she said. '*You* were the one who called me and told me the news, remember? Why else would I come?'

He stared at her, then looked away and shrugged. 'I don't know. For your share?'

Now she was really foxed. 'My share of what? I don't know what you're talking about, brother.'

He looked at her intently, his eyes watering. His nose was running too, she noticed. He wiped both on his sleeve. 'Really? But you opened the package, no?'

She sighed and got up, putting down the empty cup and wanting more. 'I told you, I don't know anything about a pack—' She stopped, turned and looked at him. 'Was it a yellow manila envelope, about yay big?' She held her hands apart to indicate the size.

He smacked the heel of his hand on his forehead. 'Sheh, budhiyillatha ... Yes, chechi. Which other package?'

'And you said *Lalima* sent me that envelope?'

He nodded, affecting a look of long-suffering misery.

'That would mean she had sent it just before she died ...' Anita trailed off.

Philip was shaking his head. 'She had given it to some lawyer in Kozhikode, with instructions to mail it out if anything happened to her.'

Anita blinked rapidly, then sat on the bed again. 'What do you mean, "if anything happened to her"?'

He spread his hands. 'Like what *did* happen, pottee. She died or what?'

'Yes, but people don't give instructions like that to their lawyers if they're expecting to live to a ripe old age and die of natural causes at eighty-nine. Are you trying to say Lalima thought she was in some kind of danger?'

He looked at her, his mouth gaping open, slack-jawed. She was sure he was on meth. Nasal intake. That would explain all the symptoms, which was good because it meant he hadn't progressed to the intravenous stage yet; he could still be treated. 'Obviously, da? Why else she was killed?'

Anita leaned forward. 'What did you just say? Lalima was *killed*?'

'Yeah,' he said sullenly, as if it were obvious. 'Naturally she was killed. She went too far. They warned her.'

'*Who?*' She almost shouted. Even said in a normal tone, he still flinched. 'Who killed her? And why? What does all this have to do with that envelope?'

Philip stared at her.

'You didn't open the package,' he said at last, uncertainly at first, as if afraid to hope. Then, with more certainty: 'You didn't open it!'

'No, I didn't. Answer my question, Philip. Why would anyone kill Lalima? She was just a social worker, wasn't she?'

'Social meddler,' he said with evident scorn. Then, seeing her reaction, he tried to make amends. 'To them! *They* said. She was meddling in things that were too big for her to handle. She should have walked away when she had the chance.' He added belatedly, '*They* said,' but with a sullenness that left no doubt about his own low opinion of such meddlers.

'But she didn't walk away,' Anita said, realizing that the best way to get it out of him was to set up a rhythm. 'Instead, she ...'

He nodded, falling in line, 'Instead she stole this data key belonging to Father Yeshua ...'

'... and ...'

'And she made copies and printouts and sent them out to god knows who, but I knew she had sent you one because she mentioned you. She said Anita would kick their asses. She said you would come here and go to town on them.' He sniggered and wiped his nose and eyes on the sleeve again. 'She thought you were fucking superwoman, MrsChristianBaleBatmandarknightrises...'

He mumbled something else under his breath, something she couldn't catch. Then he said without looking up, 'So they made me call you here for the funeral, knowing you would definitely come because you won't miss your bestfriendfirstlover's fucking funeral, would you?' Suddenly, he released a massive snorting exudation and began to cry. 'Now they have sent me to get the package from you, because that was the only reason they called you here, to get the package and make sure you hadn't told anyone else yet ...'

'... about what's in the package,' she prompted gently.

'About what's in the package,' he agreed, crying. 'So please, chechi, just give it to me and I'll give it to them and everything will go back to the way it was before ...'

'Before ...?' she asked, careful not to sound too interrogative, just a gentle uplift at the end of the word.

'Before that Greenpeacebitch came to the orphanage and fucked it all up,' he said, digging the heels of his hands into the sockets of his eyes and rubbing viciously, as if trying to erase his eyes from existence. 'Before ...' He broke down, sobbing.

Anita put her arm around him and held him for a while. From the corridor outside, she could hear the sounds of children yelling and running. Several minutes passed slowly. She held him tightly, feeling the way his body trembled spasmodically. When she thought he had calmed down sufficiently, she said softly, 'Before ...'

'Before, everyone was great,' he said. 'Father Yeshua liked me and I liked my work. Everything was so good, so clean, so pure. We were doing God's work. Jesus' work.'

'Praise Jesus,' she said.

'Praise Jesus,' he replied automatically. Then, turning his head so he could look at her. 'Sing the song, chechi.'

'The song,' she said, knowing exactly what he meant.

'Sing, no. Please.'

She took a deep breath and sang softly. '*One day at a time, sweet Jesus, that's all I'm asking of you, just give me the strength to do every day what I have to do ...*'

He sang along in the second verse, coming in late and off-key. '*Yesterday's gone, sweet Jesus, tomorrow may never be mine.*'

She continued singing until she couldn't remember any more verses and was repeating the same ones over and over again. At some point he stopped and grew still, swaying from side to side in rhythm with the tune. She sensed his breathing changing, but continued to the end of the refrain. When she stopped and looked down at him, he was asleep.

She laid him down gently on the bed. He stirred, turned sideways and curled into a foetal position, hugging his knees as if cold. She covered him with the unused sheet. He slept like a baby.

She waited until she was certain his breathing had settled into a deep-sleep pattern. Then she went to her bag and unzipped it softly, moving slowly and being very quiet to avoid waking him up.

It was right at the bottom. The only reason she had even brought it along was because it had Lalima's name at the back, with an address c/o a law office in Kozhikode. She had forgotten all about it since the time she received it.

Now, she cut open the sealed flap with the nail file from her cosmetics pouch and removed a thick stack of what appeared to be photocopied documents. A loose sheet fell out from the bottom. She caught it and glanced at it: it was just a list of dates and places which meant nothing to her. She put it aside.

Riffling through the pile of documents, she saw what seemed to be pages and pages of some kind of financial data, with notes scribbled in the margins, and figures and rows highlighted in grey – they had probably been highlighted in the original document and then photocopied, which meant these were copies of a particular printout with extra highlights and notes in the margins. There were pages of some kind of transcripts of telephone conversations. Emails – there were a lot of them. Property ownership records, car ownership documents, photo IDs of numerous people, some kind of trust ownership deed, details of bank accounts, wire transfers, mutual fund statements, and several other financial documents that she couldn't make head or tail of at first glance.

She sat cross-legged on the carpet, picking up sheets, looking over each one, then putting it aside, trying to make sense of all the raw data, figures and documents. The margin notes and highlighting helped, but it was still mostly unintelligible to her. She desperately craved more filter coffee but she didn't want to use the phone or have someone ring the doorbell. She needed Philip to sleep while she figured out what the fuck was going on here, and why the hell anyone would kill Lalima over these documents.

The rest could wait until Philip woke up.

5.2

EVEN AS NACHIKETA PULLED into the building compound, she knew something was wrong. She could hear the dogs barking and the security guard was nowhere in sight. The building was in darkness and this part of Vasant Kunj was fairly secluded and upscale. The trees added to the privacy but also isolated the buildings, creating pools of shadow that the street lights and ambient light couldn't penetrate entirely. It made the street more than a little creepy at night.

It took her a good five minutes to shift from her driver's seat to the wheelchair and get rolling, and during those minutes, the voice in her head kept urging her to call the police. But she didn't. By the time she was moving into the building entrance, she knew it was too late, that she was on her own now because even if she called them now, there was no way they would arrive in time to be of any assistance. She paused at the foyer in front of the lifts before turning down the corridor that led to her office.

Know what you're doing, Nachos? She asked herself.

Yes, came the grim reply.

She rolled down the corridor. It was pitch dark. Justice's pups were in the passageway, and they came bounding to her in the darkness. She heard their eager yelps and whining and felt their rough tongues rasping on the back of her hands as she steered the electric wheelchair. Usually she would be afraid of running over one of the puppies, but now, in the dark, there was little she could do; so she just steered until she felt the front guard bump against the wall. The closer the dogs came to her office, the more agitated they became. The pups went crazy, barking and scratching at the door, as if wanting to go inside.

'Where's your mother?' she whispered. Where was Justice? Surely the goons who had called her hadn't done something to the poor dog?

In the darkness, she could still smell the urine from the night before, on the front door of her office, and overpowering that disgusting odour, the pungent stench of something else. Something she couldn't identify.

She felt something wet and sticky beneath the wheels of the wheelchair and knew that was bad. It reminded her of wheeling her way through the aisles of movie theatres where Coke or caramel popcorn had been spilled. This felt similar – sticky and wet, yet yielding. The smell made her want to gag. Whatever that odour was, it was related to the stuff leaking out from under her front door. She used her Blackberry to see what it was and almost dropped the cell phone. In the garish bluish light from the phone screen, it looked like blood. But it couldn't be blood. There was too much of it. Moving the cell phone to and fro, bending over as far as she dared, she sniffed and immediately recognized the pungent vaporous odour: petrol. Where was *petrol* coming from? Had someone spilled a can on the floor inside the office? What the hell had happened here? And there were streaks of something darker, more viscous mixed with the petrol. Was that blood? She thought it might be. Did dog blood look the same as human blood? She couldn't remember. She didn't know whether to be more worried about Shonali or Justice or both equally. Whoever these men were, they were clearly unscrupulous.

She knocked hard on the door.

There was no response.

She tried the knob and it turned. Her breath caught in her throat.

She knew she should back out of here, get out and call Delhi Police.

But Shonali was in there somewhere. And the men who had called her. They would be here, waiting; they had said so. If she retreated and called the police, they would make a run for it and escape. This was her only chance to get them.

Yeah, sure, a cripple in a wheelchair against Punjabi thugs. That's very doable, Nachos. Great plan, girl.

It was a terrible, crazy, stupid-ass plan. She knew this. But she knew that bringing the police into it couldn't help right now. Right now, she was here and she had to do something. It was the way she was wired, the reason she was in a wheelchair today, and the reason why she couldn't turn away from trouble when confronted by it.

She pushed open the office door and rolled inside, pushing the door shut against the protesting pups before they could get in. She didn't want their little innocent lives on her conscience as well.

The stench of faeces was unmistakable. She gagged on it but regained control of herself. It almost overwhelmed the stench of petrol, but as she wheeled further into the outside office, the petrol won out, making her eyes water and her nose run at once. She wiped her face on the back of the sleeve of her blouse, blinking away the tears. Her hand fumbled with the light switch and turned it on, but nothing happened. Why were the lights off? Had the goons done that as well? Were they still here? She couldn't hear any sounds from this room – or the inside office either.

'Koi hai?' she said tentatively, her voice cracking. She forced herself to speak louder, trying to sound more authoritative. She'd be damned if she turned into a snivelling victim before them. 'Hello? Anybody there?' When there was still no answer, she asked tentatively, 'Shonali? Shons, you there?'

The whining of the pups and their claws scratching at the closed office door were the only sounds that came to her. There weren't even any traffic sounds from the street outside at this hour.

Damnit, woman, WTF are you doing here? You're no superwoman to come swooping to the rescue.

But they had ordered her to come here or else ... Shonali's life was at stake. Or so the guy said.

She sat there in the darkness for another few minutes, trying to decide what to do next, trying not to breathe through her nose – the stench was awful. She wanted to puke but controlled herself. She was convinced the office was empty; but that didn't mean she could just turn around and wheel her way out. Shonali might still be here, hurt or … or worse. Even if she was going to call the police or an ambulance, she had to know for sure.

She had to check the inside office.

The effort it took to wheel herself the few yards to the inside office door felt like the Wheelathon she had participated in once. That had been just fifty metres, but the competition had been tough because most of the other women were born paraplegics and had spent their entire lives manoeuvring wheelchairs, while she had barely been in one for a few years at the time. Still, she had been placed second and was proud of it because the other two prize winners had both been younger than her and much more athletic. She still had the trophy somewhere in the office: a trio of unisex figures raising their fists to the sky. A wink to socialistic ideology as well as bleeding-heart liberal sponsorships, she supposed. This felt much harder because there was no prize waiting at the end. On the contrary.

Finally, she reached the door of the inside office and pushed it open, entering hesitantly. That same stickiness under her wheels, but this time it was more liquid, and the stench of petrol much stronger. This part had been heavily doused, she guessed. Though why the goons would want to douse her office in petrol and then run away mystified her. Right now, she only wanted to know if Shonali was in here and if she was, then …

She fumbled with her Blackberry, holding it up. A part of her didn't want to see whatever there was to see, but she had no choice. She had come this far. *Come on, Nachos,* she told herself sternly, *you survived your marriage and your in-laws. You can deal with this.* She had to check. She had to be sure.

5.3

SHEILA WAS STARING AT an extraordinary sight. She was across the street from the gym, standing just behind a young peepal tree which, along with its neighbours, blocked the light from the streetlamps. She was invisible under the shadows, a fact that others had been aware of and taken advantage of frequently, judging from the stench of male urine on the wall behind her. She had started to raise her hand to pinch her nose when she stepped behind the tree a few moments ago but then she had caught a glimpse of what was going on across the street and had forgotten the stench.

The police were trashing her gym and office.

Thanks to the large glass facade of the gym and the fact that her office was visible from where she stood, she could see everything as clearly as if it were taking place on a proscenium stage. Some fancy set at a Bollywood entertainment awards nite, perhaps. Except that the men in white Kolkata Police uniforms weren't group dancers and there were no film stars descending from the sky suspended from winch cables.

They were really tearing things up. She watched as they picked up and threw dumbbells through the glass partitions and walls, shattering them; put their shoulders to Nautilius machines and upended them; pushed exercycles over; shoved cross-trainers on their sides; threw member cards out of the slots on the wall-mounted board; smashed the juice bar and threw metal stools at the mirrors. She winced as she watched the mayhem. They were laughing and calling out to each other as they did it, clearly enjoying what they were doing.

It was more of the same in her office. Her desk was battered with lathis, drawers pulled out and their contents emptied out, a chair deliberately thrown through the glass facade. How could they be allowed to inflict such wanton damage? She gritted her teeth in frustration, her fists clenching. They were the police; they could do anything. Besides, she could almost hear what they must be saying in Bengali as they went about their task. 'Tear down the bloody lesbian joint! Smash the deviants' pleasure palace.'

Bastards.

She saw the flash of yellow in a raised hand and all heads pausing and turning to look in that direction. A constable had found the manila envelope and was holding it up. The inspector who appeared to be in charge was standing at the far side of the gym, talking on his cell phone. He turned and beckoned the constable. The man ran across the ruined gym floor and gave the envelope to his superior.

The inspector examined the exterior of the envelope for a moment, but didn't pull out any papers from inside and look at them. Instead, he dialled a number on his cell and spoke to someone: even at this distance, Sheila could tell that he was being deferential. The call finished, he exited the building.

Her heart pounding with anger, Sheila slipped out from behind the tree and crossed the street diagonally, heading at an angle directed at the next adjoining lane. A little traffic came by and for a long tense moment, she was on the wide brightly lit street, fully exposed to the policemen on the first floor. Any one of them could have looked down and recognized her at once. But they had resumed their destructive pastime and nobody looked at her. The traffic passed by, horns blaring at the woman standing in the middle of the road, and she crossed at a steady, unhurried pace. Out of the direct view of the gym, she cut sharply back and went into the bylane that ran behind the building, the one she had left by when the police came. The wireless van was parked in the same place with the red-light car parked behind it. It was an Esteem in decent condition. That told her that the officer was not an inspector but probably an ACP. Curioser and curioser. She reached the back of the car and saw him standing by the wireless van, speaking to the wireless operator in the rear. The rear doors were open. The sound of the wireless radio giving off static punctuated their talk.

She crouched behind the Esteem, the metal of the dicky cool to her warm touch. She was trembling, not from fear but from anger. Watching the very people who were supposed to uphold the law and protect her from miscreants ruin the fruit of her hard work over the past several years did that to her. Who were these bastards? She knew now that this wasn't just about Tasneem and Marhabha. It was bigger than that. Much bigger. The way the constable had held up the yellow manila envelope told her that. The fact that the ACP had taken the envelope but not bothered to look inside her told her the rest: they know what was in the envelope already. *It's the reason why they came after me, why they're tearing up the place.*

An elderly man in kurta–pyjama and a young girl in shorts and a tee shirt walking a big happy golden retriever came by, passing her on the footpath. The old man and granddaughter didn't notice her crouching by the car, but the dog sensed her and turned, pulling at his leash. The old man and girl pulled him back and walked on, too engrossed in conversation to turn and look her way. They were chattering in Bengali about something and Sheila caught a few words. The grandfather wanted to know what 'sexting' meant and the granddaughter was trying to fob him off with a bullshit explanation. Sheila felt the ACP get into the car before she heard him: the metal vibrated as he pulled open the door and did something in the car. Then the door shut again, hard, and there was silence except for the wireless crackling with a bored voice asking about traffic movement near Victoria Memorial flyover. Sheila raised her head over the rear of the car, peering out. She saw the ACP walking back across the street to the gym's rear entrance. His hands were bare except for his cell phone.

She glanced through the rear windshield at the back of the wireless van. The constable who was the wireless operator was sitting with his legs sprawled, scratching his balls and smoking a cigarette. He wasn't looking anywhere in particular, but if she moved within his frame of view, he would see her at once, she guessed.

She duck-walked around the back of the car to the pavement side, trying to stay low so the wireless operator couldn't see her. She reached up for the car handle, praying the ACP hadn't locked it. She felt the handle yield and the door open – just as something large and wet pushed itself into her armpit.

She resisted the urge to leap up and scream.

The golden retriever's snout pushed against her neck and cheek as the dog licked her sloppily. Her found her ear and probed inside it with his tongue, slobbering happily.

'Rancchoddas Shamaldas Chanchad!' said a girl's indignant voice from behind. 'What is he *doing*, dadamoshai!'

'Rancho, putra,' said the old man's voice in the manner of Bengali men trying to be stern and failing completely. 'You will get us all arrested. That is policewoman's vehicle!'

Sheila glanced over her shoulder just as the old man and girl regained control of the golden retriever's leash and yanked him away. The dog's tail slapped her on the side of the head, hard enough to almost make her lose her balance, crouched as she was on her haunches. The old man and girl seemed to notice nothing unusual about a woman crouching beside a police car. Policewoman's vehicle indeed!

They continued up the footpath, Rancho barking an enthusiastic goodbye to her as he went. She shot him the finger and he barked one last time, happy to be acknowledged.

She glanced at the wireless operator. He was leaning over his wireless, speaking into the mike, seemingly unaware of the dog–woman encounter.

Sheila decided that this was her chance, take it or leave it.

She opened the rear door of the Esteem, slipped inside, and felt around on the back seat in the darkness until her fingertips brushed across what felt like an envelope.

Crawling back out, she pushed the door but didn't shut it. That would have required banging it loudly and even a distracted wireless operator would notice an empty car door banging shut.

She duck-walked to the back of the car again, then continued in the same manner down the lane to the cross-street she had appeared from moments earlier. No grandfathers and granddaughters walking dogs here. She reached the corner and straightened up, slipping around the side and out of sight of her gym and the police vehicles. In the light of the streetlamps, she looked at what her hands held. It was the manila envelope again, with all the papers intact, exactly as she had left it back at her office.

She started walking, away from the life she had built for herself, the legitimate decent life of Sheila Ray. She crossed over, keeping to the darker side of the street, and kept walking.

Six

6.1

ANITA AWOKE WITH THE certainty that something was very wrong, and her first instinct was to lie still and assess the situation. She found herself on the carpet, behind the bed, facing the window. She had sat that way to use the bedside lamp and avoid disturbing Philip who was sleeping on the other bed. She didn't know when she had fallen asleep, but her internal clock told her she couldn't have dozed off for more than a couple of hours. Forget the internal clock, her bleary brain told her that! The light in the room was the same as before, but there were voices on the other side of the room, near the door.

Male voices, several of them.

One of the voices was definitely Philip's and she thought that the other two were of her brothers and perhaps another man. The way they were speaking – softly but with unmistakable anger barely suppressed – must have been what woke her up. Either that, or the door opening: she had learnt since girlhood to dread the sound of a door opening at night. That and the sound of her brothers' voices was enough to send all her alarm bells ringing. Two months of unrelenting abuse would do that to a girl. Even now, so many years later, she would still wake up at night in Mrs Matondkar's flat and check the door and windows – and the sound of a particular kind of male voice always put her off, no matter how nice the guy. Once you had been raped and beaten by your brothers, days after your father's funeral, it tended to scar you for life.

She lay still, knowing that the reason they were speaking softly was to avoid waking her. She caught the drift of their conversation: they were discussing the best way to take her, which sent chills up her spine, transporting her hurtling back to that fifteen-year-old girl lying battered and bleeding and terrified in her own bed at home. The only thing missing was the sound of her mother calling the boys to have their beef mulligatawny soup. Soup! Because boys had to keep up their strength. Of course. Damn *pishaachs*! Fucking flesh-eating, blood-sucking bastards.

The papers from the manila envelope were still beside her. She had fallen asleep all over them, and one loose sheet was stuck to her arm and backside and would make a noise if she moved. She reached down and peeled it off carefully. She didn't know what to do, so she folded it slowly and carefully and slipped it into the back pocket of her jeans, with her wallet.

While she did that, she examined the window from her floor-level viewpoint. She was on the second floor and the window faced the back of the hotel. What was at the back? The parking area? The courtyard? But then she remembered: the window wouldn't do. They were the old-fashioned Kerala type – solid wooden frames criss-crossed with panes of glass. She might end up cracking it, but more likely she would crack her own ribs and break a few bones before that frame broke to let her jump through. She didn't have enough body weight to do it, or running space to gather the momentum.

Which meant she would have to go out using the door, past them.

For the first time in her life – well, technically not the *first*, but it always felt like the first time on each occasion – she wondered why the fuck she didn't carry a gun. She knew why, of course. Because she hated the damn things. Growing up watching your brothers shoot every living animal or bird that took their fancy – including stray dogs, pups, cats, kittens, birds – would do that to a girl. There were days when she felt that ridding the world of all guns and explosive weapons should be every government's first priority. Her favourite fiction was the *Change* series by S.M. Stirling, which imagined a near-future where all combustible agents stopped working: planes fell out of the sky, cars wouldn't run, guns stopped working. The world returned to bows and arrows and swords. It was even more brutal than before for a while, but somehow the absence of guns and motors almost seemed to be worth the cost. It was the only series she bought religiously in hardcover, ordering each new book online from a Bengaluru-based online bookstore.

One of the things she had learnt from the book was that if you knew what you were doing and if the circumstances were right, you could render guns ineffectual. A closed room with many opponents and obstacles – like this hotel room – qualified as the right circumstances.

Now, she had a chance to put the theory to the test.

She heard the unmistakable growl of her older brother Isaac's voice say quite distinctly, 'Enough talk. Move!' Then the voices fell silent and the sound of fabric rustling could be heard.

They were moving in.

She had crept under the bed while they talked. Now, she could see their feet approaching the first bed, going around it, then around the second bed. They were expecting her to be in the alcove between the second bed and the window, not between the two beds. That put two of them to her right, and at least one on her left – barring her way out. Three plus Philip, and she didn't know for sure where he was standing. She guessed that the first two would have guns aimed down at the spot they expected her to be in and had fingers ready on the trigger, especially after the way she had defended herself back at the house. Isaac was a vengeful bastard; he would want to punish her for hurting him, or worse. She didn't know if Graham was in on this, but he would probably do as Isaac said. But why hadn't Philip woken her? Why had he opened the door to let them in? He was the one who had called her here to Varkala in the first place, told her about Lalima's funeral. He was on her side.

Then it came to her in a flash: it was a set-up. This wasn't about Lalima's death at all. It was about the contents of the yellow manila envelope. She knew that now that she had read the papers, even though she couldn't figure out most of what they meant. The information they revealed was massively important, there was no doubt about that at all. She also knew that it had come from Lalima's lawyer after her death – the Trivandrum postmark had told her the place and Philip had told her about the instructions to send out the packages. He had also told her that similar packets had been sent to people besides her. The Matthew clan had known that one envelope had been sent to her and had Philip call her here on the pretext of Lalima's funeral, hoping to get back the documents – and get rid of her. That was why Philip had come to her hotel and told her that sob story. She had thought she was nursing him and putting him to sleep. In fact, she was the one being lulled into sleeping, thinking she was safe here for the night. Then he had called the others and hail, hail, the gang's all here, let's have a gangbang, boys. Enough soup for everyone. Let's go turn the crazywhoremysister into mincemeat.

She exploded from between the beds, a Bible in her hand. It was the room Bible which she had taken from the lower drawer of the bedside table while they were talking by the door. She threw it at the man to her far right – Isaac with a makeshift sling on one arm and a gun in the other hand. He reacted, trying to swat the hurtling object with his only free hand, which happened to be the hand in which he was holding the gun, and because his finger was on the trigger, it went off.

6.2

THE LIGHT OF THE cell phone came on but wasn't bright enough to illuminate the whole room. She held it as high as she could, turning it this way and that to throw a little pocket of light on one part of the room, then another, until she was able to piece together the whole picture in parts, like some obscene jigsaw puzzle. Her hand shook. In intermittent glimpses, all the more garish for being seen in the half-dim light of the cell phone screen, was a scene out of an Asian horror film. Something by Park Chan-wook, perhaps, or Kim Ki-duk. Some twisted tale of a plan gone wrong. Except that this was her office, not some seedy by-the-hour love hotel in Seoul or Hong Kong, and the woman sprawled naked on her desk was Shonali, poor lovely young Shonali who was a JNU pol. sci. grad with intense views about the legitimacy of some aspects of the Maoist cause with regard to tribals in deforested areas, and who liked Mojitos and long-haired, intellectual-type guys with a sense of humour. Nachiketa's hand trembled again as even the incompetent glow of the BB left no doubt that her office assistant had been savagely raped and battered and then left for dead. Nachiketa forced herself to turn her right wheel with her free hand and bumped her knee against the corner of the desk. Gritting her teeth, she reached out and checked for a pulse. The feel of human skin was the worst thing of all. It slammed home the realization that this was no subtitled film in Siri Fort Auditorium, it was, to use Shonali's own favourite phrase, 'really real'. The skin on the girl's neck felt slippery, but not with blood, with sweat. It brought home nightmarish flashes of Shonali's last moments alive. She couldn't have been dead long: her skin was still warm. But her pulse was MIA.

Nachiketa withdrew her hand, shaking, and used intellectual action to compensate for her inability to act out her emotions physically. It was a sublimation devoutly to be wished, perfected by herself to deal with her reduced state of perambulation. She looked around the office again, bringing down a curtain of calm to seal off any possibility of a breakdown. So the bastards had killed Shonali here, poor wretched thing. That still didn't account for all that blood back in the outer office as well as in this room, and the stench of shit. Someone else must have died here or been badly hurt ...

She saw a patch of something on the side of a desk that looked like cloth but which she recognized, sickened, as animal fur. It was damp and dark and had stuck there as if it had caught there in the course of some brutal unimaginable struggle for survival. She looked around as best as she could but could find no sign of Justice herself. Poor bitch. Where was she? It was impossible to be sure, but from what little she could see, Nachiketa assumed that the men who had called her when she was driving had somehow broken into the office, found Shonali here – doing what, since she wasn't supposed to come back to the office tonight? – and had attacked her in this inner chamber. Justice must have tried to defend Shonali and had paid for it dearly, but probably after causing some damage herself. Still. The blood was too much to fit even that tragic–heroic scenario. And where were the bastards who had done all this? They had called her here and then …

Frump!

The sound caught her attention. It was unmistakable, given the omnipresent stench of petroleum in the office. That was petrol igniting. She saw the room brighten at once as light from the other room spilled in. Someone had lit a fire in the front room. But she had heard no footsteps or voices.

'Kahaan ho saaley madarchodhon?' she said, not caring what might happen if they heard her and came to finish off the job they had started here. Her eyes were running with tears and she was angrier than she had ever been in her life before. 'Where the fuck are you, assholes? Show yourselves!'

The only answer was the sound of paper crackling noisily. She wheeled herself backwards through the open door, swung around in a half-circle and stopped at the sight of a small pile of court papers on Shonali's desk crackling away as merrily as a blaze in the fireplace of a Kasauli cabin. She saw a matchbox on top of the pile of papers and a cigarette in there too, crumbling to ashes as she watched. Of course. They had set a crude cigarette-matchbox timer and then vamoosed. This way, the fire would start when they were safely away. One of her activist friends had shown her how to do it: you lit a cigarette and stuck it in a matchbox full of matchsticks on top of a pile of papers in a wastepaper basket or in-tray. Five or ten minutes later, the ember would burn down to the match heads, igniting them, and the whole kaboodle would go up in flames. It was impossible to prove that it hadn't been a smoking accident: someone carelessly tossing an unextinguished fag into the basket. The activist friend, a self-proclaimed radical, the son of a pair of ex-hippy Brits, claimed to have used the trick to set a corrupt judge's chamber on fire in Thailand. She hadn't believed he'd done that, but the trick itself was genuine.

The papers on the desk flared up and the fire leapt to the books and files around it. Fragments of burning paper fell off, and the instant they touched the floor, the spilled petrol went up like a firebomb. In seconds, the entire outer office was a mass of flames. Nachiketa gasped and began to wheel herself backwards. But the trail of fire had reached the inside office and that room all but exploded when the petrol ignited.

She felt the heat of the ignition scorch the back of her head and left arm and started forward again. There was a wall of fire leaping up at the front door already. How had it spread so fast?

That's why they used an accelerant, you fool. It was a trap. They waited till you were about to enter, then left through the window. The plan was to get you in here and then set the place on fire.

That's why there was so much petrol oozing out from

under the front door. They wanted to make it impossible for her to get out. She heard the yelps of terror from the puppies outside the door and her heart sank as she thought of them being caught in the blaze, their fur soaked in the petrol. Poor wretched things!

She couldn't help them now. She couldn't even help herself. She was coughing and felt her brows and hair getting singed by the flames; even the rubber on her wheelchair tyres melted and she could barely touch the metal parts. She looked around, desperately seeking some refuge, some way to escape the demon that threatened to eat her alive.

She saw the large old metal table near the entrance, the one that had been in the office when she leased the place. It seemed to have escaped being doused by the fuel and was relatively untouched by the fire. There were a few registered A.D. packages on top, with red-wax seals over the usual hemp twine which was already smoking and starting to catch fire, but she thought the table itself was not likely to burn. The fire couldn't be hot enough to melt the table, could it?

She threw herself from the wheelchair, crying out as her bare hands touched the burning floor and were scalded. It was like dipping them in a tureen of hot oil being heated for frying samosas and jalebis – Shonali's favourite breakfast, to gorge on which the girl would slip out of office every other morning and go down to Bengali Market. She used to bring some back for Nachiketa too at first, until Nachiketa forbade her: a woman in a wheelchair had to watch herself twice as carefully, and a regular diet of samosas and jalebis was not conducive to weight control.

She screamed as her hair caught fire, and then her clothes, and then she felt as if her entire body was on fire. A flame caught her cheek in passing and she felt heat sear her left eye, turning her vision white – and white-hot – for an agonizing instant. She was somehow inside the womb of the metal table that enfolded her body inside the cramped space; the strut hit her back hard but she didn't care, the smoke made her cough and her head spin. She felt something beside her and turned and managed to see, from her right eye, the mangled bloodied body of Justice, her poor belly ripped open by the same sharp blade that had been used on Shonali, or so she presumed. That explained the stench of faeces too, and the reason why the pups had been clamouring at the front door. Justice must have tried to fend off the men to help Shonali and they must have cut her open as well. She must have crawled in here to die and breathed her last just before Nachiketa arrived. The dog was lying on a yellow manila envelope that looked vaguely familiar. It must have fallen to the floor and been kicked there somehow. She couldn't bear to look at the poor sweet bitch's snout, lips peeled back in canine rictus.

Oh well, Nachos thought as the fire began to climb the walls and ceiling and the entire office turned into one enormous mass of blazing flame, *at least I won't die alone.* She embraced the corpse of the dead dog and felt the flames eating at the back of her head before the pain overwhelmed her and she lost consciousness.

6.3

SHEILA WAS ALMOST AT the Salt Lake Metro Station when she suspected she was being followed. She had had to walk all the way because there were no taxis. Apparently, Mohun Bagan AC had played a friendly match against visiting British team Arsenal earlier in the evening and the game had drawn record crowds. After the game, the crowds from the stadium had spread throughout Biddhanagar in search of bars and restaurants and cafes, all the way upto here in Sector V. Because this entire region was an IT and BPO hub, most of the sleek, gleaming glass-fronted buildings were owned by MNCs that had their own fleets of people carriers. Taxis did ply in the area, but they wanted to stay within the area or, at best, shuttle to Salt Lake City Airport and back, in the hope of getting liberal tips from unsuspecting foreigners who didn't know tipping was not required in India.

Today, with over 120,000 football fans looking for food and drink after the game, the cab drivers were in taxi heaven. The fans were mostly young guys in groups wearing the colours of their team, all looking to cross swords with fans of the opposing team and ready for a brawl. They were everywhere, like extras in some movie about the end of the world. Sheila tried to argue with some of them when they muscled in and took a cab she had flagged down with some difficulty, but soon realized that they were more than happy to pick a fight. There were cops around, trying unsuccessfully to shepherd the traffic back towards the city, and it would be stupid to get noticed by them. Since she didn't want to go back past her lane – the ACP might have been careless enough to leave the envelope in the unlocked car but he would have realized it was missing by now and would have put his men to work scouring the area – and she couldn't get a cab for love or money, she had no choice but to keep walking uptown. Finally, she figured she might as well continue walking all the way to the new metro station and take a train to her destination.

It was while walking through the streets and bylanes, criss-crossing to get to the Salt Lake City Metro Station, that she became aware of a familiar sensation. It was her instinctive suspicious nature that made her check her rear, but it was sharp observation and good procedure that made her spot the possible tail without giving away the fact that she had spotted them. She was no amateur. She never turned her head or looked around. Instead, she waited until she saw a glass window-front ahead and angled herself towards it in such a way that it gave her a view of the entire street behind. The glass windows of a line of Qualises waiting for the end of a shift outside a BPO skyscraper, the polished side of a Volvo bus, the picture glass storefronts of a line of branded fashion stores, the facade of a McDonald's, KFC, Pizza Hut, the side windows of a Staples, and after a few blocks she was sure that there were at least three men on her ass, none of them football fans or cops.

By the time she was nearing Salt Lake City Metro Station, she was no longer in doubt. They had turned too many times with her into lanes that led in opposite directions, backtracked more than once, and now they were following her up the long flight of stairs to the elevated terminus. They couldn't all be guys who hadn't been able to get cabs and had decided, as she had, to take the metro. Besides, there was something about the way they kept doggedly on her tail in the same triangular pattern that suggested a routine: these were guys who worked together often on such jobs. They had a system, one that had worked before, and they stuck to it no matter what.

And they weren't policemen, she was sure of that too. They were rough-league, very tough dudes, bulked-up and well-fed, immaculately groomed and dressed. She was pretty sure at least two were foreigners: they had on cricket caps which hid their hair, but she was certain she had spotted the flash of blue eyes in the window of a MAC cosmetics store, and there was no doubt that the third man was of African origin yet too light-skinned to be just African. Who were these guys? What did they want with her? If they were working for the same people who had set Choudhry and his political mad dogs on her, or the cops, they would have stopped her by now. But they were just following her, keeping their distance, not making contact. That could only mean one thing: follow and observe. They wanted to see where she was going and whom she met.

The question was *why*.

She hefted the manila envelope in her hand. It had something to do with it, she was sure. Now that she had seen the contents of the envelope, she thought that maybe everything that had happened today was because of her receiving the envelope. Its contents justified the destruction of her gym, her business, her life. It warranted the use of political force – Choudhry could have tracked her down years or months earlier, why only today, after she received the package? It explained the use of the police to legitimize an illegitimate witch hunt. And now, after the politicians and police had failed to secure what they wanted, the powers that were behind this had dispatched these men. Perhaps they had been watching her gym all day, leaving the dirty work to the politicos and cops; waiting and observing in case the first two groups failed. As they had failed. And then, when they saw her about to slip out of their grasp, taking the Maltese Falcon with her, they had swooped in.

Except they hadn't swooped in yet. They were only following her. Not making contact. So they had probably decided to wait to see whom she went to meet next.

Well. Let them come along if they want. It is a free country.

She reached the metro ticket counter and bought a one-way ticket to Howrah. She actually said 'Maidan' first, being accustomed to referring to the large field – 'Lungs of Calcutta', as her maternal grandfather had called it – that was the pride of the district, then corrected herself and added, 'Howrah Station'.

The terminus was unsurprisingly full, most of the crowd wearing the familiar colours of the two opposing teams. What was surprising was the proliferation of Bengali faces wearing the British club colours. She wondered what her maternal grandfather – or her mother for that matter – would have thought of fellow Bengalis supporting a team opposing Mohun Bagan. Then again, this wasn't her grandfather's Kolkata. For that matter, it wasn't *her* Kolkata either.

The train arrived in a hushed rush, slowing as if gliding on invisible wings. The doors hissed open, the cold air feeling refreshing after the long walk. She had taken a moment to buy a bottle of packaged water and she found a seat at the end of a bogie, from which she could watch all the entrances and most of the bogie, and she sat with the envelope on her lap, watching.

The men following her got into three separate cars. One on either side, the third in the same one as her, but at the far end. He sat without looking at her, but did take off his cap to run his hands through his hair and she had the petty satisfaction of seeing that it was, indeed, dirty blonde.

This east–west metro line was still new enough to be a novelty attraction, and most of the football fans who had come for today's match were out-of-towners or from other parts of Kolkata. Large groups of young men stood and sat around chattering loudly, singing, cracking jokes, making obscene comments, and generally living up to the boisterous reputation of football fans the world over. Because Salt Lake City was built on reclaimed landfill poured over saltwater marshes and swamps, the ground was too soft and waterlogged to build underground lines. So for the first six stations, the metro ran on elevated rails. She could see the main bypass most of the way, weaving in and out as the metro line wound its way circuitously around Karunamoyee, then Central Park, the vast open darkness a visual relief after the blinding, gaudy brightness of the MNC BPO skyscrapers in Sectors IV and V. Most buildings in these neighbourhoods were two- or three-storey structures, apart from the corporate parks, of course, and the elevated line seemed to run through darkness most of the way, like a train across empty countryside, or an ocean liner on a dark passage. Perhaps it was the darkness hurtling past the polished windows, or the air-conditioning and brand-new smell of the Japanese metro coach cars, or the luxury of travelling like this in the city that Gunter Grass had once called 'a pile of shit' dropped by God on earth, but her mood began to darken, to change, and it was a familiar change, one she knew well but hadn't experienced for a long time; had hoped – foolishly, perhaps – never to experience again.

She felt something ominous in the air, and smelt the violence about to come. She knew that this was serious shit she was involved in now, maybe the most serious shit ever. This wasn't just some local police and underworld matter. These people were global, powerful, big time. They had big secrets to protect – big enough that governments and entire nations would let them do as they pleased and turn a blind eye. She was on her own now and had to do what she had to in order to survive. That would mean killing whether she liked it or not. *Not*, was her choice. Like all people who are capable of deadly violence, Sheila never desired it or liked it. Only fools and madmen desired or sought war. The truly sane avoided it – and chose to run rather than fight. She was running now. But she would have to fight soon. And when she did, it would have to be for keeps. She had to let these people know at first contact that she wasn't a pushover. If she was going to go down, it would cost them.

She waited until the train had left Salt Lake Stadium and was moving towards Phoolbagan before she made her move. The circumstances being what they were, she knew she would have only one shot at doing this right, and that meant hitting hard and fast and not caring who got hurt or how badly. She had no choice: whoever these people were, they meant business. And because she intended to come out of this alive, so did she.

Seven

7.1

ISAAC'S GUN WENT OFF as he tried to fend off the flying Bible Anita had tossed at his face. He swatted the holy book, but the corner still struck his face just below the cheekbone, probably hitting the eye–tooth nerve because he cursed in pain and blindly squeezed off another two rounds in her direction as he turned his face away, eyes watering instantly. Her 'direction' meant the place where the other two men were standing as they approached her bed, and Anita had already ducked and was ramming her head and shoulders into the abdomen of one of them, like an American football tackle. That had been the only plan she had: to come between them and get them to shoot at each other. She knew she had succeeded when she heard the unmistakable punching-bag sound of one of Isaac's shots striking human flesh and glimpsed blood splattering in her peripheral vision.

She didn't see where the other two shots went because at that instant she rammed into her target hard enough to make him fly backwards, striking the dressing table mirror with the back of his head and upper body. The mirror splintered as one of the shots hit something else that shattered too. A man screamed, but it wasn't the guy she had rammed into: he was sprawled backwards on the debris of the dressing table, head cocked at an unnatural angle. She didn't recognize him at first glance and was already turning left, using her forward momentum to propel her towards the door of the hotel room.

Behind her, she heard Isaac's gravelly voice shout something even as she saw Graham's fleshy fair face loom in front of her. He had a gun too, but was staring wide-eyed at something to his right, distracted momentarily. She caught a glimpse of a man beside Graham clutching at a spurting red geyser. It took her brain a fraction of a second longer to recognize that the spurting geyser was his carotid artery and that it was Philip and he had been struck in the throat by one of Isaac's wild shots.

She rammed into Graham, sending him lurching backwards, hands flying up and outwards for balance, the gun hand rising as well, firing a shot up into the ceiling and one over her left shoulder, the heat of its passing searing her collarbone like a red hot whip. Then he struck the jamb of the open room door and something cracked in his head or back and she saw his eyes roll up, the whites flashing as he went down. She was at the door now, and practically flew through it. Now she was in the corridor outside and there were two men standing in front of her, staring dumbly.

Both had guns, but only one had his in his hand. He raised it but she kicked it hard, missed, and hit his right hipbone instead. The impact sent a sharp burst of pain into her big right toe ,and the man lurched and fell against his partner, the gun going off, two shots going wild. The other man lost his footing and fell sideways against a room service trolley piled with discarded dinner dishes and chrome-plated dish warmers and everything went flying in a clattering cacophony.

She leapt over the sprawled body of the first man, feeling something give in her right foot as she landed. Then she was racing down the corridor and down the stairs. Mercifully, there were no more men with guns barring her way and at this hour, the Papanasam Sea Resort was deserted. She reached the lobby and ran past the reception. A man was at the desk, talking urgently on a cell phone; he pointed at her as she went past, saying her name into the phone. She went from the lobby into the courtyard, looking around for some form of transportation. Her toe was broken or hurt badly because she wasn't able to put her weight on the right foot properly. Adrenalin had got her down the stairs, but every step was agony. Broken. No mistaking that sensation. She needed to get transportation fast or they would catch her right here in another minute, and after the mess she had caused in the room, she had a feeling they would expect more than a night's rental.

She saw Philip's Norton on its stand in the car park. It was one of the old WWII models which used a push-button start instead of an ignition key. She prayed that he hadn't had it modified for whatever reason and swung her leg over the saddle-seat. Pressed the button. And grinned with sick relief when the powerful 850 cc engine turned over like butter on hot toast. Thank God for Philip and his obsessive care for Achchan's old Norton.

She put the bike into gear, fumbling a moment because her right foot was already going numb with the shock of the broken toe. Her left collarbone felt like it was on fire and bathed in hot oil. She felt wetness and assumed she was bleeding where the shot had scored her, but there was no time to waste on first aid. She fumbled through the first, then managed to get it into second gear and turned the accelerator, roaring out of the courtyard and turning onto the new road. She heard shouts from the hotel – one was definitely Isaac's voice yelling from the window of her room above, and then she heard gunshots. Something burst behind her and things whizzed and splattered in the darkness beyond the road, but she pushed the Norton into third and roared off down the road, leaving the guns and men and yelling behind, for now at least, though not for long, she knew. They would catch up with her sooner or later, that was not in doubt. The main thing was how much she could get done before they did.

7.2

NACHIKETA EMERGED FROM A miasma of pain and heat. She felt as if she had been cooked and roasted and was still in the oven. Vision swam out of the murky horizon, rushing at her like a panorama painted on the side of a monorail superfast train and reality collided with her consciousness. She gasped and tried to fumble at the object lodged in her airway but found her hands bound by her side. Hissing and pinging and other life support sounds provided an orchestra by her bedside. She sensed the sickening odours of disinfectant, pus, blood and bodily unguents, and knew she was in a hospital room. The logos of various pharma companies marched across the walls of the room, masquerading as public service messages. She gasped and choked and struggled until people in white swam into and out of her field of vision, making irritable sounds and doing things to the apparatus to which she was hooked up.

Finally, the obstruction in her airway was removed and she was able to speak. 'Police,' she said. 'Need … speak police.' Her voice sounded hoarse, like female friends who smoked too much, the kind of husky womanly voice she had always thought men found sexy. She hated the sound coming from her own ravaged throat. 'Please … urgent.' She was gasping, she realized.

'You need rest, madam. We have to insert oxygen again.' The nurse was a hard-faced woman of indeterminate age and ethnicity. Her accent was classic Dilli.

'No, please,' Nachiketa said. 'It is police matter. Urgent.'

The sound of voices from somewhere to the right distracted the nurse. She left Nachiketa's bedside for a moment. The next face that swam into view was a man's, unrecognizable with a bandage around his head. He was good-looking in a rough Jat kind of way. Nachiketa spent a moment staring at him and wondered if she had lost her memory entirely because she had no clue who he was. For a moment her heart lurched, thinking that he might be the man who had called her, one of the bastards who had raped and killed Shonali and tried to burn her to death as well. But what would he be doing here?

'Memsaab,' he said, 'yourself not recognizing? Myself Rajendra Powar, watchman.'

The security guard of her office building. What the hell was *he* doing here?

He folded his bandaged hands in front of his forehead, tears springing to his bloodshot eyes. 'I am so sorry, madam. They hit me on head from behind and go in. I was behosh all time. I wake up and see all burning.' He lapsed into Haryanvi for a sentence or three, and all she could make out was that he was describing the fire.

She tried to make sense of his words. Her brain still felt like it was on slow boil, as if the blood in her veins would start popping and crackling at any moment. 'My office ...' she asked hoarsely. 'All ... gone?'

He nodded, wiping errant tears from his face. 'Fire brigade say maybe they save building, maybe not. I take out you in time. Come in ambulance with yourself.'

She tried to keep him in focus. '*You* pulled me out?'

He nodded vigorously. 'You screaming–screaming. Kuttey bhaunk rahein the. Dog barking? I hear. Go inside. You near door, under table. I take you out.'

He showed her his hands. They were both bandaged in large swathing bundles. She realized that his hair had burned away too, and his eyelashes and eyebrows. Was that how she looked too? *Probably worse. You weren't a good-looking Jat to begin with, Nachos*. She felt something swimming to the top of her consciousness but it kept slipping away.

'Where are we now?'

'AIIMS,' he said.

As if on cue, a doctor appeared with the same nurse beside him, looking irritable and impatient. 'Ma'am, it is AIIMS policy not to treat burn victims. For humanitarian reasons, we gave you emergency treatment, but you will have to make arrangements to continue your care elsewhere.'

She tried to absorb this new twist in the tale. 'Where am I supposed to go?'

'We can have you transferred to another hospital. Your brother will have to go with you; he is also a burn patient.'

She began to correct him then realized it didn't matter. 'Right now?'

'Ambulance is waiting outside.' He turned and spoke to the nurse, then left the room. The nurse said something in Haryanvi to Rajendra Powar who answered in like fashion.

'Powar,' Nachiketa said hoarsely.

He said something else to the nurse, then turned back to her.

'My friend, Shonali ...' she asked, hoping against hope.

He raised a bandaged hand to his face, making a groaning sound. 'What to say, madam. I am lost job, don't care. Lekin goondas come into my building, rape and kill and burn office, I cannot forgive myself.'

She had been expecting that, but it still felt like a blow, as if Shonali had only just died. In the darkness of the inside office, she had still hoped that her inability to find a pulse was due to her inexperience. Now she knew. Shonali was dead. She was supposed to have died too in that fire trap, and the only reason she had survived was because of an overzealous young Jat security guard who had risked his own life to save hers.

'What about ...' she thought of her office, all her documents, court papers, passport, the detritus accumulated over the past few years that she had been in Delhi, her law practice, but that was too overwhelming right now, too much. For the moment, she had to try and figure out what had happened, why Shonali had been killed, why those men had tried to kill her. What had they wanted, damnit? Why hadn't they been there when she reached the office? The man on the phone had talked about something she had which they wanted back. But what?

Then it came to her, unbidden, along with the gruesome memory of Justice's corpse, tongue lolling, lips curled back to reveal canine fangs. 'Powar ...' she rasped. 'There was a package ...'

Rajendra Powar nodded at once, surprising her by seeming to know exactly what she meant. 'Yes, madam, you holding it saying something English. Important, na?' He left her bedside for a moment, then came back holding something gingerly between his bandaged hands. Even with the stains of the dog's blood and charred corners, she could make out the yellow manila envelope, the one that had somehow landed under the very table beneath which she took shelter. It was scorched but mostly intact.

7.3

A HORDE OF FOOTBALL fans had boarded at the sports stadium stop. They milled about now in the passenger car, boisterous and irrepressible. Sheila turned to one promising-looking bunch near her wearing Arsenal colours, and addressed the tallest and biggest among them with the harshest, most venomous tone she could muster: 'Arsenal is the full form of arse, isn't it?'

There was a moment of stunned silence into which she added, smiling, 'So what does that make you all? Arsenalholes?'

And she turned and walked away, moving quickly through the aisle until she reached the Mohun Bagan group she had settled on earlier. In perfect contrite Bengali she said, putting on her best damsel-in-distress face: 'Those men are threatening me, they say we Mohun Bagan fans are Bengali bastards and bitches. Please help.'

Then she pushed on past, as if desperately scared and eager to get away.

The sounds behind her that erupted were hugely satisfying. She heard accusations and counter-accusations, shouts and abuses, Bengali swear words and English abuses. India shining: the flat global village that God sat on and polished with his bum, as Gunter Grass might have said now if he'd visited the city in this millennium. She kept moving until she was at the end of the coach and walked straight up to the man with the cap, the blue-eyed blonde.

He glanced up in surprise as she approached. He had been briefly distracted by the ruckus, and the skirmishing passengers had blocked his view for the last few metres. She took the last few steps faster than he could respond to, and lashed out with a sideways kick that rammed the bridge of his nose into his brain and sent his head back against the glass of the coach window, where it struck with a sickening crunch. Blood spurted from his nostrils, but his eyes were already blind and he tumbled off his seat and to the floor in a sprawled heap. There was a smear on the window where his head had struck.

She turned and took stock of the chaos she had engendered. The argument had become a full-blown brawl, barely thirty seconds after she had insulted the first group. That was the nice thing about football fans. They were so dependable. Nobody had even noticed her assault of the unfortunate blonde. They were all watching the fracas with muted Bengali interest.

She had timed her move so that the train was already pulling into Phoolbagan. There was nobody waiting by the door and she got off alone, sprinting quickly to the next car and waving her arms wildly. The man in the adjoining car was already on his feet and he saw her and blinked, then ran for the exit. No more pretence, time to step up. She ran the other way, towards the exit, but only until she saw the third man get out of the coach on the other side. She stopped as he turned towards her, his hand slipping into his the side pocket of his jacket, holding something. She pretended to stop, as if afraid of him, and turned back. The other man was coming towards her from that side. They had her boxed in now, and both men had their hands in their pockets, which suggested they had either seen her attack the blonde or were willing to up the ante anyway.

She pretended to back away behind a pillar. There was only a railing this way, and a view of Phoolbagan, which wasn't much of a vista, especially at this time of night. The lights of Kolkata proper illuminated the view further ahead.

She waited for them to come to her, knowing they would, then sprinted around the pillar, throwing herself feet first at the nearest man. Because she had the package in her hand and didn't want to put it down even for a second, she could only use her feet. At the sight of her, his hand holding the gun slipped out of his pocket, barrel turning towards her. But it was off by at least an inch or two and she was already landing on his chest, feet first. She hit him with all her 57 kgs, propelled by the flying leap, and felt his ribcage yield as he was thrown back. He went sprawling backwards across the platform, gun flying out of his hand. She didn't see where it fell, and was already landing on her feet again and somersaulting, knowing that the other man had had more time and a better line of fire. Right enough, she heard the soft burr of an automatic and saw large dimples appear in the side of the metro train, stitching a pattern over the Bank of Japan and other logos. Then she was sprinting, crouched-over, behind another pillar and around it. The man she had drop-kicked continued his slide across the platform, knocking over a few passengers who in turn stumbled and reached out and pulled down a few more people. Someone cried out in Bengali, but she didn't catch the word.

She looked around. The lighter-skinned African was nowhere in sight. Smart man. She glanced around and saw a man in a suit with a briefcase standing on the ground beside him, gaping at her. He had a Blackberry to his ear and looked north Indian in that clean cut way. She grinned at him. He grinned back instinctively, absurdly. She picked up his briefcase and tossed it around the pillar, then went around the other side.

The African was caught unawares by the briefcase flying at him, firing at it in automatic response. She came around the other side of the pillar, intending to run low and catch him in the abdomen. But he was quick to adapt and the gun turned to blaze out at her, the muzzle flash blinding her for a second and she was certain she had been shot, but somehow she was still moving – and so was he – and they met in a kind of lovers' embrace, her hand clutching at his abdomen, his gun turning to follow her. She punched him low and hard before spinning around in a ballet-pirouette, trying to avoid the gun barrel following her ominously. He doubled over, going to his knees, the gun dipping low to fire off a round or two into the concrete floor. She spun and came around again, taking hold of his neck from behind in a garrote grip, and wrenched hard, the gun already turning up and over his shoulder again, about to fire, and this time at such close range, he couldn't miss. She felt his neck snap and the gun hand and everything else going limp. She let him fall to the platform, his forehead thumping the ground hard.

Then something exploded behind her and she started to turn her head, seeing an ad display kiosk struck by an invisible fist. Without completing the turn, she rolled over behind the nearest pillar. More shots followed from the direction of the train and she guessed that the man she had kicked had either found his gun very quickly or had another one handy. He was too far away for her to take at a run and there were no more briefcases to throw at him, so she did the only other thing she could: she went south.

The railing was only a metre-and-a-half high and she vaulted it easily. It was the landing she was worried about. Ten metres to the street, she estimated, give or take a metre. She fell, knowing that if she broke a leg while landing, there would be a bullet in her brain a moment later, shot from above. But as the man once said, it was the only gig in town and she would rather die trying than try dying.

Chi Kou Ri

Red Dog Day

As per Chinese customs and traditions, the third day after the Chinese new year is known as chì kou, directly translated as 'red mouth' or, when the symbol for poverty is added, as 'red dog day'. Chì kou is also called chì gou rì. Chì gou means 'the God of Blazing Wrath'. It is generally accepted that it is not a good day to socialize or visit your relatives and friends.

Eight

8.1

THIRUVANANTHAPURAM ZOO HAD BEEN one of Anita's favourite places to visit as a girl. But despite her numerous visits, she had only come once with Lalima, and they had held hands and walked around for hours and it had been one of those idyllic days that you remember forever. Unlike most zoos in Indian cities, it was a sprawling enclosed space with woodlands, lakes, large patches of lush green lawns that could have done with more frequent mowing, beautiful old museums with Raja Ravi Varma paintings that had scandalously clad women from Puranic epics, gaping at which school kids giggled while their teacher shushed them, and the animals actually looked like they were alive and healthy. Unlike, say, the Mumbai Zoo where she had felt that the beggars on the streets lived better than the animals, and where crowds stood around haranguing and harassing the creatures all day. She tried not to think about that long-lost summer day, but the image of two young girls, innocent of life and with a universe of possibilities ahead of them, refused to be completely dismissed, and around every corner she saw something that reminded her of it. The lawns were much better maintained now, and the general standard of cleanliness and upkeep was impressive. She spent a moment reading a notice that informed her that due to the increased erosion of forests and fauna, the zoo had changed its mission to focus on conservation rather than recreation. The authorities had even displayed a website URL. She limped slowly around, trying to ignore the pain in her toe that even a handful of painkillers hadn't been able to numb.

The lawyer was over an hour late and looked like a man on the verge of a nervous breakdown. His hands shook as he greeted Anita at a bench between the giraffe and zebra habitats. 'Madam, I cannot stay long,' he said in a quavering voice. He was dressed in a typical lawyer's black suit, crumpled and creased with sweat patches around the collar and arms. He was thin and short and wore steel-rimmed spectacles, and a faint moustache darkened his already dark upper lip. 'It is not advisable to be seen with you, ma'am. You are in lot of trouble. Very serious matter.'

She gestured to the bench and sat without waiting for him. 'Varkala Police?'

'Yes. There is a full-state alert for you. I am in contact with department. I enquired after you mobile-phoned me.'

'What are they saying I did?' she asked casually, watching

a group of nuns and novices by the giraffe enclosure. 'Committed murder?'

'They say you are a terrorist. Alert is under "counter terrorist" heading. It is serious matter. There are traffic blocks for you.'

She resisted the urge to quip that gee, golly, gosh, she was thrilled to bits to have traffic blocks. *For li'l ole moi? How rad!* Instead she tried to ignore the throbbing in her right toe and said, 'Lalima Mukucundan hired you?'

He hesitated a moment, then nodded. 'She was not my regular client. She was referred through an associate. I only undertook one task for her. Payment was made in advance.'

'In the event of her death, you were to send me a set of documents by courier?'

He shook his head. 'I do not know what was in the packages. They were already pre-addressed. I only had to hand them to the courier company and send them.'

Anita sat up straighter, careful how she put her weight. 'Packages, you said. How many were there?'

He frowned. 'I am not supposed to divulge details. I only agreed to meet with you, madam, because her instructions clarified that if you contacted me, I was to pass on one more item to you personally.'

Anita blinked. 'What item?'

He glanced around as if checking to see that no giraffes were peeking over the wall to eavesdrop. 'This.' He handed her a small, square envelope. It felt empty but was sealed and the neat hand-written letters were in Lalima's hand.

She slipped it into the back pocket of her jeans, wincing as the movement pulled at her neck muscles. He noticed her wince but didn't seem particularly interested in her injuries or pain. He was already starting to stand up. She reached out and caught his arm, pulling him down. He sat abruptly and looked dismayed. 'Madam, I ...'

'How many packages?' she asked roughly, keeping her voice low. The nuns and novices were drifting past. A pair of the younger ones stared at Anita and the lawyer – Anita's hand was still clutching the lawyer's elbow – and one whispered something to her friend who giggled, covering her mouth. Anita waited till they went past, then said quietly, 'Answer me.' She squeezed his forearm hard enough to hurt. It was his turn to wince.

He hesitated, then said almost sulkily, 'Four.'

She nodded but kept her hand on his arm, tight, as if he were a bird that might flit away. 'You say you don't know what was in the packages?'

He shook his head. She believed him. That was the point of using a lawyer, to keep the contents confidential. Lalima must have picked him after checking him out. The very fact that he was so scared told her he was honest.

'I need the names and addresses of the other three recipients.'

He began protesting but she punched him hard in the left kidney. A group of Asian tourists drifted past. She leaned in closer to the lawyer and smiled at them. One of the men smiled back but then noticed the bloodstain on her tee shirt collar and frowned. She waited for them to pass by. The lawyer had doubled over. When he straightened up, with Anita's help, his eyes were wet. What a fucking sissy.

'I ...'

'Shut up and write them down now,' she said harshly. 'I don't have time to fuck around. Do it or I'll tell the police that you're involved with me and we're planting bombs across Trivandrum. You'll spend the next five years trying to explain your innocence.'

That threat worked better than the violence. Reputation was more precious than a kidney in these PR-dominated times. Image was more important than truth.

'Madam, they are not in writing,' he said. 'Lalima-madam instructed me not to write it down anywhere.' He hesitated. 'But the courier company receipts are in my satchel.'

He gestured to the leather case on his lap. Anita let him open it and he rummaged through briefly before pulling out four rectangular receipts on cheap paper. She glanced at them, saw her name on one and noted that all three of the others were women too, and put them into her back pocket as well. She looked at the lawyer. He suddenly looked disgusted, as if he had done something really venal.

'What?' she asked, challenging. 'She was my friend, you know. They killed her. I'm sure of it now. That's why she hired you to send out that package to me. She knew that I would come and try to find out what happened to her. And I will. I won't stop until I find out everything and get the bastards who killed her. I don't expect you to understand that.'

The look of disgust faded gradually, reducing to a milder expression of disapproval. 'Police will catch you anytime. They say you attacked your own family and shot your brother because he was trying to stop you from blowing up a church.'

She raised her eyebrows. 'Blowing up a church? Killing my brother? Not bad. Although you'd think a terrorist would be more ambitious than that. Does anyone in Varkala even go to church anymore? What if I just ended up killing the padre and two deacons? Would anyone even cry?'

He crossed himself. 'I will pray for you.'

She sighed. Monu Varghese. Of course he was Christian. 'Alright, get the fuck out of here.'

He stood up but didn't walk away at once. After a moment he looked down and said, 'Jesus Christ will show you the way.' And then he walked away quickly with neat mincing steps, leaving her searching for a quick and dirty retort and finding none.

8.2

NACHIKETA HAD NEVER BEEN happier to see Advaita's face as she was that day. Advaita was one of those stern-faced women who wore giant black (or red) bindis high on their forehead, dressed only in Fabindia saris, and had lots of silver accessories. She had a tattoo on her right bicep – of Kali stamping on Shiva, her tongue lolling, trident raised. It had faded over time, but her intense glare had only become more intimidating as she had gained weight and age. Even the fiercest of Delhi Jats and sardars stepped off the footpath when she came striding along in her block heels, all five-feet-nine of her (plus three inches of heels), 107 kgs and as broad as a barrel. It was difficult to believe she was married with three grown children: novices to Delhi activist circles sometimes made the mistake of assuming she was a lesbian and learnt the hard way that she was not. The 'hard way' being a bitch slap delivered to the left cheek with the full force of that 'dhai kilo ka haath' and all those silver bangles. Addy, as her friends called her, was energetically heterosexual and was rumoured to have slept with half the eligible men in South Block – and most of the ineligible ones as well. Her husband, a special officer currently assigned to the law ministry spokesperson, was either an ignorant cuckold or a willing one, nobody knew for sure.

Addy breezed in and berated nurses, doctors and the rest of the burn ward staff in the hospital where Nachiketa had been shifted early that morning from AIIMS. Once she was certain that her friend was receiving the best possible treatment and care, she settled down imperiously with a flurry of hand-woven silk in a plastic chair beside the bed. Nachiketa asked her to have the oxygen apparatus removed, and with Addy giving orders, it was done without complaint. Nachiketa breathed a sigh of relief, then coughed several times, glad to be off that wretched thing even though she knew she needed it. The medication they had given her on arrival was almost wearing off and she was aware of the extent of her burns now, as she hadn't been when she had first regained consciousness at AIIMS.

'You are strong, bete,' Advaita said, reaching for her hand, then thinking better of it when she noticed the bandages. 'You will survive. It is what we women are built do to: survive the abuses of men.' She added a few choice abuses in Punjabi, delivering them in a matter-of-fact tone.

Nachiketa had once heard Advaita tell her three grown sons – they had been teenagers at the time – that all men were bastards but hopefully the fact that she had breastfed them till they were two years old each would have instilled some sense of shame in their doomed-to-be-chauvinistic heads. As it sometimes did, fate had seen fit to grant her only male offspring. Nachiketa wondered how they survived Advaita on a daily basis.

They talked for a while about Shonali and the tragedy of her death, and then about the financial and legal implications of the fire. Addy assured Nachiketa that she had already started doing as Nachos had requested when she called and was arranging for her cases to be handled by another law firm. The Collective would take over all her matters until she was well enough to resume work; although most of what they did would have to be seeking extensions and filing motions for extensions, caveats and sidebars, and so on. The Collective was a group of Delhi women lawyers engaged in their own private practices who took on a certain percentage of pro bono work related to women's issues. Only a few worked full-time on such matters, Nachiketa herself being one. They were perennially overburdened and it was all they could do to keep up with their workload. Even if they had to actually deal with or argue one of Nachiketa's cases, it would be several months before they could rebuild the files and study the cases well enough to take on the matters. And with even her computer burning down, along with all her backup disks and files, rebuilding the case files was itself the biggest nightmare that Nachiketa's practice faced right now.

'But don't worry about all that, bete,' Advaita said soothingly, patting the bed sheet in the vicinity of Nachiketa's arm in lieu of her usual patronizing thump. 'Your first priority – get well, get strong, get back in action.'

'Addy, there's something else I want you to do for me.' Nachiketa asked her to fish out the envelope that she had told Rajendra Powar to place on the table near her bed. Advaita did that, her bangles and accessories jangling and clanging as she bent over. She had a roll of fat as thick as Nachos' arm around her midriff, but despite her excess weight, she had a powerful predatory sexual aura.

She straightened up, holding the manila envelope, and dusted it off, sniffing in disapproval. 'Forget all your clients, bete. Right now *you* are the one who needs help. This is no time to think of work.'

'No, Addy,' Nachos said hoarsely. 'This isn't work. This was sent to me just before the fire. I think it's the reason why they attacked Shonali and tried to kill me too.'

Advaita frowned, her bindi dipping into the deep folds of the wrinkles on her forehead. 'So you know the attackers?'

'No. I don't know who they were or why they attacked her and set the office on fire. But I'm sure it has something to do with this package. The man who called me on my cell when I was driving mentioned it. They must have searched the office for it, and when they couldn't find it, they called me and threatened to kill Shonali if I didn't give it to them. But they had no intention of letting us go. So they set a fire trap for me, and when I was in the office, they tried to get rid of me and Shonali's body and this package as well. The only reason they hadn't found it was because it had somehow fallen under the table by the door, the same table I took shelter under to escape the fire. I must have hit it with one of my wheels somehow and knocked it there.'

Advaita frowned, weighing the package upon her large palm. 'What is inside, bete? Why so important?'

'That's what I want to know,' Nachiketa replied. 'I need you to take it and look through it and tell me what you think. Can you do that for me, please?'

'Of course, bete. I will take it home and look at it afterwards and—'

'I mean *now*, Addy. I need you to open it and look at it *now*, along with me.' Nachiketa raised her bandaged hands. 'I would've done it myself but ...'

Advaita looked at her watch. 'I have a South Delhi Women's Committee meeting at five, but there is some time. Can I not take it and look later?'

'Please, Addy. It may be important. The people who did this are out there. They got away scot-free after raping and killing Shonali and almost killing me. I need to do this now. Please? For Shonali's sake?'

Advaita nodded grimly. 'Okay, bete. Let's do it now.'

She tore the flap of the envelope open and began removing the documents from the envelope.

8.3

SHE SURVIVED THE JUMP, landing on a corporate-sponsored median about five feet off the ground. She killed a bed of flowers, rolled over some imported grass turf, and was already on her feet, jumping the railing with the brightly coloured corporate logo and into the street. She cut through the path of a WBST bus – whose driver honked angrily – and down the first turn. Several minutes later, she looked back and was sure she wasn't being followed.

She found a small hotel nearby and went in at once. If they did come after her and try to trace her flight from Phoolbagan, the last thing they would expect was for her to check into a hotel. Even if they did, there were probably two hundred hotels in Biddhanagar, all catering to the constant flow of business travellers on account of the BPO and IT boom. She found a room with a view of the street, took a hot shower, and made a few necessary phone calls.

She slept in the next day, waking late around noon. The man she wanted to see was a hard person to get through to, and when she did at last, she was told that he would see her that night. She was given a location and time. There was no question of asking it to be earlier.

She kept expecting her mobile phone to ring any time, thinking that if those pursuing her could set municipal authorities, police and trained foreign assassins upon her, they must have her cell number too. But, apart from the usual telemarketers, nobody called. This she knew because she habitually added any telemarketing caller to a contact named JUNK in her iPhone. That way she didn't have to listen to the automated recordings offering her caller tunes or the same tired call centre execs from Noida hardselling special offers. Her iPhone stayed surprisingly silent the entire day, making her wonder if even her friends were avoiding her. Then again, all her friends were people at the gym, and after yesterday, there wasn't much more to know.

She spent the day watching television and getting restless. She would have used the hotel gym but didn't want to be noticed: an Indian woman working out in a Phoolbagan hotel gym is a rarity even in these enlightened times. There was nothing on the news about her, the gym, the shootout … nothing. How was that possible? In a world with a hundred news channels chasing the most insignificant scrap of gossip, how could a shootout at a brand new metro station go unnoticed? This fact told her, again, that whatever this thing was, it was huge.

She went through the package again, several times, but didn't get much further than she had the night before. When the figures began blurring, she gave up. Finally, she settled on the hotel bed and watched an entire Arabic movie on an international movie channel, followed by half a Mongolian film.

Then it was time to get moving. She showered again, wearing the same jeans and tee shirt from the night before. She had hand-rinsed them in the sink that morning just to get the smell of the sweat out, and asked for them to be ironed. That was the other reason why she hadn't been able to step out of her hotel room all day. She had had to wrap a towel around herself each time room service came, and was glad the waiter was an old Bengali holdout who didn't seem very interested in her state of dress or undress. He didn't seem to care much about his tip either. She guessed he must be an antique piece among the young hotel staff.

Coming out of the hotel, she saw a cab going past at an idling pace and hailed it.

'Dharamtala,' she said, getting in.

The taxi driver, a young Bangladeshi immigrant with a picture of the Ka'aba on his dashboard and as much knowledge of Kolkata geography as a Patiala Sikh who has just arrived in New York, almost turned the wrong way on Chowringhee Road.

She corrected him in time. 'Lower Circular Road, turn now.'

Instead of turning, he slowed to a crawl and said, 'Jagdish Chandra Bose Street.'

She said, 'Yes, yes, same thing, turn here.'

'You want go Dharamtala, no?'

'Dharamtala Road, yes.'

'This go to Lenin Sarani.'

'Yes, that's the same thing. Dharamtala Road was renamed Lenin Sarani. I want us to turn here, please.'

He shrugged as if implying that she had no idea what she was talking about, but it wasn't his problem. She was tempted to whack him across the side of his head and tell him that if he wanted to drive a cab in another country, the least he could do was know the streets. In Kolkata that meant knowing the old names as well as the new.

He argued again when she tried to make him stop on Chandni Chowk Street. 'All closed,' he said.

She wanted to tell him she wasn't here on a shopping trip to pick up petticoat material. 'Please wait. I need to check if the person is there.'

He shrugged, but switched off the engine and waited.

She got out and looked around. The street was filled with stalls and vendors and shops selling bric-a-brac. This was a market area after all, as the Bangladeshi had rightly implied, but she wasn't here to shop. Shakespeare Bazaar – which was what the area had been called when she was a child – was where the professor lived. She was on full alert after the shootout at the metro station. Her instincts told her that she hadn't been followed but she wasn't reassured.

She had asked to meet the professor because she knew she had to do something. Sitting around in a hotel room in her bra and panty wouldn't have got her anywhere. This was definitely not about Marhabha and Tasneem or any politician with a grouse against her. This was about the evidence she had in the envelope stuck under her arm. And that meant finding a person who could help her figure out what that evidence really meant, so she could then figure out what she could do with it.

The area had changed and she had difficulty finding the place. He said they had renovated recently. It took her a few minutes to realize that it wasn't renovation but rearrangement. Some of the old vendors and stores had given way to new ones, and the owners of the shops had repainted and refurbished their places, which made everything look different. She found the shop she was looking for at last, and the narrow stairwell beside it. She had called ahead, using a public call phone after she had put a safe distance between herself and Phoolbagan Station, and he had said to look out for the green staircase. This was it, although the naked yellow bulb hanging from the ceiling turned the parrot-green into blue.

The staircase – barely wide enough to let her walk straight – creaked as she went up. Reaching the top, she went down the only corridor to the door on the far right as he had instructed. The door on the left was open and looked out on a terrace. There were dark sheets spread out across the terrace, with fish drying on them. She couldn't actually see them but the smell left no doubt. She paused, remembering her mother bringing home big jars of putimaachi and telling her how this was Shakespearan hidol-shidol. The way she used to say it made it sound like manna from heaven. The way her mother fed it to her, mixed with rice balls in just a certain ratio, it *was* manna. She still associated the smell with her mother feeding her rice balls on the veranda of their Dakshineshwar house.

She knocked on the door and it opened inwards. 'It's open,' said a voice.

She went in.

Nine

9.1

ANITA SUPPOSED SHE SHOULD be thankful that the lawyer hadn't given her away to the cops. But it was probably Lalima she ought to be thankful to rather than the shyster himself. She had picked him well. She believed him when he said he hadn't read the contents of the packages. He wouldn't have been able to lie so smoothly if he had.

She wished she had been able to keep some of the papers or better yet, the whole package. But the way things went down, if she had tried to collect all those scattered pages at that instant, it would have cost her her life. She had no illusions about her brothers. What they had done to a fifteen-year-old girl had been unforgivable. But they had justified it with religious claptrap, her mother even forcing her to pray every day, tell her rosary and go to confession every

Sunday. It had taken Anita a year or two after she left that house to figure it out completely, mainly because her young mind hadn't been able to accept the truth: her mother had known all along, had perhaps even encouraged Isaac and Graham to molest and rape her, and then to beat her when she cried and fought back and threatened to tell the world. Her mother had justified it because she had found out about Lalima and Anita, had all but caught them red-handed in Achchan's old car behind the house one afternoon, fooling around.

They had just turned fifteen then and were beginning to discover each other's bodies, and their love was pure and innocent and beautiful. But Iris Matthew hadn't seen any of those attributes of that relationship. All she had seen was two young girls making love, one of them happening to be her daughter. That was more than she could handle. She was the sort of woman who hated intensely and indiscriminately and sought the answer to everything in her worn Bible with the black leather cover and red-brushed pages. As far as she was concerned, this was the devil's work and needed to be thrashed out of a misguided young girl. When thrashing didn't achieve the results she desired, she had seethed and festered and eventually found a twisted, warped method that fit her dogmatic thinking. What better to turn her daughter back to God's path than to show her the pleasures of natural man–woman cohabitation? And how better to control such a 'treatment' than to let her own sons administer it?

To this day, Anita had no idea if her mother had come up with the sick plan or if her brothers had talked her into it. Isaac had had his eye on her and Lalima ever since her boobs had started to show and he had taken the discovery that Lalima was sweet on his sister as a twisted motivation for a personal vengeance. Anita could imagine him using the twisted logic of religion for the sake of his mother to justify what he intended to do to Anita in order to set her right. But she couldn't be sure. She couldn't even be sure if it was planned and intentional or whether it had just happened that first night because Isaac and Graham had gotten too drunk and horny and their mother had found out later and tried to rationalize it after the deed was done. She knew nothing of the truth because the truth didn't exist anymore, only fractured versions of it that varied depending on whose point of view you believed. Graham had always had a completely different take on things: he had claimed that the brothers had only been fooling around and it was Anita who seduced them. This was one of the versions that their mother had latched on to enthusiastically at first, using it as yet another piece of evidence to justify her theory of demoniac possession. Why, she had even talked Father Yeshua into coming to the house and attempting an exorcism!

The nightmare had lasted barely two months, at the end of which Anita had left the house and her family, knowing she would never return, and that they were as insane as it was possible for people to be and yet appear sane. Again, religion played a large part in that; for what else was intense fervour but a kind of insanity sanctified by society? Lesbian, gay, artist, socialist? Lock 'em up and throw away the key! Religious nutcase, fanatic, riot-instigator, bigot or racist? Why, that's just good old god-fearing morality.

Thirteen years later and she was still pissed off about it.

'What you looking at, bozo?' she asked a baboon sitting on the branch of a tree and scratching his balls. Some school children nearby giggled and pointed at the woman talking to the monkeys. Anita moved away, reminding herself that she was trying to be inconspicuous. *Yeah, sure,* she thought bitterly, *if they had a habitat here for lesbian Malayali P.I.s on the run from the cops, I would be right at home.*

She stayed at the zoo all day. Towards evening, she managed to hook a cell phone. She had to steal it, which was unfortunate, but she picked her target carefully, choosing a suited-booted type who was more involved with his Bluetooth than with his wife and kids. He was that typical thirty-something Malayali male with the thin moustache, slim physique, polished shoes, razor-sharp creased trousers, pinstripe shirt and slicked-down hair that announced **DUBAI-RETURN** in life-size block letters, Arial Black Extra Bold font. The way he carried himself when with his wife – speaking curtly, and always presenting a one-third view to her, always walking a step or two ahead, never looking back to see if she was keeping up – the sharpness with which he corrected his children, the oily obsequiousness with which he chattered away on his BT headset, all spoke of a man who had spent a decade alone in a bare apartment with ten other guys, working twelve-hour shifts and saving every rupee so he would be set for the rest of his life. She wondered how much dowry his parents had asked for him. A lot, given his Dubai-return status, the inevitable flat, car, life savings, and not to be forgotten, pliss, his Brahmin caste. What's that you say? How can a Christian be a Brahmin? Well, how can a dark-skinned man be considered inferior to a white man in America? Lawksadaisy. It's in the Constitution! All men are created equal ... except the Christians and white folk are created more equal than others. So Keralite Christians, and most other converts across India in the wake of the great rumbling-farting lorry of the erstwhile British Raj, still remembered and marked their previous caste status and that of their neighbours, because you didn't simply replace one social system or religion with another, you just layered it on top of the old one, layer after layer after layer, until bits and parts of the older layers peeked out through the new and it all made up the whole.

She flicked the phone from Mr Dubai-Return when they were in the snake farm. He had it in his pocket and was between calls at the time and his daughter needed to be held up so she could see the 'sarppam' better. Mr D-R grumbled about the crease of his trousers and the cut of his shirt, but finally relented and picked his four-year-old up by the waist and held her out, keeping her at a distance of about six inches from his body, as if actual contact would contaminate him, while she wriggled and giggled and squirmed until her bootie struck his shirt, soiling the precious fabric irreparably. It was while he had put her down and was fussing over the shirt that Anita had slipped past him, transferring the HTC from his pocket to her own, then continuing on out of the snake farm. The girl had felt ticklish, Anita knew, because she herself had felt ticklish when her father had picked her up once that way, back when her parents were still on speaking terms (and other terms that didn't involve speaking) and her mother hadn't gone all Biblical yet and he hadn't fallen into a bottle and drowned.

She found a spot near the bird habitats where it was quieter than elsewhere – in a zoo this size, with African animals and predators galore, who wanted to see birds shitting and cackling? She took out the courier receipts and checked the phone numbers on each. There was a woman named Sheila Ray in Kolkata, then herself in Mumbai, then another woman named Nachiketa Shroff in Delhi, and the fourth was a woman named Aadila Shah in Hyderabad. She had never heard or read of any of them before. She thought about it for a while, then decided to try the Hyderabad number first.

She felt oddly nervous as she dialled the number, fumbling with the city code and having to call an enquiry line to get the correct code. The HTC rang several times with incoming calls but she ignored them all, knowing that Mr D-R would have discovered the loss by now and must be using his wife's cell – if he permitted his wife to use a cell phone – to call his number over and over again. She just hoped he didn't blame it on the little daughter; his kind usually did, nasty self-centred bastards.

Finally, she got the correct code and dialled the number. It rang several times and then a cool female voice answered.

9.2

ADVAITA SET UP CAMP in Nachiketa's room. Her cell phone rang constantly, both calls and messages, and she took every single call and replied to every single message, as well as called and sent out several dozen herself. The hospital staff protested more than once, but she intimidated the nurses and bullied the doctors into submission, forcing them to back off and leave her alone. Nachiketa wondered how she could concentrate on the documents at all, but after a while, Addy settled down and read with almost no interruptions, except for an occasional glance at her Blackberry when the message tone went off.

It was dark outside when she finished. She put down the last sheet and held her head in her hand for a moment, then sighed heavily and shook her head, as if trying to clear it.

'What is it?' Nachiketa asked. She had tried to glance at a few of the papers, but between her bandaged hands and the way her medication made her head swim, it was all she could do to stay conscious and concentrate at all. It frustrated her not to be able to go through the package herself, but she had had no choice in the matter. She missed Shonali bitterly, then felt very small, realizing that she was only thinking of herself. *Sure, you miss Shonali – you miss her not being here to help you go through those documents!* Still, even in that moment of selfish need, there was an element of genuine sadness. Numbed by pain medication and still in shock from the previous night's events, she knew that she did sincerely miss her and part of what was driving her to figure out that damned package was Shonali's death. *And Justicebitch too.* A life was a life, after all. And those bastards had murdered more than one as far as she was concerned. Powar had told her that all the puppies had died, save one, the eldest female, alpha of the litter. That poor thing had lost some fur and been singed by the fire, but had survived and been taken in by an animal shelter. Nachiketa had already had them contacted and asked to care for the pup until she was well enough to take it home.

Now, she looked at Advaita's face and tried to read it.

'What?' she asked. 'I could see there are a lot of figures and accounts statements and ownership deeds, but what does it all add up to?'

Advaita spread her large hands, her bangles jangling. 'I don't know exactly.'

'Come on, Addy,' Nachiketa said impatiently. 'You're a B.Com, LLB, you must have some idea.'

Advaita sighed and put her hands heavily on her thighs. She got to her feet, slipping on the sandals she had kicked off hours earlier. One foot slipped in wrong and she had to nudge it against the leg of the hospital bed to get her foot all the way in. She walked to the window and raised the venetian blind. It clattered noisily. From the bed, all Nachiketa could see was the night sky and the deflected light of the sodium vapour street lamps, but when she had sat up earlier she had glimpsed Park Hotel. She knew Advaita must be looking at the lights of the traffic going by on nearby Park Street.

'Nachos,' Advaita said at last. 'Who sent you that package?'

'I don't know,' Nachiketa confessed. 'I told you, it just arrived.'

'And later this bastard called you and threatened to kill Shonali if you didn't give it to him. This package?' Advaita stabbed a silver-ringed finger at the envelope and papers piled haphazardly at the foot of Nachiketa's bed. 'You're sure he meant *this* package?'

Nachiketa frowned, struggling to think. 'What other package could he have meant? He said he was calling from the office. They had obviously torn the place apart searching for something already. If it had been there, they would have found it. The only reason they didn't find this one was because it had fallen under the—' Nachiketa stopped. 'I've *told* you all this.'

'Isn't it a little convenient?'

'Convenient? How?' Nachiketa didn't follow what Advaita was trying to say.

'That the package they were searching for happened to have fallen under the table and even though they "tore the place apart", as you say,' Advaita crooked one finger to indicate quote marks, her bangles sliding down that raised forearm, 'they still couldn't find it?'

'I don't know, Addy. Shit happens. What are you driving at anyway?'

Advaita sighed and came over to the bed, sitting on the window side beside Nachiketa. 'Nachos, don't you find it a little bizarre? A strange package? Jat bastards? Shonali raped and killed? Your office set on fire?'

'With me in it, don't forget,' Nachiketa reminded her. 'They probably figured they would get rid of me and destroy the package together.'

'Two birds with one stone, I get it,' Advaita said. 'What I don't get is why. Why would strange Jat men go to such lengths? For what? Even for Delhi, even for Jat men, raping and killing isn't an everyday thing, you know.'

'Of course,' Nachiketa said, puzzled and a little angry now. 'These guys were obviously criminal elements. The man on the phone sounded really nasty.'

'Yes, but still. Burning down a ... challenged person in her office? Just to get rid of a few documents?' Advaita shook her hairdo. 'I don't buy it, sweetie. It's like something out of a Ram Gopal Varma film, a *bad* RGV film.'

'Well, it happened,' Nachiketa said, a little coldly. 'Shonali's dead. So is Justice and her pups. My office is down to ashes. It's not a film set, you know.'

Advaita put her hand on Nachiketa's thigh, squeezing. 'Sweetie, I'm not trying to belittle your trauma. I know what you went through is terrible, *awful*. Whoever did this is a bloody motherfucking lauda. Shonali's death is a tragedy. NDTV is doing a special *We the People* show on violence against women and they want us both to be on it. And HT asked if they could ...' She shook her head, long earrings swinging. 'But we can talk about all that later. I'm just saying ...'

Nachiketa was feeling frustrated now – and more than a little pissed off. 'What *are* you saying, Addy? I don't get what you're saying. Can you spell it out clearly for me? I'm on painkillers, you know. My thinking is a little fuzzy. That's why I asked *you* to look at those documents for me. What do they add up to? Is it another defence spending scam? Should we take it to Tarun? What *is* it?'

Advaita sighed again. Nachiketa was getting irritated with her sighing too.

Advaita leaned over Nachiketa, her breasts pressing against the recuperating woman's feet, which of course had no sensation at all. But Nachiketa could feel the whole bed shift with Advaita's weight. She was a heavy woman. She reached out and took hold of the pile of documents, pulling them over, then realized she was pulling them over Nachiketa's feet and so picked them up and dumped them on her side of the bed. She sifted through and pulled out a sheet or three. She held it out in front of Nachiketa.

'Look at this,' she said. 'Do you see this?'

Nachiketa tried to focus. The pages appeared to be a list of names of companies. She squinted, trying hard to make her eyes coordinate. 'It's a list of ... corporates?'

'NGOs,' Advaita said. 'Indian NGOs.'

'So?'

'So the Collective is on it. So is ...' she rattled off the names of a dozen NGOs that Nachiketa and she either worked with or whose managers they knew. She ran a long fingernail – painted black with silver dots – down the side of the sheets; they gave off a rasping papery sound. 'These are most of the major NGOs in the country, and most of the minor ones too. Everyone I know is involved with one or more of these.'

Nachiketa shook her head slowly, still not understanding. 'So what does the list indicate?'

Advaita picked up another paper, and another, holding the sheets up gingerly by the corners, as if touching them would dirty her hands. They trembled in the draft from the air-conditioning vent. 'According to these documents, every single one of those NGOs is ultimately financed and controlled through a series of shell companies and other NGOs.'

She put down the pages and picked up another, continuing to pick up and drop papers to illustrate her point as she went on. 'Ultimately, if you follow the financial trail back, these documents claim that all these NGOs, which make up most of the major charities in the country, are being financed by these hedge funds and corporate investment funds.'

Nachiketa's head was beginning to throb, and so were her hands and the side of her neck and her cheek where she had been mauled by the flames. 'You'll have to spell it out for me, Addy. I still don't understand. So all these NGOs are connected financially in some way. So?'

Advaita dropped all the papers back on the bed. 'So if you believe these documents, all of them are being financed by the same interlinked investment funds in the US, Europe and Asia, and that these funds are basically using these NGOs to recycle their profits and launder them.'

Nachiketa lay back on the bed, her head swimming. She still didn't get it. 'So where are they getting their profits from, these funds? I mean, why do they need their profits laundered? Aren't these funds legitimate?'

Advaita nodded slowly. 'The funds are legit. But the source of their profits isn't.'

She was about to continue when the door of the private room opened and a man came in.

9.3

THE ROOM WAS THE way she remembered it. Though she'd been here about two years earlier, the room had looked this way even when she was a child. The same old-fashioned furniture, rolltop desk and carved wooden bed, rosewood side table and carved Queen Anne chairs, all worn from decades of use and badly in need of polish. It would have looked classy if well-maintained and viewed in a house in Alipore or Golf Links, but here, in this dingy, dimly lit room with the torn cotton mattress and cheap sheets and clothes lying higgledy piggledy, it only looked impoverished.

The professor was seated in his armchair, the one with the wooden slats that swivelled outwards so you could hook your feet on them and lie back. He was doing that now, dressed in the same old kurta–pyjama, an old clothbound book lying open on his lap, reading by the light of a single lamp in the corner. Probably reading one of the same old books she had always seen him reading, one of a set of Modern Library Classics as old as the furniture in the room. He looked older and thinner than ever, if such a thing were possible. How old was he now? She had no idea. But it had to be over ninety.

'Sheila,' he said. 'Come, come.'

'I have a taxi waiting down,' she said. 'I won't stay long. I have to see the Hakkadi also tonight.'

He pursed his thin lips as he straightened his legs, lowering them slowly to the ground. 'The Chinaman. Your trouble must be very bad, huh? Big trouble, aachey?'

She nodded slowly. 'Big trouble.' She held out the envelope. 'This is the file I was talking about on the phone.'

He indicated the bed. She put it down on the corner of the bed, then sat beside it. She respected the professor too much to just leave like that. He was one of the last links she had to her mother's family. He was her mother's uncle, her matula mama, although she had always called him 'professor'. He looked at the envelope and she could see the eagerness in his eyes. Even at this age, he relished a new puzzle, a challenge. That was why he chose to live here in this seedy rundown one-room, half-terrace flat on Shakespeare Bazaar, rereading his old classics and earning a rupee or two by tutoring a graduate student from time to time. 'One of the great economic theorists of his time', *The Telegraph* had called him – *Telegraph* London, not Kolkata, although the Kolkata *Telegraph* had printed a fair share of hyperbole about him as well over the years. *The Guardian* had blamed the commercialization of economics for the vanishing of the great economic theorists, naming him in the very brief list. But that had been twenty-some years ago. Now, he was just an old man who spent his last years rereading books and eating hidol-shidol because it was cheap and nourishing.

'You could feed the whole country putimaachi,' he had told her once. 'Every Indian would be fed daily, we would all be healthier and better nourished, and we would be able to focus our energies on more important things. Like ending war and replacing the capital-free market with a more sustainable long-term system.' She had been eleven at that time but had listened intently, absorbing every word. 'Don't take everything your matula mama says seriously,' her mother had told her in the rickshaw on the way back home – this was back when rickshaws were still drawn by men, not motors, in some parts of Kolkata, and were cheaper than trams or buses. 'He means well, but he thinks about economics so deeply, he forgets that there are other things in the world.'

He leaned forward, reaching for the envelope. She picked it up to hand it to him, then paused. He looked up at her, frowning, teeth bared because he was leaning so far forward, he was almost bent double. 'Professor, men tried to kill me for this package,' she said. 'Whatever you do, don't tell anyone you have these documents, don't discuss this information with anybody. Do you understand?'

He grinned, showing the last seven or eight teeth he had left. 'Who I will talk to, rey? You see any economic planning committee convening here?'

She handed him the package. He almost dropped it, not expecting its weight. She put it on his lap. He opened the flap and reached inside. She put a hand on his thin wrist.

The skin was cool and wrinkled like muslin cotton, it felt rougher than the frayed sleeve of the kurta he had on. 'I will call you tomorrow and you can tell me what you think this means. Okay?'

'Roger Wilco,' he said, winking his bright brown eyes at her. 'Will can do, sergeant-major!'

She paused at the door before leaving and looked back. He was already poring through the documents, examining the rows and columns of figures and computations and statistics as eagerly as a hungry child eating at a wedding feast. She hoped she was doing the right thing by involving him. She had no choice: she needed an expert to confirm her suspicions and decipher the things she couldn't understand.

The odour of putimaachi followed her down the green staircase to the street and into the taxi where the Bangladeshi sighed wearily and started the engine as if he had been kept waiting all night and a day.

The driver's attitude of sullen indifference cracked when he saw her destination. 'Burj Banglar!' he said. 'Amara sekhane?'

'Turn left off the Bypass,' she said. 'Then go straight via—'

'Yes, yes!' he said vehemently. 'I know!'

He increased speed, cutting off a dawdling Honda Civic to get off the Eastern Metropolitan Bypass. Sheila had been here only a couple of years earlier and it was impressive how fast the area was developing: the whole countryside seemed to be one vast bed of construction. Yellow metal giants towered and loomed and hulked everywhere: cranes, earth-movers, trucks and machines she didn't even know the purpose of. Skeletons of half-constructed towers dominated the skyline, rising above a forest of stunted buildings. Redwood trees in the concrete jungle. Farther back, they had already passed the four-tower cluster on Prince Anwar Shah Road, until recently the tallest buildings in Kolkata. Now, there were a half dozen others coming up that promised to be twice as tall, even among the tallest in the country. In Kolkata! Who would have believed it? It was expected in Mumbai, where even billionaires weren't satisfied with lavish mansions and raised entire skyscrapers to house their families and their egos, but not in aamaar Banglar. But Banglar had changed. Perhaps this was the new Banglar, creaking and rattling and groaning in its metal womb to rise above the stunted past of British occupation, babu corruption and Communist regression.

The Bangladeshi was actually humming by the time they turned into the road that led to the building she was visiting; she couldn't identify the tune but it was definitely not Rabindra Sangeet. She sympathized with his enthusiasm. The building was an impressive sight from afar and grew only more impressive as they approached. An elongated diamond glittering in the night, illuminated in some kind of scintillating pattern that must make Chowringhee elders snort in disgust and pull their drapes tight to avoid being kept awake by bhadralok envy. Despite the name, it was apparently not related in any way to the similarly named Burj Khalifa in Dubai, the world's tallest building. She supposed the name was aspirational rather than literal, making clever use of an existing brand word.

Something occurred to her and she leaned forward. 'Burj shobdo-ta ... ki Arabi?'

He paused in his humming without losing the beat. 'Tower. Burj mane tower.' He gestured at the diamond looming ahead.

She sat back, enlightened. Being Bangladeshi and Muslim, she had guessed he would have a little more familiarity with Arabic than she did. So burj simply meant 'tower'. That made her feel silly. Since the word simply meant 'tower' it could hardly be copyrighted. Right now, it was a lonely tower, isolated in this emptiness by its choice of location. Was this reclaimed marshland or was it the bigha owned by the royal family of Darbhanga? She couldn't recall. But it was a good kilometre from the Bypass turnoff and the road being still unfinished, it was rough going. There was a construction site on her left and large earth-digging machines were noisily at work, creating noise in a decibel level so high, she could only hear the Bangladeshi humming intermittently. The name of the song came to her unbidden: it was the title song from the new Aamir Khan movie, the one in which he played an eighteen-year-old autistic mute seeking revenge on the men who had murdered his parents and special ed. teacher.

Her cell phone rang when they were still a few hundred yards from the building. She would have missed it, except it was on vibrate-ring. She pulled out the iPhone and looked at the screen. It was a miracle it had survived her flight from the foreign assholes and the fight in the metro station, but it seemed okay, snug in its black rubber condom cover. She didn't recognize the number but the city code was one she didn't recognize either, and that was unusual. It was an Indian city, but that was all she could tell. The time was just past six-thirty though it was dark already, thanks to Indian Standard Time. Unlike the continental US which had almost the same longitudinal width as India, the subcontinent followed a single uniform time for the whole nation. That meant that the sun rose and set much earlier in the east – where she was – than on the western coast of the country. In other parts of India, it might still be working hours. This could be a telemarketer. For some reason, she didn't think it was. Out of sheer curiosity and some sixth sense, she took the call.

Ten

10.1

'HELLO, COULD I SPEAK to Aadila Shah, please?' Anita said. She glanced around. It was nearing closing time, judging from the way the crowds were heading in the general direction of the exits. She would have to leave too, unless ...

'Who's speaking, please?' said a very cultured voice with a perfect English accent.

'My name is Anita,' she replied. Security guards were genially waving the crowd on. They were a few dozen yards away but weren't looking in her direction yet. She remained seated on the bench. 'It's important.'

The voice told her to hold on for a moment. She could hear music playing somewhere in the background. It sounded like jazz. Something by Coltrane, though she couldn't be sure. She had never been a big fan of jazz but had briefly been involved with a woman who was a blues singer and had made her listen to all the classics, especially when in bed. It brought back sweet memories. Where was Charmaine now anyway?

Someone came to the phone. Only now did she realize that the cell phone call had been forwarded to a landline. A younger voice said, somewhat breathlessly, 'Yeah?'

'Aadila?'

'Aadila's on a trek.' The younger voice shouted something over the Coltrane and someone else answered in the background. 'She'll be back Sunday night. You can reach her at her office Monday morning.'

'It's a bit urgent. Hasn't she carried her cell?' Anita asked. The security guards had reached her and one of them was gesturing to her to move on. She nodded to him, trying to smile around the HTC.

'She has, but you know those hills; no signal,' said the girl. 'If it's urgent you can always try Sadia's cell.'

Anita didn't want to get into who Sadia might be. 'Is this ... her sister?' she took a wild shot.

'Um, no, this is her daughter Aasma speaking,' said the girl, not particularly bothered by the question.

She sounded so helpful, Anita decided to brave another, more foolish question. 'Err, Aasma, this is going to sound a bit dumb, but could you tell me what your mother does?'

The answer came pat without any hesitation, 'Yeah, she's an accountant, na. A.S. Shah & Associates. Are you a client?'

The security guard was gesturing to her to get up. Anita nodded and started to rise from the bench she was sitting on. Her foot cramped with the pain and she almost doubled over in agony. It had been fine so long as she was walking around but she had spent the past few hours just sitting here, eating peanuts and sipping a fruit drink she had bought at a vendor's stall, and it hurt like hell now when she tried to step on it. *Son of a* ... '... Bitch,' she whispered.

'What?' the voice on the HTC sounded shocked. 'Hey, who is this?'

'Sorry, sorry,' she said apologetically. 'I didn't mean you. I hurt my foot, that's all. Yes, I'm a potential client. Your mother was recommended by a mutual friend, another client. Is there any other way I can get in touch with your mother this weekend?'

The girl sounded a bit dubious now. *Way to go, Anita. Call a teenager a bitch and expect her to tell you all about her mother.* 'I don't know. Maybe you should try the office on Monday, okay? I have to go now. Bye.'

'No, wait—' Anita said, but the girl had already hung up. She didn't blame her.

The security guard was looking at her doubtfully. He had spotted the bloodstains on her neck and shoulder and seen the way her foot hurt. 'You are wokay, madam?'

'Yes, I'll be fine,' Anita said, then in a fit of mischief, 'just put my foot in the crocodile's pond, that's all.'

She limped away, grinning inanely.

The grin vanished after a few yards.

Her foot hurt with each step. Finally, when she was by the rhino habitat, she knew she couldn't make it this way. Even if she managed to limp out of the zoo in this state, she wouldn't go fifty yards before being noticed. There would be police outside the zoo as always. She had mingled with the crowds when coming in this morning, but now, the crowds had thinned out suddenly, and a woman fitting the description, limping this way, moving at a snail's pace, would be easy picking.

She stopped and leaned against a concrete wall. In a field of wet mud, a pair of rhinos stood and munched grass. The air smelt of rhino shit and wet mud. She tried to think. What were her options?

Not much, if I don't get some medical help fast.

She had a sudden burst of inspiration. Seeing a security guard coming towards her from the opposite direction, she waved him down. He came up, smiling in the friendly Malayali way. 'Closing time, madam,' he said.

She pointed to her foot. 'I think I stepped on a broken bottle. My foot is hurt,' she said.

He lost his smile and clicked his tongue. 'You want me to call ambulance, madam?'

'No, no need for ambulance. I need first aid,' she said. 'You have first aid?'

'Yes, madam, we have doctor and first aid.' He pointed in another direction, past the tiger section. 'Animal hospital.'

'Please, could you help me there?' she put on the sweetest smile she could manage, raising her arm to indicate she needed to lean on him.

'Yes, of course, madam,' he said, offering his shoulder. He was a thin skinny chap, but strong enough to take her weight. She grunted as his foot kicked her injured toe accidentally. It felt like it had swollen ten times its size although there was no swelling visible with the shoe on. She leaned on him and together they limped in the direction he had pointed.

The first aid clinic was a proper emergency facility. A doctor and a male nurse attended to the patients who came to the single-room clinic attached to the zoo's main animal hospital. The authorities clearly gave it the importance and facilities it required. There was a boy with a gash in his hand and his mother and aunt there, and an elderly man lying on a cot who appeared to have got too much sun. The doctor examined her foot and looked up at her through his brown-rimmed spectacles, frowning. He was a youngish man about her age in his early to mid-thirties.

'This injury is from today?' he asked, his tone suggesting it wasn't.

'No, doctor. I stubbed my toe last night before going to bed. It hurt when I put my shoe on in the morning but I thought if I walked on it, it would be okay. Why?' she asked, keeping her face straight. 'Is something wrong?'

'Toe is broken. I think foot is also fractured.' He looked at his watch. 'We will need X-ray. I'll have you taken to the hospital.'

'Can't you just bandage it or something?'

He looked up at her, frowning. 'You need an X-ray, madam.'

'Please. Just bandage it, then you can have me taken to the hospital.'

He shrugged. 'Okay, but you will have to sign release form.'

'Of course.'

'Wokay.' He gave her the form and watched her sign.

Fifteen minutes later, he had finished. 'I will call the ambulance now.'

She nodded. The other patients had left by then, the boy being treated to a constant barrage of admonishments by his mother and aunt for some hare-brained stunt he had pulled, the old man taken away in a wheelchair by his daughter and her husband. She was alone for a moment in the clinic. Even here, the smell of animals overpowered the odour of disinfectant. An elephant trumpeted in the distance. A lion coughed in response.

She decided to use the time to make another call.

She consulted the receipts and dialled the woman in Kolkata named Sheila.

The phone rang.

10.2

NACHIKETA KNEW SOMETHING WAS off the instant the man stepped through the door. He was chewing gum and had a cap on, pulled low over his forehead, but there was something about his eyes that was hard and cold. He was white, not just fair but really light skinned, and the hair visible on his sideburns and arms was reddish brown. He was wearing a denim jacket over a white tee shirt and jeans. His eyes found her the moment he came through the door.

'Nachiketa Shroff?' he said in a distinct north-European accent, either Germanic or Nordic. *Natch-ee-quetta Schrauff?*

'I'll deal with this,' Advaita said, getting up and stepping around the bed. One foot didn't fit into her sandal again and she paused by the foot of the bed to bend and fit it properly. 'Visiting hours are over, and she's really in no condition to receive—'

The man's hand slipped into his jacket and Nachiketa cried, 'Addy, look out!'

The hand emerged holding the very object she had feared – a gun. It was short and snub-nosed and with a black matte finish, not like the guns in RGV movies. The man pointed it at Advaita and shot her.

But she was bending over sideways at just that moment, and the shot went through the folds of her Fabindia sari pallu, ripping the fabric, zipping on past her matronly bulk, and shattering the glass of the window she had been looking out of only moments earlier. She reacted to Nachiketa's scream more than the shot – she hadn't even seen the gun yet – leaping forward, straight at the man. Typical of Advaita: when attacked, fight back. It didn't matter that the man had a gun.

Advaita crashed into the man like a football tackle, losing her balance on the half-worn sandal and tripping as much as hitting him. The man wasn't expecting it and fell back with Advaita on top of him.

In that same moment, Nachiketa used her hands to pull herself off the bed, rolling to the right and falling heavily to the ground. Her shoulder hit the ground hard enough to hurt and her hands screamed in pain. Yes, the medication had worn off. *I'm sober now, girls.* Her dead feet got caught up in the tucked-in sheets and she found herself hanging half-in and half-out of the bed. She pulled hard at the sheets and they came free with an effort. Her hands felt slippery inside the bandages, as if they were bleeding, and she thought that the burn sores must have split open. The doctor had warned her about that. She screamed at the top of her voice.

Under the bed, she had a clear view of the floor by the doorway. Advaita was on top of the European guy, wrestling with him. She bitch-slapped the man twice, then tried to reach for his gun. 'Lauda madarchodh,' she roared in her full-fledged tigress mode. 'Bloody rapist–murderer ...'

The man's gun barked once more, then a third time. Advaita stopped short, lurched forward, and collapsed, gasping.

The man pushed her aside with an effort and stood up, looking at the bed where he expected Nachiketa to be.

Nachiketa threw the bedpan at his foot from under the bed. It was full of her piss and the dark yellow fluid splashed everywhere as the shiny kidney-shaped chrome pan struck the gunman in his shin. That must have hurt like hell because he exclaimed, mouthing an abuse even she recognized from the German movies she had watched: 'Scheisse!' And his gun went off, the bullet hitting the frame of the bed and producing a loud pinging sound with a vibrating echo that Nachiketa felt in her bones and inner ear. He fell over again, landing on his knees, clutching at his shin, and his gun hand landed in the pan full of Nachiketa's urine. 'Scheisse!' he yelled, louder this time. He shook the gun, spattering piss everywhere as he rubbed his hurt shin with the other hand.

Nachiketa was already searching for something else to throw at him. One advantage of using a wheelchair for years was that it built upper body and arm strength, and she took hold of the only thing available, upended it, and threw it. She was hampered considerably by the fact that she was lying on the floor, only able to move from the hip upwards, and her lower body was still entangled in the bed sheets, but she used the strength of desperation.

The object she threw was the IV stand beside her bed, drip and all. The other end of the drip was in her hand and she forgot that momentarily. The stand itself was solid aluminium with a steel or iron base and it probably weighed 5 kgs. It went top first at the gunman and struck him across his torso, hitting his elbow and jaw and then his chest. He was knocked to his rump, landing hard. He yelled out and fired again, the shots whooshing into the ceiling and one hitting the television set on the wall in front of the bed, the LCD screen shattering with a sound like metal crumpling. Physics caught up with the IV line trailing out behind the stand, and the needle of the IV, still embedded in Nachiketa's hand, was yanked out with a ripping sensation and she cried out in pain, the needle tearing free and pulling out the white plaster holding it in place.

She began trying to crawl away, not caring where, just wanting to put something else between her and the assassin. Traffic sounds from Park Street and polluted warm Delhi air from the broken window came from above her head, and she struggled with the bed sheets like a beached mermaid desperate to get back into the ocean. She could see Advaita dying from under the bed, her mouth wide open and gasping in air with furious effort. Blood was pooling across her belly and on the floor beneath her and her eyes were filled with rage.

The man cursed again, this time exceeding Nachiketa's one-word knowledge of German vulgarity, and kicked the IV stand away from him. Still seated, he had a clear line of sight beneath the bed and could see Nachiketa still struggling with the sheets. His cap had fallen off and he had one of those stylish haircuts that looked like you had bed head all day long. He was young, no more than twenty or maybe in his early twenties at the most, and looked very fit and well-trained. Something about him gave off the air of being a professional, someone who had gone through shit like this before and survived. He was still focused on finishing his job and his gun hand was already rising, dripping with her piss, the dark hole of the barrel on a vector that could only end with her body or brain.

He brought the gun to bear on her and fired.

Something crashed down on the German gunman's hand as he fired. Nachiketa recognized it as an upturned wooden stool. It smashed his hand, the fingers cracking like walnut shells, and he screamed, already turning to deal with the new threat. Nachiketa assumed it was Advaita at first, fighting with her last breath. But it was someone else entirely, someone who had come in from outside and flung the stool at the killer's hand. She had no idea where the shot went, although she saw the muzzle flash and it looked as if it was aimed directly at her. She watched as the person who had hit the German with the stool raised it and smashed it into his head this time. The impact produced a sickening sound, breaking several of the young man's teeth, and blood and teeth spilled on the shiny tiled floor. The stool came down one more time, then the German lay still. Beside him, Advaita was still jerking and rasping.

The hand holding the stool whose corner was now bloody, came around the bed and the saviour saw Nachiketa still struggling with the sheets. She screamed instinctively, holding up her hands, and saw Rajendra Powar's bandaged hands and head. He looked like a Sikh, or a Jat with a bad toothache. He dropped the stool and fell to his knees, untangling her legs from the bed sheets. She gasped, half in relief and half in shock, and tried to convey to him that she wasn't the one who needed help.

'Advaita ...' she managed as he pulled the sheets down, exposing her paralyzed lower body in the hospital pyjamas. 'Usse help karo ...' She pointed.

This time he got it. He leapt up and ran out of the room, jumping over Advaita and the German to reach the door, which was still jerking spasmodically as the door closer tried to shut it. Nachiketa had a moment of panic when he left, thinking, *No, no, no, bastard, don't go, don't leave me alone here ...*

Then she saw Advaita gasp one last time, issue a copious amount of blood – trickling down the side of her fleshy face and neck like viscous red vomit – from her mouth and lie still.

Nachiketa stared into her friend's wide-open, dead eyes, kohl smudged and running with the tears she had shed as she died in agony, and thought: *Another one down.*

And she was still alive.

10.3

'HELLO?' SHE SAID, AND could hear just the faint tones of a human voice because of the earth-digger about fifty yards to her left.

'Hello?' she repeated. 'I can't hear you, hold on a sec, will you?'

She rested the iPhone on her shoulder and leaned over the front seat, tapping the Bangladeshi's shoulder to get his attention – the noise of the construction was that loud. 'Ekhane thamuna, please.'

He didn't hear her the first time, so she repeated herself, literally yelling and pointing to the side of the road farther down. It took a third time before he finally got it – showing him the phone did the trick – and he pulled over to the right a little ahead. The noise was still annoying but at least now she could hear a little better. She got out of the taxi on the far side from the construction, using the car as a shield.

'Hello, who is this?' she asked.

'You don't know me,' said a female voice with a faint accent that Sheila couldn't identify. 'My name is Anita, I'm a consultant from Mumbai.'

Sheila was silent for a moment.

As if reading her mind, the woman on the phone said, 'I'm calling from Kerala right now, but I'm based out of Mumbai.'

'What kind of consultant?' Sheila asked.

Another pause, this time at the other end. 'An investigator. Private.'

Sheila raised her eyebrows. 'Really? So then there are *two* of us in that shithole of a city?' She paused. 'Well, I'm not in Mumbai anymore. I meant, when I was based there. So how come I never heard of you back when I was in Mumbai?'

'Because I'm not officially licensed by the police. I mostly do corporate work. For law firms, a little forensic accounting, that kind of stuff.'

Suddenly, Sheila got the connection. But she didn't want to say it herself. So she asked, acting casual, 'What's this about?'

'About a package you received a day or two ago. Probably yesterday? At your ...' a pause like she was reading off the address, '... Salt Lake City, Kolkata address ...'

'Yes,' Sheila said, abruptly.

At that instant, the construction site machines stopped. Just like that, all at once. The silence that followed was almost deafening out here, with nothing else around for kilometres except the distant burr of traffic on the E.M. Bypass.

'I got that ... package,' Sheila said. 'Did you send it to me?' She recalled now that the address of origin had been Thiruvananthapuram. And the caller had mentioned she was in Kerala at the moment.

'No, but a friend of mine did. Lalima Mukucundan. She had left instructions with a lawyer to send out four packages by courier if she happened to die.'

'So technically the lawyer sent it, not your friend,' Sheila said a little more sharply than she intended, then realized what an ass that made her sound like. 'Sorry, I didn't mean to correct you, it's just been a long couple of days here.'

'Tell me about it,' said Anita. 'Get shot at much?'

Sheila looked around. The Bangladeshi had got out of the taxi too and was crouching in front of his taxi, staring up at the diamond-bright tower ahead as if it were a religious symbol. The light from the tower reflected off all the windows and windshield of the taxi, even the dusty metal body, making it somehow look glamorous by extension. She herself was bathed in the blue–green light, her skin tinted by it.

'Actually, yes,' she said, deciding she would have to trust this Anita long enough to at least find out what she wanted. 'You too?'

'Yes,' Anita said, then nothing further.

Sheila found herself liking the other woman. An amateur – or a man – would have described the encounter, maybe exaggerating a little, definitely using it to promote himself or herself a bit. By simply admitting it without comment, Anita had told Sheila a whole lot about herself: she was a woman who did what she had to in order to survive, taking no particular pleasure or satisfaction from violence, and fuck the ego trip.

'Interesting,' Sheila said. 'And this is because of the package?'

'I think so. My friend was probably killed because of it. Because she tried to gather the information and pass it on to someone who might do something about it.'

'Is that what I'm expected to do? Why me? I could hardly make sense of it all. Have you seen those documents?'

'I got one too. That's why I came to Kerala. Though I found out it was a trap. I wasn't supposed to come here at all. I was supposed to do something with the documents.'

'What?'

'If I knew, I wouldn't be calling you now.'

'Well, I'm still trying to figure it out myself, Anita. While trying to stay alive in the process. In fact, I'm on my way to see someone right now. I think he might have some answers.'

'An accountant, maybe? Or a lawyer?'

'Not that kind of help. Not with the actual documents, I mean. This is a guy who has powerful connections with ... with all kinds of people. I think he might be able to find out who the men were who tried to kill me earlier. Or who's behind them and behind the police and bureaucracy that's harassing me too. Because this thing is big, Anita, I hope you know that? Whoever these people are that your friend Lalima pissed off, they have great resources. The fuckers shut down my business and ruined my life, all in a couple of hours. Now I'm a fugitive on the run trying to figure out what the hell I did to get into this mess. I thought I was done with this kind of shit.'

Anita was silent a moment. 'Were they Malayalis?'

Sheila frowned. 'Who? The men who tried to kill me?' She grinned despite her anger. 'No, Anita, they were definitely not Malayalis. I think they were Americans.'

'Americans? Really?' Anita sounded confused.

'Like I said, this is bigger than either of us may know. Listen, do you have a number where I can reach you?'

'I lost my cell phone when I ... I have to get another one. When I do, I'll call you.'

'Okay. But don't text or email. Those are easier to intercept and track.'

'I know. I'll be in touch. I hope your powerful shady friend can give you some info.'

'I hope so too.' Sheila thought of mentioning the professor, poring over the documents and analyzing them even now, but for some reason decided against it. 'You take care, girl. Survive.'

'It's what I do,' Anita said, then was gone.

Sheila stood for a moment, holding the iPhone in her hand and leaning against the car. A little dew had started to collect on the metal top but it was absorbed by the construction dust. There was an enormous old banyan tree – bathed in the same blue–green glow from the tower – bang in the middle of the construction site she was looking at. *The Burj.* It looked like some tree out of mythology, yggrdrasil. Or parijata. She wondered how leaves could breathe in that environment. She supposed if people could survive, they could too. Probably better than people. She liked the sound of this woman Anita's voice and her attitude. She felt better just knowing she wasn't alone in this thing, that there was someone else out there going through the same shit. It also gave her more information than she had before. That could only be good.

She got into the taxi and told the driver to take her to the tower.

Eleven

11.1

ANITA FELT BETTER AFTER she had spoken to Sheila. She liked the sound of the woman's voice, her discreet yet matter-of-fact attitude. She hadn't said more than she needed to, yet she had been frank and open to a stranger. She wondered what Sheila looked like, what she was wearing. She put the HTC down on the examination table and when her fingers touched the steel table, it felt ice cold. She felt her neck and forehead with the back of her hand. Yes, she was feverish. Not just feverish. Really, really hot. Maybe it was something the doctor had given her; maybe it was just the past couple of days and her injuries catching up with her.

I got Philip shot. He's dead. It's my fault.

She realized it had been too long since the doctor had been away. There were no other human patients in the clinic, but should he have left her alone this long? Where was the male nurse she had seen earlier? They were a regular doctor and nurse, not vets, she had heard the injured boy's mother or aunt say earlier. So they couldn't have gone back to the main veterinary hospital to treat the sick animals. Maybe they had gone off duty for the day. It still didn't explain why the place was so empty. And quiet.

Something's wrong. It's been more than half an hour. If he called an ambulance it would have been here by now. So would the police.

A woman moaned loudly with pain, the kind of moan a delirious malaria-ridden woman makes in a hospital bed when she's racked by the shivers that accompany the disease.

Anita realized with a shock that it was her. *She* was the woman moaning.

She looked down. She had put her foot down on the ground. That was what had elicited the moan.

Bastard gave me something. Some kind of sedative or tranquilizer.

And then he had called someone.

She had to get the fuck out of here, fast.

She tried to take a couple of steps but the pain was excruciating. Yet there was a layer of numbness between her and the pain. So the doctor had given her something, but the fracture could probably not deal with having her weight on it anymore. The memory of the day was doubtless making it scream in agony. No more.

But she *had* to step on it. She *had* to walk. She had to get the fuck out of here before Isaac and Graham and whoever else they were mixed up with came to get her. Because this time there would be no Bibles, no mistakes. They would *get* her.

'Come on, bitch. Man up,' she said, then snorted a burst of laughter, spraying mucus from her running nose. Her eyes and nose and throat were all running because of the pain and because she was literally weeping with the pain. She had laughed because of the incongruity of her being a woman telling herself to 'man' up. 'Woman up, bitch,' she corrected herself. That sounded better. Toughness wasn't an exclusive male privilege.

If women can have babies without epidurals, I can fucking walk on a broken foot.

She gritted her teeth and limped towards the entrance of the clinic.

By the door, she spotted a crutch, leaning against the side of a medicine cabinet with a glass front. There were two or three of them. She almost cried again with relief.

'Give me that, fucker,' she said aloud, not even aware she was speaking aloud.

She tried on and discarded the first one for being too high. It was taller than her head. She tossed it aside. It fell against the front of the cabinet and cracked the glass. She didn't care. She tried the second one. It was a perfect fit.

'Howzzat!' she cried, shooting up a finger in the universal gesture of a cricket fan.

She fixed the crutch under her armpit, happy that it was padded. She hopped a step or two on it and was so pleased to have the weight taken off her broken foot, she cried a little more out of relief.

She turned and hopped out of the entrance, into the main zoo.

Except for the distant sounds of various animals, it was quiet outside. She sniffed at the raw stench of manure, piled somewhere nearby in the darkness. She hobbled down the pathway, trying to remember the way she had come with the security guard. Not a soul was in sight, and from down here, she couldn't see a thing. She might as well have been in the backwater swamplands. The zoo was heavily wooded and she guessed the trees and animal habitats blocked the light and the view.

She saw a few glimmers of light here and there in the darkness, but they seemed very far away. Still, there was light enough on the pathway to see by, so she decided to stick with it and put as much distance between herself and the clinic as possible. Once she was at large in the zoo, it would be as difficult for them to find her as it was for her to see anything. She hopped until she found a divergence in the path and turned right without thinking about it. Either the painkiller was kicking in now or the activity was making her feel better. She wasn't moaning any more or crying, and damn, she loved this fucking crutch.

She continued for what seemed like kilometres and hours. Finally, she stopped, exhausted and feeling as if her joints were stiffening from the exertion. She hobbled close to a wall and leaned against it. She was afraid to sit because she knew it would hurt like hell when she had to get up again. She didn't know what the security system was like in the zoo; whether the guards did regular sweeps or searches or just went home for the night.

Yeah, sure, it's a concentration camp. They have searchlights sweeping the walls and sentries in towers with precision rifles. It's a fucking zoo, Anita. The only occupants are in cages or behind high walls.

She shook her head at her own stupidity, knowing it was the continual pain of the injury and then the medication that were clouding her thinking. But that was dangerous. It could get her killed. She had to stay sharp.

Nobody came, no voices yelled out in the night, no gun shots rang out, no police sirens – or even the wails of an ambulance.

She leaned against the wall more, letting almost all her weight rest on it. It felt so good just to be still and to have the weight off her feet. Foot, actually. Damn, she loved this crutch.

It was dead quiet in this part of the zoo. She had no idea where she was. With its labyrinthine turns and slopes, the layout of the place eluded her. But she thought she would be able to hear anyone approaching. She decided to chance making another call. By the light of the HTC, she fumbled with the courier receipts, searching for the phone number of the last recipient.

11.2

RAJENDRA POWAR RETURNED WITH a doctor and a nurse. The nurse looked terrified witless, eyes darting this way then that. She saw the man on the ground and Advaita, and reacted as though they were the first dead bodies she had ever seen. Rajendra Powar pointed emphatically at Advaita, then jumped over her body and came towards Nachiketa. The doctor bent and began checking Advaita with a stethoscope. The nurse just stood staring around her as if expecting gunmen to leap out of the corners and start shooting. She chanced on Nachiketa across the room and stared at her wide eyed. Nachiketa raised her hand to Powar and the nurse started, as if shocked that Nachiketa was not a corpse. Powar pulled her legs free of the last bit of the bed sheets – damn, these hospitals really tucked those sheets and blankets in tightly – and began to pick her up.

'Wait, wait,' she said. 'Tehro.'

He paused, bent over in an awkward angle. The whole thing was taking place in a pantomime, she felt. The doctor was still examining Advaita with the stethoscope. Couldn't he see that her eyes were open and she wasn't breathing and she had vomited gouts of blood? The nurse was still standing there doing nothing but gaping, like a character in a black-and-white slapstick comedy. The Three Stooges, or Abbott and Costello, or Laurel and Hardy. Nachiketa reached out and grabbed the sheets on the bed, trying to align them by hitting them on the floor so she could get them into the yellow manila envelope. It was difficult with the mittens on, but she managed somehow. She thought there might be a few pages strewn here or there, the ones Advaita had been holding up to demonstrate the point she was making before the gunman came in, but she didn't want to search for them. She just wanted to get the hell out of here and so put the envelope on her lap and nodded to the security guard.

'Okay,' she said to Powar. 'Uthao.'

He took hold of her and picked her up with almost no effort. He was trying to avoid holding her with his hands, not out of modesty but because of the burns on his palms. She could identify with that. Her own palms felt awful and she didn't know if it was the ointment inside the bandages or blood or pus or what-the-fuck. He carried her around the bed just as the LCD TV's screen, hanging together like a glassine spiderweb, came crashing down in pieces on the side table with the flower vase. A little glass fell on his shoulder and she brushed it off with her mittens – that's what the bandaged hands looked and felt like, hands in oven mittens – without thinking about it. He continued around the bed, then stepped over Advaita's body to get to the door.

The doctor raised his head from the dead body of Nachiketa's friend just as Powar stepped over it, and Powar's knee struck the doctor's forehead a slight glancing blow. The doctor fell back on his bum, landing heavily. The stethoscope, not anchored to his ears at that instant, fell somewhere behind him on the floor with a metallic clatter. The nurse made a sound and stared down at the doctor who was sitting with his head exactly between her legs, looking up her skirt without intending to. Beside him, the German gunman lay on the ground, his head, mouth and hand smashed by the stool Powar had wielded.

The security guard carried Nachiketa out of the private room into the main burn ward. There were doctors and nurses and ward boys milling about. Some of them crouched behind stretchers and tables when they saw Powar emerging, ducking to avoid being shot. They were all staring wide-eyed, but one very old ward boy with his cap perched at a jaunty angle on his almost-bald head was grinning for some inane reason. He grinned at Nachiketa as she was carried past him down the corridor.

Powar picked up speed as they approached the door to the stairs.

'Nahi,' she said firmly. She had no intention of being carried down several flights of stairs by the man. 'Lift se chalo.'

Powar let the door to the stairs swing shut and turned and ran heavily to the lifts. There were more nurses and doctors here. Interns. They stared at them as if trying to recognize them. Nachiketa realized they thought they might be celebrities of some kind, either criminal or Bollywood or political – there wasn't much difference between the three anymore, was there? – and were hoping to recognize one of them. A Dubai don's moll, maybe? A Bollywood producer who had refused to pay extortion money to gangsters? A politician's son who had shot a socialite in a snack bar because she wouldn't serve him a hamburger with beef? Any of the above.

Powar tried to reach the lift call buttons but couldn't do so without banging Nachiketa's head on the wall, so he jerked his chin at the intern standing nearby. 'Bhaiya, button dabaoge?'

The intern reached out and pressed the button.

They waited for the lift to come up.

Nachiketa was suspended sideways in space. From her angle she could see all the way back up the corridor down which they had come. The doctor and nurse were coming out of her room, both looking dazed. The doctor said something to a ward boy nearby – the same old dude who had grinned at her like a madman – who turned and began pushing a stretcher towards the room. Other doctors and nurses were turning and looking at her, then back at the room and at the doctor–nurse pair, as if trying to figure out if the action was over or just beginning. She realized it couldn't have been more than a few minutes since the German had entered her room. It felt like an hour.

The lift arrived with a young man in a wheelchair pushed by a very overweight middle-aged woman. Powar exclaimed in Haryanvi, then used his elbow to hold the door of the lift open. The woman stared at them.

'Hattey kattey ho, utar jao. Isey bithana hai,' Powar said to the young man in the wheelchair. The man looked up at him dully, then at Nachiketa. She smiled at him without thinking about it.

When neither the young man nor his mother responded, Powar propped Nachiketa with one hand against the wall, reached out and grabbed the collar of the young man's kurta and shoved him out of the chair. He went stumbling but found his feet with surprising ease. He stood, looking dazed. His mother stared at him then at Powar, trying to understand what had just happened.

Powar put Nachiketa in the wheelchair, slapped at the mother's wrists to make her let go of the wheelchair's handles. The mother realized what he was doing and tried to grab the wheelchair again. Powar slapped her hands away – they were immensely thick with heavy rolls of fat, and wobbled gelatinously when he slapped them. She made a sound of Punjabi outrage. Powar rolled the wheelchair into the lift and the doors rolled shut, leaving the woman standing and making her noises of indignation.

It was quiet and peaceful in the lift. Muzak was playing on a speaker somewhere. She recognized the song, the title song from the new Aamir Khan movie, the one in which he was a ...

The lift doors opened again. They were still on the same floor. The Punjabi woman was holding her son by the shoulders. The contrast between mother and son was like an image from a burlesque film. She was so much bigger in size and proportion that he resembled a belan she was about to roll over chapatti dough. The boy saw the lift doors open and looked directly at Nachiketa. She smiled at him again. The mother's head started to turn but the lift doors shut again.

This time Powar jabbed his mitten at the lift buttons and the lift began to move downwards. Downstairs in the lobby, everything seemed as normal and chaotic as usual. Nachiketa couldn't make out if there was more activity because of the shooting or if nobody even knew it had taken place.

Minutes later, Rajendra Powar was wheeling her out of the hospital's emergency entrance and down the wide concrete ramp. It occurred to her that she needed to tell him where to go.

Some place safe. Some place where men won't come after me and kill all my friends.

Where on earth could she find a place like that?

'Aapko gaadi chalani aati hai?' she asked him, then realized it was foolish question. Jat men probably grew up driving tractors from the age of six. When he nodded, she pointed in the direction of the parking area. Advaita had gone to Nachiketa's office building and picked up her car for her, leaving it in the hospital parking until she was ready to leave. She had remembered to snatch up the keys and dump them in the manila envelope as well. Now, she took them out and used the remote to locate the vehicle. The familiar beep-beep of her Civic came almost immediately, a few cars to the right. Powar wheeled her there at a half-run, taking the keys from her.

He had just placed her in the car and strapped her seatbelt on her instructions when her cell phone rang. She fumbled and pulled the Blackberry out of her pocket. It had miraculously survived the fire, buried in her blouse pocket as it was, smothered by her when she crawled under the table. She looked at the screen. An unknown number flashed on it, with a Kerala code. She recognized the code and thought of the only person who could be calling from Thiruvananthapuram.

'Drive,' she told Powar who shut her passenger side door and went around the car.

She clicked with her mitten-encased hand, glad that her BB was set to be answered with any button. 'Hello, Lalima?' she said. 'What the fuck is going on, woman?'

11.3

SHEILA TRIED NOT TO let herself be intimidated by the Burj. Driving up the entranceway itself made her feel like a character in some Hollywood film. *The Towering Inferno*, she thought wryly. She didn't try to look up and see how the building looked from right below. She left that onerous task to the Bangladeshi who was more interested in damaging his upper spine than in what she had to say. She had to repeat herself twice before he heard her. 'Hahm, hahm,' he replied dreamily. 'Aami apeksa karaba,' he added as she began to walk away. 'Apanara samaya niye.' Of course he had no issues waiting and had plenty of time on his hands. She wondered if he would have been as patient if she had asked him to wait near Howrah Bus Stand. But as she walked away and looked back before entering the atrium, she thought he looked sweet standing there and staring up, like a child looking at a mountain. That sense of wonder, that simple amazement at humanity's achievement was what differentiated him and her. Where she and her fellow Kolkatans saw only a rich man's monstrous monument to greed, he saw something extraordinary and inspiring. She made a mental note to ask him his name later.

The lobby was like something out of a science fiction film set. The ceiling went up so high, she couldn't see the top without craning her neck, so she didn't bother. She walked across a polished floor so sharply reflective she could see herself walking upside down in it. There were vaulting flights of glass flying this way and swooping that way, and she thought that the architect must have been an Ayn Rand fan, Howard Roark by way of Hafeez Contractor. There was an artificial body of water outside with vaulting fountains that weren't switched on at the moment, and the glass picture windows, rising several dozen yards high, had water cascading down on one side, which produced a dreamy surreal effect. She found herself wondering what it would be like to sit on those lush calf-leather upholstered sofas on a hot afternoon, sunlight streaming in through that cascading waterwall, and read a book while sipping hot Earl Grey tea. *Yeah, sure, and you're wearing a Sabyasachi outfit and flirting with a Tollywood star. That's so* you, *Sheila ... not.*

The security officers wore suits, or maybe they were just security guards but wore suits. They looked neatly groomed, well paid, and hard as nails. Not the usual uniformed backwash from standard security agencies. They tapped her name out on a touchscreen computer – shades of *Die Hard* – and politely told her to 'take Elevator P to the penthouse suite, the last one on the right'. She was glad they guided her to it, because there turned out to be about two dozen elevators, and even though each one was neatly marked with which floors it went to, she would have spent ten minutes searching for the right one. 'P' was in an alcove by itself with a lobby and reception desk with an attractive Chinese Indian woman – dressed like a hostess in a swanky Chinese restaurant, in a dark red gown with beautiful gold embroidery and a slit all the way up to her lovely waist – behind it. Sheila admired the leg the slit revealed for its muscle tone. The hostess indicated the elevator door and pressed the button for her.

'I love your gown,' Sheila said.

'Thank you,' replied the hostess politely.

'The embroidery is fantastic. From back home?'

'No, actually, it's done right here. China Town.'

Sheila nodded, raising an eyebrow. That was impressive. She had no idea there were still Chinese artisans that good left in Kolkata. The old Chinese Indian population had long since dwindled, their traditional leather tanning and restaurant and beauty parlour businesses long since sold out to other communities. That was why she was meeting the Hakkadi here rather than in Chinatown.

The elevator arrived and the hostess held the button while Sheila walked in, feeling very down at heel and embarrassed about her crumpled sweat-stained shirt and faded jeans. The doors closed and she was treated to an orchestral symphony for about thirty seconds before they opened again on the most glorious view she had ever seen of the city. She had expected a typical penthouse suite with glass picture windows, an extension of the luxurious interiors she'd seen in the atrium lobby, but this was far more extravagant. There was an entire garden here, with pathways and fountains and marble statuary. At one end was a dining space with buffet tables and white-liveried waiters and gowned hostesses, a bar, several Jacuzzis and a heated infinity swimming pool, and at this end, where she stood, was an atrium with marble tiling and all-white decor, so bright and gleaming she was afraid her Converses would leave footprints. There was another lift and a marble spiral staircase that led up somewhere. A hostess who could have been the sister of the one in the lobby downstairs greeted in traditional Chinese style, then added a delicately performed namaste as well. Sheila was aware of herself speaking the Hakkadi's name, and of being escorted by a marbled, covered pathway that led around the garden and directly to a lounge area not visible from the lift. This was also done entirely in white, with gold piping and flourishes. About thirty distinguished and very wealthy looking men and women and couples lounged around, drinking, talking quietly, eating finger food and generally being rich and self-indulgent. Sheila felt certain that if she went around and looked at every face in the place, she would have a list of stars and celebrities and a Who's Who of influential people whose names or company's names were more famous than their recently exfoliated faces.

The Hakkadi was seated on a luxurious white couch that seemed to extend sinuously around the entire room. She realized it was meant to represent a Chinese dragon, right down to the magnificently carved head at the end, but all in white, with gold touches. Seated by the head, resting his hand on its flaring nostril, was the Hakkadi, looking as handsome and suave as ever, surrounded by a half dozen people she vaguely recognized. One was definitely an *Indian*

Idol winner and host, a Chinese Indian singer. Another was a Chinese Indian badminton champ. She didn't recognize the others but they all looked very glamorous and rich. The hostess bent strategically so her slit side was in view of the Hakkadi and whispered to him. He looked up and saw Sheila.

'Sheila,' he said, standing up. 'Sheila Ray. I should shoot you at sight.'

Twelve

12.1

ANITA WAS TAKEN ABACK by the woman's tone and by her use of the name 'Lalima'.

'Um, excuse me,' she said. 'I'm not Lalima. I'm a friend of hers. My name's Anita. Is this Nachiketa Shroff?'

'Yes, lady, you just called me, don't you know whom you called?'

'Yes, but how do you know Lalima?'

'We met at a conference on violence against women in Delhi last August. We were both speakers and we co-chaired a panel. Haan, idhar se chalo.'

'What?'

'Nahi, woh one-way hai. Park Street se chalo, Powar.'

'I'm sorry, are you driving right now?'

'Yes. I mean, no. I mean yes, I'm driving but he's the one

driving and he doesn't know Delhi roads. I don't think he has a license. So I have to guide him.'

'Have you had men trying to kill you today?'

Silence for a moment. Anita could hear traffic sounds in the background and someone using a car horn liberally while mouthing abuses in a north-Indian accent. Punjabi, she thought, or maybe Awadhi or Haryanvi or something.

'Hello, Nachiketa? Are you still there? I said—'

'I'm paralyzed from the waist down, suffering from second-degree burns on my hands and face and neck and back, my pain medication has worn off, I've seen one friend raped and killed, another friend died trying to save me from a German gunman, my office and all my case files were set on fire, and Justice and her pups are all dead, all except one. Where the fuck else would I be, Lalima?'

'Um, I'm Anita, not Lalima,' she said, feeling dazed. 'Did all that happen today itself? I mean, I'm so sorry—'

'Fuck sorry, Anita. Put Lalima on the line. I want to know why the fuck she sent me that package. What does it mean? What am I supposed to do with you? Nahi, nahi, yahan se right nahi, flyover se lo. Ring Road se chalenge.'

Anita's head was beginning to swim. She was trying to absorb what the woman had just told her. Who the hell was Justice? And her 'pups'? Was that some kind of metaphor? The woman in Delhi still sounded as if she was personally angry with *her*, Anita. So she decided the only thing to do was to shock her back.

'Listen, Nachiketa, listen to me. Lalima's dead. She was killed by my brothers, I think, and then they tricked me into coming to Kerala and tried to kill me too. I got away but I'm pretty sure my brother Philip's dead. He got shot while I was escaping. Now I'm in Trivandrum Zoo with a broken foot and I know they're coming for me. I don't have much time, so please, just try to keep it together and let's talk for a few minutes, wokay?'

There was silence at the other end. Traffic sounds. Honking. More abuses in some north-Indian dialect. Then Anita heard the Delhi woman tell her driver something and a few moments later, the honking and abusing ceased and the traffic sounds receded to the background.

'Okay, Anita,' Nachiketa said, still sounding upset but less pissed off. 'I told him to stop by the side. I need to get my brains back into my skull anyway. I don't know how to deal with stuff like this. We can talk now. Go ahead.'

Anita began by briefly telling her what she'd told Sheila and the little she'd learnt from Sheila, and about Aadila's call being a dead end. Then she fell quiet, letting Nachiketa sort through the info. Nachiketa had already asked her what she did and told her that she was a lawyer, and they exchanged a few other bits of basic info.

Anita looked around as she waited in the darkness. She thought she heard voices somewhere but it was difficult to tell. Nothing close by, that was for sure. And if they did come this way, she would see or hear something, wouldn't she? She hoped so.

'Okay, okay,' Nachiketa said at last. 'My friend Addy said something about NGOs, lists of NGOs ...'

'Yes,' Anita said, 'I remember seeing that.'

'Something about their being funded by illicit profits ... and hedge funds are diverting those profits to the NGOs here?'

'Yes, that's what the paper trail shows, that someone has set up a long, convoluted paper trail of companies owned by other companies, ultimately funded by corporations through various capital market funds under legitimate corporate brand names, with legit banking and financing ties, but is mixing profits from illegal activities and using the NGOs to launder some of them and turn it legit.'

'What illegal activities?'

'I don't know for sure,' Anita replied. 'The thing is, nothing's really spelt out clearly. These are all mostly raw data grabs from all kinds of sources. There's no index, no outline, nothing to help figure out the big picture. Now, I've done some forensic accounting before, so I know my stuff. But this is out of my league. There's stuff on international double taxation avoidance treaties, proposed legislations, government regulations on investments and monopolies, insurance regulatory bylaws ... it's really complex stuff.'

'So what does it all add up to?'

Anita paused, thinking. 'Look, I can't be sure exactly, but I think Lalima got hold of these from someone else. I don't know who. She was a whistleblower, if you know what I mean. A troublemaker. She'd worked for Greenpeace, travelled the world, taken part in demonstrations, been arrested in a dozen countries, been extradited from a couple, banned, been arrested in India. I was out of touch with her for years, but the last I saw of her was a picture of her in a protest march against a dam in Madhya Pradesh, with a bunch of tribals and Arundhati Roy and Medha Patkar.'

'I know,' Nachiketa said. 'She got into trouble at the conference last year because she tried to explain why Maoism was rising in the country and why so many tribal women were taking up arms to defend themselves and their families against army and police brutality. She was making comparisons with Kashmir and the north-east and she really raised a ruckus. We had to shut down the panel before time and cancel her next session. All she did was go straight to the press room and talk to the media till she found someone willing to cover her story.'

Anita grinned. 'That sounds like my girl alright. But she wasn't a publicity hound. She just wanted to fight for the underdog.'

'And the underbitch,' Nachiketa said. 'Look, Anita, are you saying that the package she sent us is evidence against some hedge fund financiers on Wall Street?'

'I don't know for sure, but yes, I think that's partly it. I think those documents were all public records and can be obtained by anyone. Lalima or someone associated with her pulled them together over time and was building a case against these people, and they found out and had her killed.'

'So how does your family fit into this? Your brothers?'

Anita didn't have an answer. 'I don't know. That's what foxes me. My brother Philip,' *who is dead now, by the way*, 'said something about the church here in Kerala being involved. I don't know what that means, but obviously there's a connection. My brothers are really pissed off with me, to the point where they want me dead. But there's also government authorities involved, I know, because the lawyer said that the police and state police had listed me as a terrorist and that they were after me.'

'So,' Nachiketa said, as if ticking off points on her fingers, 'there's Lalima, a radical activist, hedge funds in the US and Europe and Asia being used to launder illegal income from some criminal activity, there's Kerala, and possibly the church, and your brothers, and the police and authorities, and NGOs and German assassins are involved as well. And everyone who received the package is being hunted down and killed. So whoever is behind all this is willing to go to any lengths to keep the truth from coming out. So what does it all add up to? What is the truth?'

Anita lowered the HTC for a moment. Someone was coming. She could hear the monkeys going crazy in their cages, shrieking and chattering, and a boar or some other creature snorting and grunting unhappily. She could also see lights bobbing in the darkness and, fuck, was that a chopper with a searchlight approaching over the horizon? *Hey guys, I was only joking about the concentration camp thing!* Then she heard the roar of an engine and saw headlights moving through the trees on the other side of what she guessed must be the crocodile swamp and knew the jig was up: they were here and they were heading towards her, or at least the general area in which she was located. 'Listen, Nachiketa, I think they've caught up with me. I have to go now. I'm going to try and text you Sheila's and Aadila's cell numbers too. No other option, let's hope they don't trace it, wokay? Bye.'

She disconnected and adjusted the crutch under her arm. Time to run again.

12.2

'HOLD ON,' NACHIKETA SAID. 'Is ...?'

But the call was dropped. She looked at the BB and thought of storing the number, but how was she supposed to press those tiny buttons with these mittens on? She needed a phone with a bigger screen. An iPhone 4G. No, that needed finger touch. It wouldn't work with cloth on your fingertips. Something with a stylus? But how would she grip a stylus with these mittens? An iPad? No, you couldn't make calls with that, only VoIP, Skype and email. An Android device, then?

'Chalo,' she said aloud to Rajendra Powar. He was leaning forward on the steering and staring out at the traffic streaming past. With mittens covering their hands, they looked like characters in some bizarre NSD play. A children's play at Nehru House on 14th November. He put the car into gear and took them back into traffic, not bothering to signal. Angry horns blared and cars screeched behind them, one Merc narrowly missing them as they cut right across its path at a sharp angle. It reminded her of the many times she had been cut off exactly like that by highway truck drivers.

'Aap pehle truck chalate the?' she asked casually.

'Hanji,' he replied, then glanced at her, frowning. 'Aapko kaise pata chala?'

'Just a lucky guess,' she said and turned to the window to hide the smirk she wasn't able to suppress.

They were on the flyover when she got the idea. 'Aisa kartey hain, Daryaganj chalenge.'

He frowned at her. He was so tall he crouched over the steering wheel of the Civic and made it seem like a Maruti 800. 'Daryaganj?'

'Yes. I want to meet someone there. You know the way?'

He shrugged noncommittally. She gave him directions, carefully, and told him where to turn after they descended from the flyover. Then she used her cell to make a call. Before she dialled the number, she saw that she had a whole list of missed calls. When had they come? Apparently, all day. She hadn't bothered to even look at the cell once the pain had got too much to bear, and once the pain medication had kicked in, she had forgotten about it. She was more involved with Advaita and the documents they were poring over by that time, and that was about all she could handle at the time.

Advaita's dead, she told herself glumly. She didn't even know how to feel about that. Horrible, of course. But also guilty. Was it her fault? Had she been partly responsible because she had told Addy to read the documents and stick around? She berated herself. *You're thinking like a victim, Nachos. Like women who get battered by their husbands and blame it on themselves. 'I shouldn't have provoked him, it was my fault ...' Bullshit!* It was never their fault and it wasn't her fault now. Nobody had the right to use violence against anyone else, whatever the provocation.

If a German with stylish hair and a gun comes in and shoots your friend, it's not your fault, Nachos.

Yeah? Well, what about Shonali? And Justice?

She shook her head, trying to clear it. That woman Anita had sounded like she was in trouble, just as deep as Nachiketa herself. And she had mentioned two other names ... what were they? She didn't recall. Anita had said something about texting her the names and numbers. She hoped she would.

She struggled with the BB's interface for several moments, trying to find the number she was looking for, then trying to dial it. 'Fuck! Fuck! Fuck!' she shouted, hitting the dashboard angrily.

Powar glanced at her. 'Why don't use voice activate feature?'

She looked at him dully. Her head throbbed; her hands felt like they were on fire – hitting the dashboard hadn't helped – and her entire body was racked with pain. 'Thanks. Should have thought of that myself.'

She managed the voice activation, feeling like a rustic idiot herself. Then used it to call the number she wanted. The person answered on the second ring, sounding distant and distracted as always. 'Shama.'

'Shama, it's Nachiketa. Nachos.'

Dead silence for a moment. Powar took a wrong turn

from CP but it was too late to correct him. She gestured in the other direction, he slapped his forehead, realizing his mistake, and nodded vigorously, swinging the Civic around to the right lane with an ease that speedboats on the open sea would have envied. She had no idea how he managed to do it without hitting a single other car in the thick of traffic but she guessed that drunks and Jats must be just plain lucky.

'Nachos. Wow. Wow wow wow. Mind blowing.'

Nachiketa rolled her eyes. Typical Shama. 'Yeah, I know. What have you heard?'

'Basically ... you were blown up, burned, shot, run over ... the works? No, I'm sorry. I don't mean to sound flip. Are you okay? How are you? *Where* are you?'

'On my way to see you. Just passing CP. I have something to show you. I think ...' she hesitated, knowing that if she took this next step, there was no stepping back. It was either follow the yellow pulp road all the way or the house fell on you, hard. She thought of Shonali lying sprawled naked, semen on her thigh; Justice with her lips curled back, belly slashed open; Advaita with her eyes wide open, kajal smeared, vomiting blood; and she thought, *Fuck it, let's go for broke.* 'I think it might be a story,' she said. 'A pretty big one. Is Tyron there?'

'He's on his way. We're closing tomorrow, so it's the usual all-nighter.' Shama Kidwai was the editor and her significant other Tyron Bose was the publisher/co-editor of *Pink*, an almost-fortnightly magazine that had once broken a major news story about government corruption in a telecom scam that made both of them famous for a while – and unemployable ever after. They had a hard time getting sponsors or advertising, and eked out a living on subscriptions and donations from well-wishers. They survived because Tyron came from a moneyed family with political connections and they ran the magazine out of a rented place in Daryaganj with the money he got from renting out his own bungalow in South Ex. to some MNC on a long-term lease. The lease brought in enough to cover expenses and they managed to survive from issue to issue. Enough of their stories got picked up and commented on and talked about for them to have some clout in Delhi hifi circles. Firebrand journalist–politician Arun Shourie had once called *Pink* 'the liberal conscience of India'. The line ran beneath their logo on the masthead, with a credit line at the bottom of the masthead.

Shama was referring to their usual all-nighter before closing an issue. That was a bit of luck, the fact that they were closing an issue the very next day. Just enough time to change the cover, maybe. Perhaps even redo the whole issue. But that was getting ahead of herself. First she had to get there and show them the documents and see what they made of the whole pile.

'You guys sit tight, okay? I'll be there in twenty minutes. Tell Tyron it's big, really really big.'

'Fuck me,' Shama said. 'Yeah, sure. We'll be here. I'll tell him. TC, TTYS.' Shama was forty-four, with two teenage daughters, but she was still sixteen at heart, a perennial hippie.

Nachiketa disconnected the call and looked around. Where the hell were they? Was that Nirula's?

Rajendra Powar raised both hands despairingly, taking them off the steering wheel. 'I know, I know,' he said. 'Don't shout, madam. I go wrong way. Please to guide now.'

12.3

THE HAKKADI'S NAME WAS Stanley Wu. He was in his early thirties, handsome in a glamorous Eurasian Tony Leung kind of way, dressed suavely in immaculately tailored suits, smoked herb cigarettes that lent him an old-world ambience without the tar and nicotine punishment of real tobacco, and was the last Chinese Indian tycoon in the country. Some said he ran the Triads from Kolkata and she guessed they might not be far from the truth. Others said that over the last hundred years, his family had helped the two hundred thousand Chinese Indians settled in Kolkata migrate farther west, to the US and UK and Europe, and in exchange they had 'inherited' all the properties and establishments the emigrants left behind in the subcontinent. His great-grandfather (or was it his great-great-grandfather?) had perfected the blending of Cantonese cooking with Indian ingredients and spices that came to be called 'Hakka' after the predominant clan of Chinese immigrants that first settled in India. Over time, by inheriting, buying out, or simply taking over establishments, the family had come to possess a chain of Hakka restaurants across Kolkata, then across India that became the spearhead of his family's growth in fortunes. Adding the word 'di' to a Chinese name conveyed great respect, elevating the person thus titled to the stature of a great being or God. Hence, Hakka-di. There had been many inheritors of the wealth, the fortune, the power and the title over the last hundred-odd years, but they were all just 'Hakkadi' to the world.

Stanley was enough of a gentleman to rise when greeting Sheila. For a man of his stature there were no small or big people, only people or not-people. He had told her this the first time they met, when she expressed surprise at the same thing. If you didn't fit Stanley Wu's definition of a person, you didn't exist, period. If he acknowledged you, he would give you his full attention. He was a man who either did or didn't. There were no greys with him.

He bowed graciously to her and she bowed as well, feeling ridiculous in her faded jeans, muddied Converses and wrinkled tee shirt. Fine way to meet a billionaire.

He excused himself from the company without offering to introduce Sheila, for which she was grateful, although he didn't do it out of consideration for her, she knew.

'Please,' he said, gesturing to a hostess, 'go ahead, I will join you in a minute.'

Sheila turned her head to watch him go around an undulating curved wall and out of sight. She tried not to gawk at the celebrities in the party crowd, and to make herself as small as possible to avoid being noticed. She felt shabby and cheap in this environment. She shouldn't have cared a damn, but damn it, she did. Why hadn't she put on some lipstick at least before coming? Brushed her hair. Lined her eyes. Maybe slipped on a pair of earrings. Something to identify her as a woman.

Because you were more concerned about staying alive and that meant staying out of sight.

Yes, but damnit, she had gone to Shakespeare Bazaar to meet the professor. She could have picked up a few things right there. Would it have killed her?

Well, yeah, it might've!

She hadn't known she would be seeing him at a swanky party for the Who's Who of Kolkata high society. She had thought the address was an office in an under-construction building off the E.M. Bypass – that was what it had been the last time she had come to see him here. How was she supposed to know that the construction was done and *this* was going to be the scene?

She told her feminine side to shut up and followed the hostess. The woman's tantalizing length of thigh played peekaboo beneath the generous slit as she led Sheila up the marble spiral staircase that she had passed earlier, by the elevators. She couldn't help but be presented with an excellent close-up view of the woman's bum clenching and unclenching beneath the body-hugging sheath, and took a professional interest in the view. Based on the gluteal definition and muscle form visible, Sheila concluded that the woman must do a lot of lunges and pullovers but not enough squats. Swimming would be good too, or maybe kickboxing. Still, she sniffed mentally, they weren't that great, just better packaged. She resisted the urge to pat herself on the backside: she wasn't in that bad shape herself. Just not dressed as showily.

They reached the top of what seemed like two or three storeys worth of winding spiral stairs and found themselves in a palace of white and gold with flourishes of emperor's purple and empress red in the form of paintings and wall hangings and objets d'art. The ceiling was easily ten metres high and the entire floor was one vast open luxuriant jewel box encased in crystalline glass. It was breathtaking. Sheila was still staring when the hostess smiled and bowed and began descending the staircase. She took several moments just looking around, trying hard to be casual and failing.

She reacted with a start when Stanley Wu said, 'You've been a bad girl, Sheila.'

She turned and saw that he had been standing by a pearl-encrusted bar, smoking, since before she had arrived. He must have another way to get here, a private way, because he had been heading in the direction opposite to the stairs that she had taken.

Reading her confusion, he gestured behind himself. 'Private elevator. Runs through the whole building. On its own power generator, separate from the building, the grid, everything else.'

She felt her brows twitch. That made sense. A man like him would make sure his lift would run even if there was a war, a riot, the end of the world. 'So this is what you used to call your "new project" back when we used to meet?'

He shrugged. 'I told you I was getting into real estate.'

He gestured to a couch lined with what looked like panda fur, in black and white. 'Please.'

She sat, he sat.

He offered her nothing, she asked for nothing.

He smoked and watched her.

She waited.

They sat that way for a long minute.

Finally he nodded. 'Nice job, the way you handled the American shooters.'

That didn't surprise her. It was the reason she had come to see him. 'You heard?'

He gestured vaguely towards a wall. 'I saw. CCTV footage grabbed from the KMRC cams.'

She realized he was indicating a wall where there must be a screen. It probably popped out or slid down when activated by remote. Right now, though, it was just a blank space on a pearl wall. 'So the police have the whole thing on camera?'

He shook his head, smoke blurring his face. 'Only me. I had the discs wiped. Nobody but I saw.'

'How—' she began, then remembered.

He watched her remember and smiled, nodding. 'The Chinese built the railways across the world. Now, we own a few too.'

She knew he didn't mean that literally. He didn't actually own the KMRC. His name probably didn't appear on any paperwork anywhere, nor did the names of any companies he owned. But somehow, through a series of shell companies or ghost entities or proxies and surrogates, he owned a piece of the metro. Enough to call it his own. Enough to have a CCTV flash drive's contents dumped, then wiped. It had been another of his 'new projects' only a few years ago. She was impressed by how much he had achieved and how far he had come in that short time.

'Who were they?' she asked.

He smiled. 'She comes to my house and interrogates me. My men would have anyone else chopped and minced just for that.'

Again he gestured with a slight nod, again she saw nothing.

She guessed he meant the men who were watching them, just out of sight, somehow positioned so they could see him, or her, or both, without being seen themselves.

She smiled back while using her peripheral vision and tactical knowledge to guess where they might be positioned, keeping her eyes on Stanley. 'It's the reason why I came to see you, Stanley Wu,' she said.

He released a carefully timed burst of laughter and herb smoke, revealing a perfect pearly thirty-two, a pink tongue and a beautiful tapering throat. 'She calls me by my name, informally! Even the chairman of Lehman Brothers doesn't dare call me by that name. He says "Mr Stanley", so careful to use the correct formal form for a Chinese. But you, you say "Stanley Wu" as if you are my relative … or my …?' He gestured, inviting her to finish the sentence.

'Your one-time fuck-buddy?' she said casually. 'Your dial-a-cunt? Your friend-with-a-benefit? Your pussy pal?'

He laughed full-throatedly, slapping both his thighs, shaking his head and torso vigorously like a character in a Jackie Chan movie whose automated suit had gone out of control. 'She blasphemes in church! She is a potty-mouthed slut! She is a bad, bad girl. Oh, I love this woman.'

She got up and walked over to his couch, unbuttoning her shirt. She yanked the shirt out of her jeans and slipped it off her shoulders, reaching back and unhooking her bra. Her breasts spilled free, hot and sore from being kicked or punched the day before, she didn't remember what. She kicked off her Converses, the lush white pile carpet feeling like she was walking on water. Then she unzipped the jeans, and peeled them off, the end of the left foot getting tangled in her toes, then coming free. She stood before him, presenting herself in just blue bikini briefs, pushing her groin forward until it almost touched his face. She could smell herself. She knew he could.

He had stopped laughing by then. He was watching her with a lingering smile and a light in his eyes. She had seen that light before. She liked that light.

'Prove it,' she said.

Slowly, delicately, almost reverentially, he peeled off the panties.

Thirteen

13.1

ANITA WAS IN DEEP shit. Not figuratively – although that was true too – but literally. Emboldened by the kicking in of the sedative the zoo doctor had injected her with, she had decided to climb a wall. So long as she stayed on a walkway, they were bound to find her. She didn't know how many there were, but judging from the torchlights waving around, there were enough to hunt her down and nail her ass. 'Bitch!' It came out louder than expected in the quiet of the zoo and she clapped a hand over her mouth. Somewhere to her left, in a row of cages with long vertical bars on the front, something growled. It occurred to her that she had just said the word aloud in an environment where it might be taken literally. 'I meant myself,' she clarified, even pointing at her own chest in the darkness. Yup, those sedatives had kicked in with a vengeance, no doubt about it.

She was on a concrete wall now, lying face down on the top. The wall was really massive – probably two feet thick and about six feet high – which set off warning bells in her head. Whatever lived behind this wall must be a tough ammepanni. But the men chasing her were worse motherfuckers. She heaved herself over the side of the wall. Given a choice between men and predatory animals, she'd take her chances with animals any day. Using the crutch to support her descent, she relinquished hold slowly until both the crutch and her good foot were on solid ground. Then she began shambling through the darkness, away from the growing sounds of approaching men and footfalls. In moments, she was plunged into a darkness deeper than night, or so it seemed at first. And moments after that, her good foot plunged into a shin-deep pile of what felt and smelt like only one thing in God's own country. She had played enough football in muddy Varkala fields in the rain as a schoolgirl to know that this wasn't wet mud. She was in deep shit. Animal shit. She took another step, the ooze sucking at her lovingly, reluctant to let go. *Please, please stay. I promise I won't be clingy.* After at least a half dozen steps, she realized this wasn't just any deep shit, this was an entire fucking land mass composed entirely of compost. How turdilicious. Something sparked in her pain-exhaustion-and-drug-addled brain and she found the words of an old poem springing to mind, one she had discovered with ... *who else?* Lalima, and liked the sound of so much, she had gone around reciting it every time a boy was mean to her or just plain *boyish.* It was a way of saying 'Fuck you!' to boys and men, of slut-walking through their world, of raising her feminine voice deliberately to match and outmatch their loud masculine tones. There was something about this poem that was so deliciously offensive without actually saying anything that she remembered every single line word-perfect.

'Call the roller of big cigars,' she said now, wading through her private shit field, 'the muscular one, and bid him whip/ In kitchen cups concupiscent turds.' The original poem said 'curds', of course, but she had changed it just now – it was that play on words that had brought the poem to mind. She took a moment to grin in the darkness at that witticism, disgusting though it was – *but then again, so is life sometimes, Lalima, isn't it?* – and wondering what creature produced offal in such copious quantities and had a fondness for depositing it in the same spot each time. Somewhat like a capitalist free market wealth-builder, building a bigger pile and relishing the aroma of sweet shit each morning. Man! I love the stench of crap in the morning, ain't free markets great? 'Let the wenches dawdle in such dress/ As they are used to wear, and let the boys/ Bring flowers in last month's newspapers/ Let be be finale of seem/ The only emperor is the emperor of ice-cream.'

She was loud now, really loud. Loud enough to be heard across the whole habitat, for sure, probably even beyond that wall no more than a couple dozen yards behind her, quite likely loud enough to be heard across half the fucking Thiruvananthapuram Zoo, and she didn't give a damn. If anything, she began reciting louder, at the top of her voice, as if challenging God in His Heaven to do his worst.

Send my brothers in to rape and beat me when I was fifteen? Why not! They're good Christian boys!

Force me to choose between staying and enduring their

nightly rapes and beatings and become their bitch–whore or run away from home and eke out a living any which way I could in a city that considers lesbian minority girls to be a blot on society?

Sure, Father dearest, I'm just a perverted Christian dyke, why don't you make me suffer some more!

Take my best friend Lalima, the sweetest, most god-fearing, humanity-loving person that ever lived, and kill her for godknowswhat reason?

Of course, because every bloody sundae needs a bright red cherry on top to make the Sabbath Special complete!

She was out of the shit pit now and moving across solid ground, but it was still hard going in the darkness. She stumbled more than once, almost fell but caught herself and kept going somehow, anyhow. All she knew was that she had to keep going, to get away from them, make them chase her if they wanted to get her, make them work for it, damnit. She had no illusions anymore. She had been up shit creek enough times – though not as literally as tonight – to know when things were beyond salvaging. This time she was going to bite the big one. She was going to buy the farm. Kick the bucket. *There's a hole in the bucket, dear Liza, dear Liza, a hole in the bucket ...*

'Take from the dresser of deal,' she yelled, raising her fist in the air as she hobbled fast enough to qualify for a Special Olympic event. 'Lacking the three glass knobs, that sheet/ On which she embroidered fantails once/ And spread it so as to cover her face/ If her horny feet protrude, they come/ To show how cold she is, and dumb.'

'Lalima's dead,' she whispered in the middle of the second, and last, verse. 'She's dead, and these bastards killed her. Fucking bitch!'

She could hear voices behind her now, sounds of men jumping the same wall, their feet thudding as they landed inside the animal habitat. She didn't look back. She had come too far now. There was no turning back. *You killed your brother, Christ will judge you for it,* her mother's blotched face raged at her, swimming out of the darkness ahead. What had that fucking doctor given her anyway? LSD? She hobbled on, feeling the pain return to her broken foot like the zombified shambling corpse of a long-loved friend. *Chakkare,* Lalima said, dressed in the same sari she had worn the last time Anita had seen her, two days before she had left Varkala. *Chakkare, come to me, let's go down to the beach. It's Papanasam.* It was Lalima's first sari, sign that she was a young woman now, no more a girl, a beautiful hand-woven Balarampuram sari, deep red in colour. Blood red. Symbolizing the maturation of a young woman, her coming of age.

'Let the lamp affix its beam,' Anita cried, loud enough to be heard across Kerala. 'The only emperor is the emperor of ice-cream!'

If God really was residing in His Own Country and happened to be visiting at that moment, he didn't answer.

But something else did. Several somethings.

13.2

PINK'S OFFICES WERE A hive of activity. There were more young men and women in indigo blue jeans and dark coloured jackets coming and going than at a St. Stephen's literary group meet. Nachiketa was taken aback at first, then processed it. 'Must be some internship thing,' she said, mostly for her own benefit. Rajendra Powar was pushing her wheelchair and wasn't really listening. He manoeuvred her clumsily up the entrance of the three-storey building and somehow managed to get her into the lift without any major mishap. She was glad she had kept this spare chair in the dicky of her car all this while, just in case. Today was a bloody just-in-case day through and through, that was for sure.

Surprisingly nobody really paid much attention to her – the woman in the wheelchair with blood and urine all over her and bandages on her hands – or to the hulking Jat with matching bandages around his head and hands. Glancing at herself and Powar in the mirror of the cramped old cage lift, she saw that the two of them made quite a sight. Wheeling her through into the office, guided by her directions, Powar managed to improve his technique slightly, which impressed her. The man had actually learnt how to wheel someone around in just a few minutes. She had friends who had kept banging her elbows and knees for weeks. Maybe all Jat men weren't assholes, after all; just the ones from that colony in GK-II.

And the bastards who did that to Shonali.

Except ...

She was no longer certain they had been Jats.

Well, maybe the guy who called her had been a Jat but not the people behind this whole mess. There was something else going on here, something non-Jatty that she was still trying to figure out. The call from that woman in Kerala ... *Anita?* had helped put a few things in perspective. Just knowing that Lalima had sent her the package had helped. But she needed some more brainpower focused on this problem. And *Pink* was the best brains trust she had access to right now.

She steered her own brain back on track as she caught sight of the familiar glass-encased cabin at the far end of the office. The whole top floor of the building was just one big open space, the kind of media office one saw in old Hollywood movies. Desks littered with files and papers – and laptops, of course. Shama and Tyron occupied a large cabin at the end, with glass walls as befitted their 'open' policy. But from the looks of it, they were moving. The office was bustling with young men and women in dark jackets and blue jeans, carrying boxes of papers and files out. And Shama and Tyron themselves appeared to be in some kind of meeting with a bunch of people in dark suits. What was going on? Had they finally lost the last of their financing? Were they being shut down for non-payment of dues? Those dudes and dudettes looked like bankers. Even the young men and women carrying stuff out seemed internship or post-master's age. The other thing was, all the young south Delhi Golf Links post-grad-types were carrying identical banker's boxes, the kind made of heavy corrugated cardboard with cut-out holes for handles on either end. And all the banker's boxes had the same logo on all sides. She recognized the logo as belonging to a major MNC accounting firm, the one that had taken top dog spot after Arthur Anderson's bright star had waned in the wake of the post-Enron post-sub-prime double whammy. The odour of MBA finance degrees was so thick in the room, she could barely breathe.

She was stopped by a lady in a suit-and-skirt, a combination she had always hated and which, for some reason, always reminded her of FBI agents in B-grade action serials on a TV channel, one of those where the channel logo and English subtitles (for English serials) seemed to occupy most of the screen's real estate. The lady in question was a dark brunette with lovely brown eyes and had about ten years on the post-grad types milling about her. She was quite lovely, actually, and when she saw Nachiketa, she smiled and Nachiketa smiled back at once, instinctively, like this was just a regular day and she was a regular visitor here on usual business.

'Hello,' she said in a distinct European accent that for some reason reminded Nachiketa instantly of the man who had come into her hospital room only a couple of hours ago, looking to kill her. Nachiketa's smile slipped off and fell to the floor like a piece of dropped cutlery. 'You must be Nachiketa Shroff?'

'Er, yes,' Nachiketa said, even more chilled by the similarity in the pronunciation of her name. *Natch-ee-quetta Schrauff?* The way he had said it would probably haunt her forever ... or at least as long as she lived, which at the current rate, wasn't expected to be very long. 'Shama and Ty are expecting me.'

'Yes, yes,' the lady in the FBI-ish suit said, still smiling. She said something softly to the young groupies – adoring of and awestruck by her – and they dispersed reluctantly but efficiently. That left the woman alone with Nachiketa and Powar in this part of the office, Nachiketa realized. For some reason, the day's events had made her hyper-aware of every detail of everything happening around her. She supposed near-death violent encounters had that effect. That, and the fact that she was probably suffering from post-traumatic stress disorder.

'I have heard so much about you,' said the European woman. 'I am an admirer of your work. You are an inspiration to women in law everywhere.'

She looked down at Nachiketa's legs as she said that, which implied that she was praising Nachiketa's ability to overcome her physical handicap and still achieve all that she had as a lawyer. Somehow, that didn't make Nachiketa feel very loved. She didn't like people who patronized her. Either she was a lawyer who had done her bit, or she wasn't. The fact that she was in a wheelchair for life, or a woman, or both, were really beside the point as far as her achievements were concerned. Unless this was a self-empowerment seminar, which it wasn't.

'You have me at a disadvantage,' Nachiketa began with less than good humour, still trying to be polite. 'I don't even know your name, Miss ...'

'Kylliki Kolehmainen,' she replied, pronouncing it in a way Nachiketa could never hope to pronounce without a year of language lessons reinforced with rigorous incarceration.

'Um,' Nachiketa said, momentarily at a loss. This was usually the moment when the person smiled and proffered a more easily pronounceable alternative. 'Can I call you ... Klickie?'

The woman's attractive face lost some of its beauty. 'You may not. In Finland, we are very proud of our names. If you wish to continue living in a global economy, you must learn to pronounce such names.'

Nachiketa didn't know whether to smile disarmingly or just tell her to go fly a Finnish kite up a fabulous fjord. She settled for trying to be civil. She had enough enemies already today. 'Look, ma'am, I really don't have time to sit and discuss international linguistic geopolitics. I'm here to see my old friends Shama and Tyron on urgent business.' She used her elbow to nudge Rajendra Powar who moved the wheelchair an inch or two forward, preparing to roll by this hardass Nordic female once she moved her iron butt.

'You have no business with them,' said Finnish Hardass, looking across the office with a gaze that would not have seemed out of place in the sentry tower of a Nazi death camp. 'They can do nothing for you here.'

And she moved to bar Nachiketa's way completely, making it impossible to roll past her to reach Shama and Tyron's office.

This really pissed Nachiketa off. It was one thing to be a typical high-and-mighty DIC – Shonali's private short form for Diplomatic Immunity Cats, with 'Cat' actually standing in for another far more offensive word – but this was taking Nordic fascism a step too far.

'Listen, Kyllicki Delicki or whatever your name is, I'm going through what you might term a crisis and I really need to see Shama and Tyron right now, not that it's any of your business, so for the last time, I'm asking politely, kindly move and let me pass.'

Those lovely brown eyes looked down at her. 'Did you not hear me? They cannot help you. Nobody can. Nobody except—'

Nachiketa held up a bandaged hand. 'Look, lady, I'm really not—'

But before she had finished speaking, the woman was leaning over, holding her open dark hair back with one practised hand, close enough to put her lips near Nachiketa's ear, and said in her curt Finnish accent, 'I can help you if you let me.'

13.3

SHEILA SIGHED, STRETCHED AND swung her feet off the bed. The lighting had adjusted itself when they were making love and it adjusted again now, also reducing the tint on the floor-to-ceiling windows by maybe 10 per cent (she guessed), just enough to provide her light to find her panties and jeans and slip them on. She stayed bare-top for the moment, knowing that Wu was watching her. She knew her scars were visible and didn't care: he had seen them before. It was because he had seen them before that she felt so comfortable with him. Once you've shown someone your deepest scars, you don't need to hold anything back. She sat and basked in his discreet attentiveness, liking the way the blue luminescence of the external lights limned her naked body.

She supposed that his invisible bodyguards must be watching too, and had been all this while, but she really didn't care. She had long since got past things like coyness and shyness, shedding them along with the myriad illusions most people retained in order to continue living a hypocritical life. It was the reason why she didn't have a religion and didn't give a damn about it: stuff like religion and spirituality were for people who believed in good and evil, grace and sin. She believed in survival, love, and Kung Pao chicken with egg noodles – in that order. She felt the air-conditioning grow a tad cooler to compensate for the reduced tint and increased lighting, and felt her nipples grow hard again. She sat a moment, looking at the table which had borne the food they had eaten after making love a while back, still feeling like she could eat another bowl or two.

'Hungry, kya?' Wu's voice said from the bed, mimicking McDonald's Indian advertising slogan.

She turned her head just enough that he could see her profile and she could see his legs beneath the satin sheets. 'You know what they say about oral sex with Chinese women?'

'What?' he said in a pained we've-heard-these-before tone.

'One hour and you're hungry again.'

He sighed. 'That's racist.'

'Of course it is. All jokes are either racist, bigoted, or culturally insensitive. That's why they're funny, just like toilet and sex humour. We laugh at the things that make us uncomfortable.'

'Chinese jokes don't make me uncomfortable,' he said. 'Bad Chinese jokes do.'

'So tell me a good one.'

He came over and sat beside her. She felt the tips of his fingers trace the outline of her scars. So he *had* been looking at them. Well, what the fuck. It wasn't like she was a *Playboy* playmate: real women didn't get the luxury of airbrushing. This was all her in the flesh.

But his touch was arousing something within her, something deeper than sexual arousal. She could feel him feeling, and knew he was remembering the time she had spilled her guts to him, told him all the things that had been done to her – by men, of course. And how he had held her and loved her and she had loved him back. She had especially loved the fact that he hadn't commented or analyzed or explained her past abuse away; he had simply tried to wipe it away with his lips, his hands, the stroke of his erect penis within her, his warm breath upon her vulva …

'You know what they say about Chinese torture,' he said softly.

'What?' she asked, in a barely audible tone.

'One hour and you're ready to talk again.'

She didn't laugh. He didn't either. But in the fluorescent blue light, they looked at each other and something passed between them. *It's okay*, he seemed to say to her. *You were fucked up by men in the past, but I won't fuck you up.* And the incredible thing of it was: she believed him. She trusted him.

After a while, he moved away. She heard the click of a lighter and smelt the fragrant aroma of a Chinese herb cigarette. He came crawling up to her on his knees and sat on the side of the bed beside her. He was naked and his cock was semi-erect. She liked the fact that he didn't shave his pubic area. He was hairless enough as it was.

He offered her the herb cigarette. 'Herb fag? Specially made for me.'

She took the cigarette and took a small drag. It was pleasant, not in the choking throat-throttling way of tobacco, more like the second-hand smoke and aroma of good pipe tobacco when it lingers in a room. She took another, deeper drag, filling her lungs, and was amazed that not only did she not feel like coughing, she actually felt as if it was warming her lungs and chest in a pleasant, soothing way. '... Fuck is this?' she asked, holding it up so he could take it back.

He gestured and produced another one seemingly out of nowhere, already lit. 'Keep it. They're harmless. No nicotine, no tar, nothing. It's like marijuana, except it isn't a drug.' He took a drag and released it, saying, 'Unless you want a joint, in which case ...'

'No,' she said. She wanted to keep her head clear for whatever lay ahead. 'These are fantastic. Why doesn't everyone smoke them?'

He shrugged. 'Because there's no market for harmless vices? If alcohol and adultery weren't bad for you, would anyone still want them?' He gestured. 'Have you seen the show *Mad Men*? The one with all the dudes in '60s get-ups and suits and do's and all?'

'Yeah, why?' She had caught an episode or two while surfing the TV in the gym office and been struck by the looks of the main lead. What was the character's name? Dan Draper? *Don*. It was Don Draper. 'Sexy dude.'

He nodded, agreeing. His cock twitched. 'We supply them.'

'You're shitting me.'

'No, seriously. California has a legislation that prohibits smoking or drinking or consumption of any controlled substances in a work environment. That includes movie and TV show sets. So everybody has to smoke herb cigarettes and drink fake liquor.'

She thought about that for a moment. 'All of them? All the shows?'

'All of them.'

She looked down at the herb cigarette. She had smoked it almost down to the butt. 'No wonder everybody on that serial smokes and drinks all the time like that without anything happening. I wondered how they did it.'

He spread his hands. 'Well, technically speaking, the characters are supposed to be actually drinking and smoking that much, so ...'

'Yeah, yeah,' she said. 'I get it.'

They smoked the rest of their cigarettes in silence. He held out another one for her but she shook her head. A guy came with ashtrays and took the butts away. He didn't look at Sheila's boobs once – she would have known if he had, she always knew when a guy looked. That was one of the things men never seemed to realize: women always knew when you were ogling their tits. That was why she didn't feel half-naked (or fully naked, earlier) in Wu's place, even with a dozen men watching her every move. They were watching her as a subject of potential threat, not as a woman, not as a sex object. She supposed that must be the only time men could watch a woman without sex as the primary motive: when they viewed her as a physical threat or target of violence.

She slipped on her bra and then her shirt, but she didn't button it up. It was her way of saying, *maybe we could still have a bite or two more, maybe I might still be a little hungry, kya.* Stanley never asked or demanded sex from her, he always waited for her to offer – or not offer, as she pleased. It was the reason why she had become involved with him earlier. Because he understood that she couldn't be had by his choice, only by her own choosing. It was also the reason why she had walked away one day and never come back, just to make the point. The truth was, she liked him as a lover. He was the best she had ever had. Maybe it was the fact that there was nothing else between them; he didn't expect or need anything else, nor did she. That made it almost perfect.

'Tell me,' she said. 'What's going on with me? Why are they out to fuck up my existence? Most of all, who are they? What do they want?'

Fourteen

14.1

WHAT HAPPENED NEXT HAPPENED mostly in darkness, lit occasionally by the light of an Eveready torch waving wildly, at other times by the pools of light from the lamps on the pathways, and once by the light from the helicopter overhead. For some reason there were no lights in the heart of the habitats themselves, probably because there was no reason for humans to venture into those parts at night. Also because bright electric lights might not be conducive to creating the illusion of a natural habitat. The zoo management definitely hadn't designed the place for a desperate chase and shootout at night.

Anita heard grunts and snorts from something nearby. *Very* nearby. Close enough that she thought she could make out dim shapes hulking in the darkness, and feel the thud of their treads as they came towards her. She froze, thinking that this time she had really stepped in it. The smell of the animals wasn't catty or furry, or even canine, but of course, she was no fucking expert on animal odours. Still, she thought this smelt more buffalo-like, or elephant, maybe. Though the dark shapes moving towards her seemed too big and bulky to be buffaloes yet not big enough to be elephants. Then there was a succession of sucking wet sounds to her right and the unmistakable sound of water dripping in great fat drops and streams from a leathery hide onto grass and she knew what they were at once.

She began moving as quickly as she could to the left. She had a vague sense that the far wall of the habitat was in that direction. She now knew that the water was to the right. It was a miracle she hadn't gone into the water because if she had, with her leg, she would probably never have got out alive, crutch or no crutch. She kept to the left, moving slowly and trying to be as quiet and non-menacing as possible.

She felt the creatures approaching her, then passing by. One bumped her and the nudge almost knocked her down. The stench was overwhelming, yet the water dripping from their hides suggested that they had just bathed. She couldn't imagine what they must smell like when they hadn't bathed. But then she recalled that they needed to immerse themselves in muddy water virtually all the time to keep their fatty bodies cool. She felt hot odorous breath wafting across her, redolent with the smells of some kind of half-digested substance and almost puked thanks to the stink. She had an image of an enormous open pink mouth and knobbly teeth the size of her fists. If that creature had taken a bite off her ...

Then they were past her and moving left and behind, towards the wall she had just climbed over. She didn't know why they ignored her. Maybe because they felt more threatened by the larger group of invaders coming over the wall after her, or perhaps they smelt her injuries and sensed she was no threat to them; maybe it was for a dozen different reasons, but she liked to think it was because she was female.

She paused a moment, turning her head to try and figure out what was happening. She saw the herd, or group, or whatever they were called in large numbers, shamble in the direction from which she had come, saw the flashes of torches in the darkness, glimpsed backs and shoulders and arms of men with guns revealed in those flashes, saw the silhouettes of the men, moving purposefully after her, only one goal in their minds: to kill. She knew her brothers would be with them. They would want to be there to finish her off. She knew that she probably wasn't going to get out of this place alive. *This zoo!* She thought, issuing the mental equivalent of a deranged cackle. Gadzooks, this was like some crazy surrealistic film. Only the Marx Brothers were missing. Or her perennial favourites, Abbott and Costello. *Yup,* she thought, *Abbott and Costello meet the Matthew family in Trivandrum Zoo. Yuk it up, kids.*

She knew she should run. Or hobble away at a rapid pace. Make some attempt to escape. But she felt strangely compelled to watch. Just as her mind kept repeating that last glimpse of Philip, his throat exploding, his artery spouting blood like in a zombie horror film. *They're coming to get you, Philip!* And she paused and watched.

The men coming after her seemed to have forgotten that they were in an animal habitat. Or they didn't care. She had seen from personal experience that guns tended to do that to men. They tended to assume that a gun in any situation was like a magic kavach – invulnerable armour gifted by a Hindu deity. That all they had to do was hold the fucking phallic symbol and nothing bad could happen to them. From the way the torchlights moved and the glimpses and flashes of illumination, she saw that the hunters were breaking into a run, coming directly at her – and at the charging animals.

Because by then that's what the animals were doing: charging straight at the invaders who had entered their habitat uninvited. They had built up a little momentum after bypassing Anita and their bulk was such that they really didn't need to build up a lot of speed. The ratio of weight and size to each of the oncoming men was probably five to one or something like that, not to mention the fact that they were built like brick walls on legs. The impact was a no-contest.

She heard the sounds of hippo hide and bone thumping into human bodies. The unmistakable cracking of bones. The loud lowing of a hippo cow as she attacked the invaders that she probably felt were a threat to her calves. She glimpsed a great pink maw open and snare a man's upper body, closing like a vice. The light turned away in a continuing arc but not before she caught a glimpse of blood and gristle exploding out of the man's body as those gigantic teeth and jaws closed upon him. There were other sounds as the other men were either trampled or struck down or bitten or butted.

Two men managed to let off shots. But she had the impression that they went wild, probably up into the night sky. The helicopter hovering overhead seemed to grow aware that something was seriously wrong and shone its light downwards. But just then a third shot went off and Anita heard a distinct metallic *ping!* The chopper's light wavered and veered away in a sharp arc, flying away from the habitat and out of sight.

In the instant the chopper's light had been trained on the habitat, she had seen the hippos killing the men. It was a sight she would probably remember all her life.

She had a scattered recollection of the next few moments, either because of the drugs, or because she was so shocked by what she had just seen, shocked at her near escape as well as the almost-miraculous elimination of her pursuers. The next thing she knew, she was at the far wall of the habitat, struggling to get over.

A hand caught hold of her shoulder and pulled her over. She reacted instantly, trying to raise her crutch and strike out. But another hand caught the crutch and pushed it down. 'You're going to need that,' said a male voice. It didn't sound menacing or threatening and she realized the hand was helping rather than trying to hurt her. She accepted the help conditionally and let the unseen man in the darkness lower her to the pathway on the other side of the hippo habitat. There was a lot of shouting and screaming and yelling from behind. She glanced back.

'They will send more men,' said the man who had helped her over the wall. 'They won't stop until they catch or kill you. You have to keep moving.'

He started moving, still holding her arm on her good side. She stopped him.

'Who are you?' she said, trying to see his face in the light from the nearest lamp about ten yards farther down the path. The trees and foliage drank most of the light, but from the little illumination that got through, she could see that he looked youngish, fair-skinned, and blonde. He wore a dark coat and trousers with a dark-coloured tee shirt.

And a white collar band.

'I'm Father Francis,' he said. 'I was a friend of Lalima's. I'm here to help you.'

14.2

RAJENDRA POWAR'S HAND SHOT out instinctively, pushing the Finnish woman's shoulder away from Nachiketa. Perhaps he was rougher than he needed to be, but to be fair to the guy, he had seen people try to kill her twice already, and the gori memsaab, as he had named her, was being more than a little menacing. Klicky Koalmine or whatever her name was, wasn't expecting the push. She reared back, lost her balance on her high heels, tottered for a moment, then fell back, landing on her ass with an audible thump.

Nachiketa winced. That must hurt. 'Oops,' she said, grinning. She wasn't one to take pleasure at a pratfall but it had been a bitch of a day.

The Finnish woman glared up at her with such venom, Nachiketa lost her grin. 'You stupid cow,' the woman said, her accent overwhelming her Etonian English – or Helsinki English or wherever the hell she had learnt the language – making her sound as if she were gargling with marbles in her mouth. 'Who do you think you are?'

The fall of the queen of Finland attracted the attention of everyone in the office. All the groupies in their dark jackets and indigo jeans turned and stared and looked shocked. Several came to help up their goddess, glaring at Rajendra Powar and Nachiketa as if wondering what monsters would do such a thing. Even the meeting in Shama and Tyron's office seemed disrupted and the suits all looked around, trying to see what was happening, their view hampered by the partitions and groupies.

'Chalo,' Nachiketa said to Powar – god bless him – who understood at once and wheeled her to the office, right past Miss Finland International, who was getting to her feet aided by two able-bodied male groupies and a female one.

The office door was glass but it was shut.

Nachiketa's hands were bandaged, which made them useless for knocking on doors; so she used her elbow, banging the door a little harder than intended. The glass rattled in the frame, making a row of perfect haircuts and well-groomed faces turn and gaze at her speculatively.

Shama's head popped up from amidst the circle of management degrees, and after a moment, so did Tyron's bearded face. Tyron vanished as quickly as he'd appeared, resuming his seat before Nachiketa could finish her wave and 'hi, guys!', but Shama remained standing, leaned over and said something to the top of Tyron's head, then made her way through the suits and to the door.

'Hi, Shams,' Nachiketa said, 'I'm really sorry to barge in on you like this but ...'

'Nachos,' Shama said, glancing around at the outraged Finnish goddess and her equally outraged devotees. 'What are you up to? Listen, it's not a good time.'

Nachiketa gestured at the suits in the cabin, then at the office in general. 'What's going on? Did the Finnish Embassy take over the place?'

Shama frowned, as if puzzled by the reference. 'I really can't talk much, Nachiketa.' She glanced at her friend's bandages and then at Powar, her frown deepening. 'It's ... unfortunate you're going through such a hard time, Nachos. But I really can't talk to you now.'

Nachiketa felt as if someone had physically assaulted her. 'What? But we spoke just a while ago. I told you I was on my way here. You said you were closing an issue.' She looked around. 'It looks more like you're moving out.'

Shama glanced around then gestured to Powar to bring the wheelchair to the far corner of the office. There was a small alcove there with a pantry and a door leading off to the toilet. It was empty now. She walked to the pantry platform near the microwave and tea machine and turned back, waiting for Powar to wheel Nachiketa up to her. 'Nachos, we're merging,' she said briskly.

'Merging?' Nachiketa stared up at her. 'What do you mean, merging?'

'Don't you know what merging means?' Shama said with more than a trace of irritation. 'Look, I really don't have time to explain every concept to you.'

'Okay, okay,' Nachiketa said, trying to pacify her. She had never seen Shama like this before, except maybe the time when Shama's father had had a heart attack and died in the middle of Daryaganj while driving his grandchildren – Shama's and Tyron's son and daughter – to school one morning. Shama had gone to pieces when she got the call and Nachiketa had happened to be around. That was back when Nachiketa's legs still worked and she hadn't even met Jignesh Shah yet, let alone married him. She had held Shama and comforted her when she cried, then had driven her to Daryaganj Police Station to pick up her car and her children. Shama had told her a few days later, after the cremation and the initial mourning period was over, 'You were there for me, Nachos. I'll never forget that. Sisters for life.'

Now she looked away grimly, hands folded over her ample bosom, as if she blamed Nachiketa for her father's heart attack.

'What's really going on?' Nachiketa asked, a seed of suspicion sprouting in her heart. 'Did all this happen after I called? In the past one hour?'

Shama rolled her eyes. 'Of course not. It's been in the works for a long time. We just happened to say yes now.'

'So it *did* happen in the past hour? The saying-yes part?'

Shama looked at her sharply. 'Are you a director of *Pink* Publications? It's none of your business, Nachiketa. Unless you're asking in your capacity as a lawyer. Are you?'

Nachiketa knew something was very wrong now. Shama had never spoken to her this way, would never speak to her this way unless ...

'Shams,' she said. 'Tell me the truth. What have you heard about me since I spoke to you an hour ago? Who's been filling your head with nonsense about me? Don't deny it because I know you well enough to know someone has said something. Who was it? What did they say to make you behave like this towards me?'

Shama looked down at Nachiketa with a look so cold, Nachiketa felt she would rather die right there than have to see a friend as dear as Shama look at her that way, whatever the reason. 'So you want me to believe that Shonali's dead? Raped and killed in your office?'

Nachiketa spread her bandaged hands. 'Yes, exactly, that's what happened to her. I was there, I should know, but that was only the beginning ...'

'Then Addy was attacked too? By the same people?'

'Well, yes, I guess. That's what I'm trying to figure out.'

'And you were awarded a huge payoff from your in-laws in your compensation case today, and they went berserk, threatening Shonali and attacking her in your office? And then they burnt your office down, trying to trap you and kill you inside?'

Nachiketa felt her mouth fall open. 'My in-laws? Is that what you heard?'

'And then, when you were in hospital being treated today, Advaita was with you and they came again and attacked you both, and a German tourist who tried to help was killed in the attack?'

'Tourist?' Nachiketa almost tried to get up from her chair, something she did very very rarely, and only when she was upset enough to forget, momentarily, that she was physically challenged. 'He was no tourist. He was an assassin. He tried to kill me. Addy tried to protect me and he shot her. If it wasn't for this guy,' she pointed to Powar behind her, 'saving me both times, I would have been dead too by now, too.'

Shama shook her head, looking disappointed. 'Really, Nachos, I thought at least you had your head on your shoulders. Really, you need some help. These are really terrible things to go around saying about your friends. Think of Shonali's family. What will they think when they hear you spouting these stories? And Addy.'

Nachiketa shook her head. 'Look, I agree it sounds bizarre but it's all true. Shonali really is dead and so is Addy. I wish they weren't, but they are. That's why I came here, to ask you for help.'

Shama sighed wearily, pushing a half-grey half-black bang off her forehead, tucking it into her hairline. 'And what is the motivation behind all these shootouts and car chases and killings and murders and rapes?'

Nachiketa was ready to explode but controlled herself. 'You're blowing it all out of proportion.'

'It's already way out of proportion, Nachos. I know the judgment came against you; that you lost in court. Deal with it. Appeal. If you want support, we're here for you. But don't do this. Don't throw away your career like this.'

Nachiketa was speechless. She didn't know what to say. Then she remembered and held up the envelope that was lying in her lap. 'Look, forget all this. Don't believe me. But look at these documents. See for yourself.'

Shama nodded. 'I know about that too. All of Delhi does. Our industry at least. Media persons.'

Nachiketa stared up at her. 'Know what?'

'That you're on some kind of crazy vendetta, blaming the NGOs for not helping you during the time you were suffering abuse at your in-laws'. You have to be realistic, Nachos. You can't blame the world for your problems. Okay, so you lost the case. Fine. Move on. Get on with your life. But don't take it out on those collectives. Those organizations helped you after you escaped from that hellhole; they helped you put your life together, get your law degree, gave you cases, recommendations, helped you build your practice. How could you repay them this way?'

'What way? What are you talking about?'

Shama shook her head again. 'Advaita called and texted several people. Those of us associated with those NGOs, people who are trying to do some good here. Positive-thinkers. She told us you had concocted some wild story about NGOs being involved in illegal activities, being used to launder money from some kind of criminal activities ...'

'Not some kind,' Nachiketa interrupted, waving the thick envelope. 'Human Trafficking. Disguising it as legitimate businesses. Adoption. Orphanages. Child welfare. Charities. Schools for special children. It's all here, in this package. This is the reason why these people are after me. Why Shonali was killed. Why my office was burnt down. They were after these documents, this package. But they didn't get it. I still have the evidence. And that's why I came to you, so you could read it and judge for yourself. If you don't agree with the conclusions, fine, don't print it. Don't write a story. But at least look at the facts for yourself. I got a call from Kerala earlier, from this woman ... she says her friend sent it and was probably killed because she found this stuff out. Lalima. You probably remember her from that seminar last year we went to together. Look at these documents. Show it to Tyron, to anyone else. See for yourself.'

Shama looked at Nachiketa for a long moment, then at the package in her hand. 'I won't even touch that garbage,' she said. 'Let alone read that pack of lies. You can take it with you when you leave. And you can do that right now. Please get out.'

She began to walk around Nachiketa, but Nachiketa reached out and caught hold of her hand – or tried to. It was impossible to actually get a grip with the bandage on. But she managed to sort of press her hand against Shama's. She looked up at her. 'I don't understand. This doesn't make any sense. Why are you angry? With me? What is it you think I did wrong here? Can't you see that I'm the victim? That people are trying to kill me? I came to you for help, for god's sake, Shams. Why are you behaving this way?'

Shama looked down at her and something changed in her face at that moment. Nachiketa saw it and latched onto it.

'Please, Shams,' she said. 'For old times' sake. Sisters forever, remember? Tell me what's really going on here?'

Shama looked down at her sadly. 'Addy contacted us and told us you would be coming around with a crazy story. She told us to watch out; that you would say exactly this kind of crap.'

Nachiketa stared up at Shama, speechless for an instant.

Shama turned and walked away, towards her office.

With an effort Nachiketa found her voice and gestured to Powar to wheel her. She called out to Shama, loud enough to attract the attention of Miss Finland and her disciples. 'But you don't understand. Addy's dead. She was killed in the attack by that German gunman. She *died* trying to protect me.'

Shama turned and looked at Nachiketa with something bordering on outright pity. 'Addy emailed me after you called. We're on the same BB group, remember? So are you? She's been contacting everyone in the media, warning us about you and your conspiracy theory. She said you would say something like that. That you would pretend she was dead and make up some bizarre story about Shonali being dead. Shonali backed her up too. They both felt you had taken the loss in court really hard and gone off the deep end. They said you need help and I agree. Look at your condition, Nachos. You need help. Medical help. Maybe even psychiatric help. Do yourself a favour. Check yourself into a good place. I'll come visit you and hope you get better soon. Right now, I have a life to get back to and a business to run.'

She opened the glass door and went in, shutting the door behind her.

14.3

HE SLIPPED ON A red silk robe with beautiful Chinese embroidery – a purple dragon running all the way around. He belted the sash loosely, his male package still making a bulge at the front because of how thin his body was overall and the way he stood, head leaning back and perpetually tilted a little. He stood looking out at the breathtaking view. Finally he turned and said, 'What do you know about the way the capital markets function?'

She shrugged. 'What everyone knows. People follow the progress of companies and buy or sell their shares to make a profit.'

He shook his head. 'You're thinking of equity markets. And individual investors. That's for suckers. It's the equivalent of pickpockets at bus stops and purse snatchers on bikes. I mean the real markets, the big bucks.'

'Yeah. So?'

'So it's a game of kings. The big barons, feudal lords who already own the world, what do you call them here?'

Sheila frowned. 'Thakurs?'

He gestured. 'No, that's Bengali. I mean the general word. They used the word in an RPG game I played.' He snapped his fingers. 'Zamindars.'

'Zamindars are land owners.'

'Yup. These are the people who own the world. Institutional investors. Multinational corporations and conglomerates so massively tentacled and sprawled out, they encompass the global village, which means they provide succour to it and strangle it both at once.'

Sheila tried to follow his imaginative metaphors. Stanley Wu's private obsession was CGI, computer graphic imagery. He owned a VFX studio based in Hong Kong, and apart from the work they did for movies, both Asian and Hollywood, they designed and developed games, their speciality being MMORPGs which, she had learnt during a night-long post-coital session, stood for 'massively multiplayer online role playing games', *World of Warcraft* being the most famous and successful one of that genre, and one that he was always trying to emulate. He played around with the designs himself and she had seen some of his stuff: it was pretty damn good. So when he gestured and waved his arms about like this, his penis flip-flopping unenthusiastically inside his gown like a disinterested participant, she understood that he was visualizing these things more extravagantly than she could ever imagine.

'Okay,' she said. 'I get that, obviously. I know the big dudes own everything and run everything. So what does that have to do with anything?'

He looked at her, hands frozen in mid-gesture. He was still doing the octopus embracing the globe thing. 'Everything. The rich want to get richer. That's their own raison d'être. It's what they do.'

'So?' she shrugged. 'Get richer. The fuck do I care? I don't even invest in the stock market.'

He lowered his hands, grinning. His hair was dishevelled just a little. It was too short to ever get really funky. She liked him this way – out of his immaculate suit, away from his celebrity guest parade, letting his hair down ... as much as it could be let. He was almost human at such times. Not a man who had a stake in every major illegal operation run out of the subcontinent, with ties to the Triads, Yakuza, Jopok and every other Asian mafia in existence. Apart from his billion-dollar legitimate business interests, of course. Or was it the other way around? Was there a difference anymore?

'So where do the rich get more money from?' he asked.

'Each other? Through competition? By outdoing each other at business or service or even just making money? Isn't that the basis of capitalism, free enterprise?'

He shook his head. 'That was true maybe a hundred years ago. When the capital markets really were used to raise capital for legitimate business and fuel growth. Back when the so-called "developed nations" were still growing, populations and consumer buying expanding. But all that changed once the First World markets peaked. Population went into negative growth. So did consumer spending. You name the sector, the industry, the business, the service, it's all in a downward spiral.' He used his finger to follow an invisible graph vector in the air, taking a gradual declining path that increased in the negative gradient of the Y-axis. 'Fewer people means less spending, which means negative growth, and the basic rule of business is the same as nature: "Grow or Die". The older industrialized countries went through a similar graph. The British Empire. Towards the end, they couldn't consume as much as they were producing – as much as they *needed* to keep producing and selling in order to keep growing. So what did they do?'

She sat on a beautiful shaped thing that was either a futon or a very well-cushioned statuette. She almost leapt up again when it moved and adjusted its contours to her body posture, weight and angle of incline. Intelligent furniture, fuck. 'They sold their shit to their colonies?'

'Yes, and what substance did they use initially to trade and set up the distribution network for those sales?'

She shrugged. 'You lost me there.'

'Opium,' he said, with a touch of sadness that he rarely displayed. 'The drug they used to subjugate the most powerful nation in the world.'

'China,' she said. 'Of course. They manufactured and distributed opium legally across the Cathay belt at the time. I read Amitav Ghosh's trilogy.'

He spread his hands. 'I read his bibliography, the list of books Ghosh took his information from. Half a dozen of them were written by my ancestors.'

Sheila kept silent. She knew better than to say or do anything when Wu spoke of his family. He continued on his own.

'Did you know that opium was sold legally in India until 1947? It was only after we formed our own government and took charge that we outlawed the drug and its manufacture, sale and distribution. But the damage was done. The groundwork had been laid. Once they had created the distribution system and market with opium, they used the same system to market other, legitimate products. The British basically laid the railway tracks for the same drug distribution system that continues even today, now selling a hundred other substances in place of opium. Bastards built the Drug Railroad of the World.'

She ventured an aside. 'And your family runs quite a few trains on that railroad.'

He turned and looked at her sharply. 'You're one to talk, Sheila Ray.'

She smiled. After a moment, he smiled back. That was another thing she liked about him: unlike the stereotypical movie cliché of powerful ganglords – especially Asian ganglords – Stanley Wu's emotional intelligence quotient and self-esteem were high enough that he could take criticism and not have you double-tapped on the spot or taken out back and have the shit beaten out of you. At least that was true of her and of the few instances when she'd taken a potshot at him.

'It's true,' he admitted. 'The British started the fire, but we kept it burning. No denying that. But now it's a different world, a different ball game. After the sub-prime-mortgage fallout and the crash, the big boys needed a new cash cow. Something they could milk for at least a few decades without the well running dry. Something big. Something that feeds a need that won't go away anytime soon.'

'Drugs,' she suggested.

He waved that away, flapping his hand like a Tai Chi master. 'Drugs are already in the mix. So are Ponzi schemes, legal as well as extra-legal. Counterfeiting. Arms dealing.

Extortion. Identity theft. Prostitution. Money laundering. The small-time stuff like fraud, forgery, illegal immigration, larceny, murder-for-hire, armed robbery …' he gestured. 'All that small-time shit. But all that was already around and already pushed to the limit. There is only so much juice you can squeeze out of an old litchi.'

An attendant in a traditional Chinese Hanfu brought in a tray and handed Wu a tiny scroll of paper so discreetly that had Sheila even glanced away for a moment, she would have missed the exchange. She followed the attendant for just a second, the richly brocaded Hanfu catching her eye, and when she looked back at Stanley, the scroll had already been read and disposed, she didn't know where. He gestured to the tray, but she shook her head, declining. He picked up a tiny bone china cup adorned with delicate artwork and sipped steaming hot jasmine tea as he talked.

'There was only one business left that hadn't been fully exploited yet and was still profitable enough to assure the zamindars of the free market the certainty of guaranteed profits for decades to come. Something big and widespread enough that it would always be in demand, and for which there would always be a plentiful supply. What was more, it was a self-replenishing supply.'

'Self-replenishing?' She frowned. 'You mean, like cocaine?'

He wagged a finger slowly, holding the tea cup high in the other hand, at face height. 'Cocaine needs to be grown in secret, processed in secret, packaged and distributed in secret. They needed something that could be supplied through legitimate channels, under protection of law, using borderline-legal methods. It would never go out of demand and keep rising in price, and they could control the supply and quality of it.'

Sheila shrugged, giving up. 'Diamonds?' It did sound a lot like the way the original cartel had built the diamond trade, exploiting native African labour and lack of legal sophistication to create a trillion-dollar empire through the use of legal technicalities and loopholes. 'Blood diamonds?'

Stanley Wu smiled, the steam from the tea swirling around his high cheekbones and only slightly slanted eyes. She loved his eyes. They were dark, intense, trustworthy eyes, Chinese eyes. 'People,' he said simply. 'Human trafficking, to use the correct term. Or to use an older unfashionable term, slave-trading.'

Fifteen

15.1

FATHER FRANCIS HELPED ANITA off the main pathway onto a narrow overgrown grass path that had evidently not been used much in years. She guessed it was one of the older paths, before the zoo was renovated in 2005, because she remembered them from her childhood visits. He had a plastic yellow flashlight which he used discreetly, keeping it pointed downwards. The sound of shouting and yelling faded behind them, but didn't die out completely. There were police or emergency vehicle sirens in the distance too. The path wound at a genial angle, culminating in a mossy side wall of a building that looked abandoned.

A man was waiting by a side door. She recognized him as the doctor who had given her the injection earlier and stopped at once. Father Francis's chin collided with the back of her head, probably hurting him more than it did her. 'He's with them,' she said. 'He has to be the one who called them.'

Father Francis put his arms on her shoulders, steadying her. 'Dr Jayawardhane called me, not them. That's why he sedated you and agreed to keep you in the clinic instead of following procedure by sending you to Trivandrum General Hospital. He will probably lose his job for it.'

She thought about this and realized he was right. Besides, she was trusting Father Francis for the moment, so she had to go with what he said.

The doctor looked her up and down, his gaze lingering on her leg. He looked very pained to see the muck and grass stains all over the dressing. 'You must be careful to not get infected,' he said, reminding her of a character in a zombie movie. *Too late, doc,* she wanted to tell him. *I'm already one of the living dead.* 'I will give you some drugs for her,' he said to the padre over her shoulder. 'Make sure she has them on time or the foot could become septic.'

He led them into the building which turned out to be some kind of extension at the back of the same animal hospital building she had been in earlier. They passed cages with injured or sick animals lying in various states of discomfort, some bandaged, others asleep, their chests heaving. A lioness with a bandaged paw and an enormous plastic Elizabethan collar around her neck lifted her head and growled a greeting. Anita growled back, drawing a look from the priest. They kept moving.

The doctor had a van waiting with the zoo's name painted on the sides. The engine was idling. He opened the rear doors. There was a cage inside, with blankets and a lot of straw. 'Get in, cover yourself well, stay quiet.' He went around to the front and got into the cab of the van.

Father Francis helped her into the cage, covered her with the blankets – which stank to high heaven of some unidentifiable animal's sweat and urine – then sprinkled handfuls of straw strategically. He leaned over and whispered, 'I'll be up front. Don't worry, we'll get you out of this, Anita.'

He began to step back, to shut the van doors. She reached through the bars of the cage and caught his jacket. 'Padre, about Lalima, just one question. Who murdered her? Was it my brothers?'

He patted her hand, 'I'll explain later. Now just relax and lie still.'

He shut the doors, leaving her in darkness. She couldn't hear his footsteps going around the side of the van but after a moment, she heard the passenger side door open and then shut and the van began moving.

She lay down, intending to play sick-lioness for a while, even thinking mischievously of growling a bit if anyone tried to check her cage, but before she knew it, she had conked off. The next thing she knew, she was awake and being carried on a stretcher into some kind of old British Raj-era building. High vaulted ceilings and stained glass casement windows floated high above. There was an ancient chandelier with the biggest cobweb she had ever seen and very dark oil portraits of stern-looking Jesuit-types. She registered the fragrance of jasmine blooming and it reminded her of jasmine tea which she loved to have after a Chinese meal at one of the last surviving genuine Chinese restaurants in Mumbai. Her favourite, when she could afford it, was Baba Ling's. Though she still missed Frederick's.

They brought her into a room with stone walls and high vaulted ceilings, and she felt certain she was either in a church rectory or a convent. She glimpsed a habit or two floating about and thought of the goddamn beautiful irony. She who had turned away from God and the Church for so many years was now being given refuge in a house of the Lord by a deacon of His faith.

She was still smiling when they settled her into an iron spring-cot with a window over her head, slightly to the right. There was a carved dark wooden table and a chair for visitors by her bedside. From the sound of their footfalls as they carried her in, the floors were stone. She could see rows of beds to either side and on the other side of the room. It was like a hospital ward in an old WWI movie. Except that she was the only patient.

Dr. Jayawardhane spoke with Father Francis for a moment, mostly about medications and diet and rest, from what she could catch. Since he used mostly English, she assumed that the American didn't know her language, but he surprised her at the end when a nurse or nun came up and he addressed her in fluent, if slightly limited Malayalam. So he'd been here awhile. Interesting.

The nurse administered a drip which Anita hated because she had had them before and they sucked big time. But she endured it, waiting until the nun had finished, even managing a 'thank you, sister' before turning to Father Francis.

'Lalima. Tell me about her,' she said.

'You should rest,' he said. 'The drugs will make you sleepy.'

'Time enough for sleep in the grave,' she replied.

He smiled. He was handsome when he smiled. 'What is that? Ecclesiastes or Doxology?'

'*Conan the Barbarian*, the first movie, with Arnold.'

His smile vanished. 'I see you're not as sick as you appear.'

'I'm sick of my family trying to kill me. I'm sick of not knowing what's going on. Tell me, father. Tell me, how have I sinned? Against who?'

'Whom,' he corrected. 'Sorry, I majored in English. Boston U.'

'Good for you, college boy,' she said, trying to sit up and regretting it instantly. What the fuck was that at the end of her right leg, a foot or a piece of lead filled with ground glass? Damn sedative must have worn off. She hoped the fresh ones would kick in fast. 'Please explain what this is all about and where you fit into this picture.'

He saw the hostility in her eyes and softened. 'Anita ... Lalima told me about what you went through with your brothers after your father's death.' He shook his head, his fingers touching the rosary around his wrist in a gesture she knew was instinctive: her grandmother used to touch her rosary the exact same way. 'It was un-Christian behaviour. Such things are greatly offensive to any good person on God's earth.'

She bit her lower lip to keep from saying more than she should. 'Your commiserations make me feel all warm and toasty inside. But right now, this isn't about me. I want some answers and I'd like them fast, please. We can talk about my good old days later.'

He frowned. 'Haven't you read the documents? We thought you would have figured it out by now. You did call the others, didn't you?'

She stared at him. 'Jesus, padre. No disrespect, but you're freaking me out now. Who are you? How do you know whom I called or didn't call? How do you know about the packet?'

He shrugged. 'I'm a priest of the Catholic Church. I was at the parish of St. Bartholomew's in downtown Boston for two years before choosing to join this mission. I'm not CIA or some government agency spook. Lalima told me, remember? I know what's in that package; I know she left instructions with the lawyer to send it to the four of you. You're a detective. It's perfectly logical that you would have found out who the others were and called them by now. What's so sinister about that? It's the reason why Lalima chose you, apart from the fact that you were her dearest and most trusted friend. She knew you would take it up like a righteous cause and do what had to be done to stop them – or try, at least.'

Anita drew in a deep breath and released it slowly. 'Okay, I get that part. Crystal. But who's "they"? My family? Philip—' she paused, experiencing a moment of utter despair and fighting it back with kung fu fists of fury, *not now, damn-dog*. 'Philip said something about Father Yeshua, our parish priest in Varkala ... It made me think the Church was somehow mixed up in this too. And going by the Catholic Church's record in the past few decades, I somehow came to the conclusion that you were the bad guys. No offense.'

Father Francis sighed and looked down briefly, grappling some inner demon of his own before nodding. 'It's true, we have had our share of problems. But don't paint the whole barn with the same shade of dung, Anita. It's true that there are some members of the Church mixed up in this, but we excommunicate them the instant we are certain of their complicity. Please know that nobody involved in such sordid dealings is authorized or associated in any official capacity, or operates with the complicity of the Roman Catholic Church, so help me God.'

He signed the sign of the cross, even muttering the standard 'In nomine Patris et fils et spiritus sancti' sub-voce as he did, out of habit.

She was starting to like this Father Francis. He was a straight guy. Or at least seemed to be. 'Okay, I'll bite,' she said, feeling a subtle easing in her foot. Was it the pain medication or the benediction? *Oh yeah, Anita, girl, you've been saved! Hallelujah!* 'Then who are the bad guys here? What do they want? What's this all about really? Why did Lalima send us four women those packages? What do those documents really prove? What did she expect us to do with them?' Anita gestured. 'I don't even have my package anymore and the bastards still tried to kill me. At Trivandrum Zoo, of all places. What is going on, father? Please tell me. Treat me like I'm stupid. Or American. Break it down for me.'

He smiled at the American jab, and she liked him even more for that, for not getting uppity and all nationalistic about it. 'It's about the business of human trafficking. That's what it's about, to put it simply and stupidly in Americanese. The documents prove how legitimate banking and insurance and financial institutions are earning profits from enterprises with "dirty" sources and simply turning a blind eye to where the money is really coming from.'

'And they're using NGOs and grant funding and charitable trusts to funnel and whitewash the dirty profits from these illicit activities before rerouting them back into the system, is that right?'

He made a gesture with an upturned palm, tilting his head and smiling. 'There you go. You have it in a nutshell.'

'And now they want me dead because I know this?' she asked, looking puzzled now. 'That doesn't make sense, father. I don't have the documents anymore, so I can't really prove anything ...'

'No,' he said, looking surprised. 'They want you dead on general principles, yes. But the real reason why they're after you is because of the schedule, of course. I thought you knew that already.'

Now it was her turn to look surprised. 'What schedule?' *Ah, the painkillers have kicked in. Man, that feels great!*

'The one that spells out the next round of terror attacks in India.'

'What?'

'It's a tabular list on a single sheet, right at the end. It just has dates and place names, just cities, no neighbourhoods or specific details.'

She stared at him. 'And this is a list of terror attacks in *our* country?'

'Impending terror attacks.'

She reached into the back pocket of her jeans, pulling out the sheet she had folded and put into her wallet right at the beginning. The sheet that had slipped out of the package when she pulled out the pile of papers and which was stuck to her face when she woke up in Papanasam Sea Resort. She opened it out now. It was a list of dates and places, that was all.

But it was no longer meaningless.

She stared at it for a long moment.

'What is it, Anita?' Father Francis asked, leaning forward to look at the page.

She turned it and showed it to him, jabbing her finger at the topmost entry. He took the sheet from her, looking at it in a way that told her he had never actually laid eyes on it until that moment, even though he had known of its existence.

'That's today's date, isn't it?'

'Yes,' he said, his face paling. 'Damn it, we thought we had at least another week.' He looked down the list and his face grew even more troubled. He genuflected silently with his right hand, presumably because of the 'damn'.

She caught hold of his wrist, making the paper rattle. 'And the first attack is ... when?'

He finished crossing himself and lowered his hand, two fingers still joined and crooked as if about to anoint with holy water.

'Now,' he said. 'In a few minutes. It starts in Delhi ...'

15.2

NACHIKETA WAS TOO STUNNED to do more than simply sit in the wheelchair as Rajendra Powar wheeled her out of the office, watched by the condescending eyes of the MBA brigade. She told the Jat to wait a moment as she made a quick phone call to a clerk she knew at the Delhi High Court, a Chennaiite who had been in an abusive marriage and had expressed sympathy for Nachiketa's ordeal and admiration for her fighting back. The clerk was still at the courthouse and looking up a judgment on record was simply a matter of opening a page in an Internet browser these days. She confirmed what Shama had said back in *Pink's* office: the judgment on record was declared against Nachiketa, not *for* her, as claimed by Judge R.K. Jain just two days ago.

How that was possible, Nachiketa had no idea. But by now, it didn't surprise her that these people, whoever they were, might be powerful enough to alter court judgments – perhaps even have a judgment rescinded and a fresh one issued. Or an incorrect one filed. It didn't matter how they'd done it or whether Nachiketa could appeal against it or overturn it on various grounds; the point was the judgment presently stood against her, and that lent credence to what the 'living dead' Advaita and 'undead' Shonali seemed to be telling every journalist and columnist in Delhi. As Powar and she waited for the lift, she had taken a moment to check her messages and emails on her BB and had seen that she had forty-seven unread messages and/or emails, and about twice as many missed calls, almost all from media publications and channels. Whoever these people were, they were thorough as hell. They had come up with a story that fit what could be presented as 'facts' and there was nothing she could do to change that now.

She was silent in the lift all the way down and in the street while Powar pushed her back to where they had parked the car in a Pay and Park zone. She hadn't fully recovered even after he had decanted her from the chair to the car, packed away the wheelchair and seated himself in the driver's seat. He fiddled with the keys of the Civic for a moment and put one into the ignition but didn't start the car. Finally, he turned slightly so he could see her better, his right elbow banging the side of the steering wheel.

'Who is persons doing this to madam?' he asked indignantly. 'Who is behind all so much shitness?'

She glanced at him, intrigued by the choice of words more than the outburst. But she said nothing. She could think of nothing to say.

He reached towards her, his bandaged hand like a fat white rabbit on a hairy stick, and she reacted. 'Sorry, sorry,' he said, then jabbed the bandage downwards. She realized he was trying to point. 'I am wanting see envelope. Lifafa?'

She took hold of the package with both her bandaged hands, lifting it up. As delicately as possible under the circumstances, and with the awkwardness typical of Indian men forced to be in close proximity with women yet trying to avoid actual contact, he managed to take the envelope in both his bandaged hands and towed it over to his side, propping it against the steering wheel. The horn went off once, alerting the parking attendant who assumed they were leaving and started towards them, pulling his notepad from his DMC coat pocket and jotting down the figures.

Powar struggled with the documents for a moment, then finally managed to pull the wad of papers out of the envelope. Because he was pressing the envelope against the steering wheel, one paper at the end got caught inside and tore as the rest were pulled out. He looked sheepishly at the torn sheet, then heaved the rest against his chest, tucking the sheets under his chin to hold them in place while he struggled to free the last sheet with his white mittens. Just then the parking attendant knocked on the closed window and slapped the parking receipt against the glass, just in case they were planning to drive off without paying. Powar nodded at the attendant who couldn't see him from that angle – Powar was so tall, the attendant would have had to bend down and look inside the car to see his face properly. Nachiketa watched this with a detachment that was yogic in its quietude. Nothing seemed to matter anymore.

What was the point of taking any action at all? Shonali

was dead, her office was burnt to ashes, her practice destroyed, Advaita's death in vain too, and somehow, incredibly, the forces at work here had altered the verdict in her case, putting a 'Denial of Claimant's Petition' in place of the finding for the plaintiff that had been announced in open court. *How the hell did you do that anyway? How did you get the Delhi High Court to reverse a declared verdict?* She could guess, of course: they had got to Justice R.K. Jain somehow, either coerced him or killed him, and since it took a day or so for the verdict to be entered into the system's records, they had been able to enter the altered verdict. So in a sense they hadn't changed the official record, just the verbally declared one. Even so. What arrogance! What power! What hubris!

And now, every single one of her friends believed she was a raving lunatic, that she had gone off the deep end at last. She could almost hear them chatting on their BBMs now: 'I saw it coming for some time. You have to know how to read the signs.'

Even the dog was dead, that poor thing. Along with her poor pups.

'Justice is dead,' Nachiketa said. 'And so are her children.'

The attendant knocked again, still unaware that Powar was otherwise occupied. Rajendra was struggling with the pile of documents which was slowly slipping down his chest. Nachiketa sighed, deciding to rejoin the real world, and reached out. She took the envelope from his hand, indicating the pile of papers with her eyes. He made a sound of acquiescence and used both hands to grab the slipping pile, settled them on the steering wheel – another blast of the horn – then rolled down the window to pay the attendant.

Nachiketa had the envelope in her hand now. The half-torn sheet was still in it, but it had come almost all the way out. She was about to stuff it back inside when she happened to see the tabular rows of dates and times and places. It was fairly simple. Her eye happened to notice the word 'Daryaganj' because that was where they were right now, in a Pay and Park almost within sight of Delhi Gate. The words beside the Daryaganj entry simply said 'Jama Masjid'. There were some numbers in the right-hand column which she read easily as twenty-four-hour times. The time entry for Daryaganj–Jama Masjid read 21:11. There was something about that time that caught her attention – twenty-one hours was 9 p.m.. She glanced at the digital clock on the Civic dashboard which had come on just that instant, as Powar, having paid the attendant, turned on the ignition. The time display was accurate – it was a lawyer's car, after all – and read 9:10 in bold, blinking digits. That would be 21:10 in 24-hour time, a minute before the time listed here, which meant that whatever was supposed to happen at Jama Masjid, Daryaganj, Delhi, was going to happen in less than a minute. At the precise time of ...

'Nine eleven,' she said aloud.

Rajendra Powar glanced at her as he used the paddle shift to put the Civic into gear to reverse out of the parking space. 'Aapne kuch kaha, madamji?'

She looked at him. 'Something is supposed to happen at nine elev—'

That was as far as she got before the car shook as if hit by an invisible fist and the world turned white.

The digital clock on the dashboard had just turned to 9:11.

15.3

AN ASSISTANT OR BODYGUARD – was there a difference? – whom Sheila had seen often before, came up to Stanley with a cell phone and said something briefly. Stanley took the cell and listened to it for barely a second before handing it back to the assistant. The assistant's eyes met Sheila's as he turned to leave and he acknowledged her without making any visible gesture or action: for a well-mannered Chinese, merely making eye contact *was* acknowledgement. The man left as discreetly as he had entered, receding into the shadows. She saw that a change had come over Stanley. He turned back to look out at the view, but he had lost all interest in it. He turned to look at her, then came over. From the way he walked she knew that the news must be really bad for him to be taking it this hard. She hadn't known him long enough, but had seen him in his most intimate moments and in the throes of intense emotional release, and she felt sure he had revealed more to her in those instances than he did to people he did business with or socialized with all his life.

'What is it?' she asked.

He made a gesture of resignation. 'Chi.'

'I don't understand.'

'It is the reason you are here. Why you came to me.'

'I came to find out what that package means. Why people are trying to ruin my life – *have* ruined my life. Why they're trying to kill me. Who they are.'

'Yes,' he said. 'And this is why.'

He gestured at the view, at Kolkata in the dark night, a sprinkling of lights. 'It will begin soon. It has already begun in Delhi.'

She had no idea what he was talking about. 'What has begun?'

'The same thing we have been talking about all this time.'

She tried to connect the dots. 'Slave trading? Human trafficking?'

'That's part of it, yes. That is the ongoing business, the bread-and-butter part. It's a big business, the fastest growing in the world. But this is bigger than that and they use this to drive that business and others. This is the whip they use to keep the sheep in line.'

She shook her head. 'I don't know anything about this shit, Wu. Please explain it to me.'

He came over and sat beside her on the futon. 'Capital markets. That's the heart of the whole thing, right? Business, manufacturing, trading, services, everything can only give you so much return, no more. There are expenses, rules, regulations, limitations, taxes. But capital markets are unlimited. Once you've put together a pile from whatever sources – legitimate, illegitimate, it doesn't matter – you have only one place left to invest it, if you want it to grow.'

'The stock market.'

'Yes. In 1992, in a single day, George Soros short-sold UK Pound Sterling currency worth $10 billion. He was exploiting a weakness in the Pound Sterling which he had been talking about openly for years before that. The Government of England knew what he was doing, knew it was possible to do just that, and tried to counter him by pumping as much as $15 billion to prop up the Sterling. But by the close of business, when the accounts were squared, the Bank of England couldn't afford to meet its short calls for the day. Soros basically broke the Bank of England in that one day. And in the process, he pocketed a neat $1.1 billion for himself.'

Sheila raised her eyebrows. 'That's a lot of fish and chips.'

'He did it again, in 1997 during the Asian financial crisis. He killed the Thai Baht and Malaysian Ringgit just as he had done the Pound Sterling. Mahathir Mohamad was PM of Malaysia then. He's a close family friend, and insisted that Soros deliberately chose that time to attack the Asian market because the Association of South Asian Nations or ASEAN had just inducted Myanmar, formerly Burma, as a member.' Stanley smiled wryly, without humour. 'Mahathir was accused of being anti-Semitic. Of course. You can't accuse a Jewish billionaire of anything without being anti-Semitic. Mahathir later recanted his allegations publicly, but in private anyone who knew the Asian markets knew that Soros and his gang of European–American billionaire bullies had set out to crash Asia. In barely fourteen months, over 1997 and '98, they caused losses of over $125 billion to ASEAN countries. Nobody knows for sure how much Soros personally profited from that raid, but that was when he went from being just a punk opportunist to a billionaire hedge fund manager. A player. Today, he only manages his own family's investments of almost $30 billion.'

Sheila still hadn't understood a thing. 'So are you saying that George Soros is behind this?'

Stanley Wu laughed. 'I wish. It would be so nice and simple, wouldn't it? Like a Bond movie. The villain with the eyepatch and the Siamese cat with the diamond collar. Or a glass eye and a cigarillo. But there are no individual villains here, Sheila. That's what I'm trying to explain to you. It's the whole system. The reason I brought up Soros is because he's written some interesting books on global capital markets that really make a lot of sense, if you're interested.'

'I'm not, actually,' she said. 'So I'll take your word for it.'

'Okay,' he said. 'But he has a theory he came up with a long while back, based on the work of philosopher Karl Popper. It's called Reflexivity and it's quite simple to understand.'

'For you, no doubt. For me, probably not so simple. I don't dine and wine prime ministers and finance moguls, Stanley. I run a women's gym. I work out. I read a little, watch some TV. Costume historical dramas are my favourite. I don't know shit-all about capital markets or what the fuck they have to do with human trafficking. You're still not making a whole lot of sense here.'

He nodded. 'Bear with me just a few moments longer.

Reflexivity, okay? It's really simple. It's a philosophy that says that the very act of observing a stock market closely influences the market.'

Sheila raised her eyebrows. 'That's heavy. Like spectators watching a game affecting the game's outcome?'

'No, not spectators. Participants. The actual investors whose money is in the market, the more intently they observe the market, the more they influence its valuation.'

'For better or worse?'

'That's the point: it throws them into a vicious cycle of ups and downs which can never be corrected completely.'

'Because they can't stop watching?'

'Yes and because the market can't stop being influenced by their watching. Soros says that is the current state of the world economy. It's in a death spiral from which it can never recover. There will be occasional stabilization, bubbles that make it float upwards – he claimed that we now have super-bubbles in which our speculation fuels more speculation which in turn influences further speculation, thereby causing the market valuation to shoot up to unsustainable heights – but in the end, what goes up must come down.'

'So the world economy is in a tailspin,' Sheila said. 'Great, I'll make sure I don't put all the cash I withdrew from the ATM last night into a hedge fund. But how does all this economic philosophy connect with trafficking humans?'

'The big guns, the kings who run the world of big finance, the hedge fund managers, the tycoons of Wall Street, the MNCs, the mega-accounting firms, the insurance conglomerates, all those guys, they know that there isn't any business or trade left that can give them new bubbles of growth, especially the super-growth they now want, that they're addicted to.'

'The greed economy.'

'Yes. Money for the sake of money. As an end in itself. That's the only purpose of a corporation. Not to build or manufacture or serve or provide. Simply to make money. It's a machine. And the machine must be fed.'

'So they turned to illegitimate means of earning more bucks? Like slave trading, you say? Human trafficking?'

'Yes, but that's only the bread and butter.'

'So you said. What's the jam then?'

He looked at her. 'Terrorism.'

She didn't get it. 'What do you mean, terrorism?'

'The business of terror.'

'Yeah, duh, I know what terrorism means, I know it's run like a business now, but what's that got to do with—'

'Not *like* a business, it *is* a business. The fastest growing and biggest business today, matched only by human trafficking. The two go hand in hand. The countries that are the epicentre of human trafficking are the ones that suffer the most terror attacks. It has to be that way. That's the system.'

'Which country is that?' she asked, then stopped. She raised a hand to her head. 'You mean ...'

He nodded. 'India.'

'But how the fuck can terrorism be good for business? I mean, terrorism kills confidence in a country's security, affects everything, even the stock market crashes ...' She stopped. 'Crashes ...'

'What else was Black Wednesday for the UK in 1992? It was a day of pure terror for the British Government. That was the day that made them realize they were fools to have stayed out of the EU. It led to a complete overhaul of the British banking and financial system. Which was just what

Soros and his gang wanted. The same thing in Asia in 1997–98. And those are just two examples of legitimate trading and market raids. There are a hundred, no a thousand, or thousands of such raids and manipulations happening all the time all over the world, some by groups, conglomerates, temporary partners, even governments and public sector undertakings, individual or family investment funds … it's a melee, all the time, 24/7, 365.'

'But that's legit. Now you're talking about terrorism. Actual bombs and killings of innocent people. Random attacks.'

He shook his head. 'Not random. Never random. Always planned carefully. Targets pinpointed, debated, discussed … bid upon. Decided by mutual agreement. Chosen for maximum impact. But to what purpose? To promote Islam?' He grinned and shook his head. 'That's the biggest myth of all. Islamic terrorism doesn't do a thing to help the Islamic cause, it only demonizes Islam further. Or like Anders Breivik, the Oslo gunman, whose manifesto proposed that each country return to nationalism and killed his own countrymen to publicize his cause! Talk about breathing in your own ass fumes for too long. No, Sheila, terrorism today is a planned and calculated affair. David Headley, the man who did the reconnaissance and planning of the Mumbai 26/11 terror attacks, was CIA-trained and FBI-supervised, yet he planned an entire terrorist operation allegedly without their knowing what he was up to. In collusion with Mumbai authorities and Bollywood celebrities, who later claimed, as the FBI and CIA did, that they did help Headley but without knowing what he was doing.' Stanley shook his head. 'The fact is, religion has nothing to do with it. The people pulling the strings at the highest level don't care if a Muslim does it. Or a Bollywood actor. Or a Christian fundamentalist in Oslo. Or Al Qaeda operatives in NYC. Or a madman in a Tokyo subway. All that matters is the timing and location. That's the key.'

'Because their goal is to use the fallout from the attacks to manipulate the capital markets.'

'Yes!' he said. 'You *do* have something up there besides a beautiful head of hair, Sheila Ray. That's what this is all really about. Terrorism as a tool of manipulation of stock markets, of currency valuations, of indices and ...'

His assistant approached again, stopping several feet away at a discreet distance, waiting to be noticed and summoned closer. Stanley beckoned him. The man leaned forward and said simply, 'Shijian'.

Stanley took Sheila's hand and stood up. He led her forward until they were a foot away from the glass wall that was all that separated them from a view of Kolkata from eighty-five storeys high. He squeezed her hand tightly. 'It is time.'

She turned to look at him, although her heart was pounding and she already knew what was coming. 'Time for what?'

'Time for the next one, the big one. The one listed in the package sent to you. The reason why they wanted the package back, why they were trying to kill you. Because it lists the locations and times and dates of the next cycle, the biggest one in India yet.'

And Sheila remembered the last page of the pile of documents, the one that had made least sense to her at the time, which she had actually looked at, puzzled over briefly, then set aside with a shrug because it seemed so inane. She had assumed it was a schedule of meetings or appointments or something.

Delhi – Daryaganj – Jama Masjid – 21:11 and today's date.

Mumbai – Dadar – Shivaji Park – 21:17 and today's date.

Bangalore – M.G. Road – Chinnaswamy Stadium – 21:23.

Although the fourth line on the list had held her attention briefly:

Kolkata – Salt Lake City – Salt Lake Stadium – 21:27.

And she remembered the football fans swarming across all of Biddhanagar and remembered that she had seen something on a poster about today's big game. That was why the fans hadn't dispersed and were still milling about the area. They were waiting for tonight's game, the big event of the season. A major film star was coming to inaugurate it.

Her breath caught in her chest as a brightness flared in the eastern sky, blazing out of the darkness. The sound wave struck a moment later, hitting the glass tower like a blow from an invisible dragon's tail. She felt her bones jarred and Stanley squeezed her hand tighter. And then she saw the plume of flame rise in the distance.

Author's Note

THIS IS A WORK of fiction. As are all the characters, events, and even the locations which are depicted purely in a fictional context. However, human trafficking and profiteering from such illegal enterprises is very much prevalent and possibly the greatest threat to the world today. Information is freely available online and in numerous studies, including many valuable ones conducted by non-governmental organizations (NGOs) which require many brave individuals to put themselves in positions of threat. Further studies in this field are encouraged. The more we know, they less they can hide it. Shine the light of knowledge in the darkest corners.

I'd also like to thank the usual suspects: V.K. Karthika who has been the greatest supporter of my work and vision that I've had the good fortune to find in my entire career. I honestly couldn't have done it without her. If you like anything I write, no matter how little or how much, please send a wish her way. An author proposes, but a publisher disposes – or promotes. Karthika's untiring faith and appreciation of my work has more than partially made it possible for me to fulfil my vision of an Epic India Library. May she thrive and the vision be fulfilled all the way – in time!

Prema Govindan, a rare editor who actually edits well, is a wonderful person to interact with, and enjoys her work as well as the books she publishes. Too many editors outside India (and in India too, sad to say) have chosen to become glorified marketing and administrative tools of a corporate structure. Prema is a book editor and a great one. I'm lucky to have worked with her on ... is it really six books so far? Wow. May we work on sixty more!

The wonderfully talented Ermisenda Alvarez, who even at nineteen, with a working knowledge of Photoshop and no formal graphic design training, has turned out amazing cover designs for my e-books. It's a thrill to have her work featured on this print edition. I feel proud of having played some tiny part in discovering and encouraging her talent to flourish, even across continents and through only email communication. Hope to meet you some day, and until then, keep up the great work!

Arijit Ganguly and Shuka Jain made working on this cover design a pleasure. Look forward to working with them on the rest of the Kali Rising Series!

P.M. Sukumar, Sameer Mahale, N.S. Krishna, Lipika Bhushan, Neha Punj, Amit Sharma, Rajeev Sethi, Girija Padmanabhan, Mohit Mehta and all else at HarperCollins India who devote their lives to not just the business of book publishing but the sharing of knowledge itself. You are great at your jobs. Please keep it up!

Biki, Yoda, Yashka and Willow, my homies: I love y'all. 2gether 4ever, awright!

My constant readers: You may not have wanted this book, so shockingly, profanely different from my epic retellings, but an author is more than one story, and in this case, more than a genre or several genres. I love storytelling and writing and sharing stories about all kinds of people everywhere and everywhen, and this is one that I truly loved telling. I hope you loved reading it as much. But whether you did or not, it's all good, because stories are like people: they're not in competition with one another, not really. Just with themselves. I hope I was able to do justice to this very challenging project and hope that you will follow me to the books that succeed this one. The great news is that the sequels are not only complete, they have been turned in to the publisher already. They're titled *Burnt Saffron Sky*, *Rust Black Heart* and *Silver Acid Rain*.

From my heart and mind into your hands. Peace, only, and love always. Happy Reading!

ASHOK BANKER
Mumbai
November 2012